She wasn't alone

"Is anyone there?" she whispered.

No words were spoken in reply, but she felt...
confronted. She imagined a warm breath ruffling
her hair, a hand urging her to get up off the floor.
She followed the curious instinct, and reached out
in front of her.

She felt what had to be a door. But there was no
handle, no way out. Searching for a hidden release, she traced the wall to the left with her hands.
Then suddenly there was nothing and she pitched
forward, banging herself on what felt like a stair.

They were narrow and dangerous, but she started
to climb, exploring the walls with her hands. Another door met her touch... another door with no
way out. And still she felt the malevolent presence
behind her.

Trapped! She felt faint and chilled all over. Why
was she here, and who was this presence she felt,
but couldn't see?

Dear Reader,

What better time to snuggle tightly with the one you love than on All Hallows' Eve—when things truly go bump in the night!

Harlequin Intrigue is ringing your doorbell this month with "Trick or Treat," our Halloween quartet—filled with ghastly ghouls and midnight trysts!

Halloween was always Patricia Rosemoor's favorite holiday. Even today, she and her husband dress up as creatures of the night to partake of Chicago's Halloween treats: watching the costumes parade on Rush Street, visiting the Lincoln Park "pumpkin house"—with hundreds of jack-o'-lanterns—and checking out what ghoulish additions her neighbor Marybeth has added to her yearly haunted house!

Be sure *you* check out all the TRICK OR TREAT quartet this month.

Regards,

Debra Matteucci
Senior Editor & Editorial Coordinator

Haunted

Patricia Rosemoor

Harlequin Books

TORONTO • NEW YORK • LONDON
AMSTERDAM • PARIS • SYDNEY • HAMBURG
STOCKHOLM • ATHENS • TOKYO • MILAN
MADRID • WARSAW • BUDAPEST • AUCKLAND

For Veronica Mary, who led me into the world of fantasy that is the heart of every fiction writer; who expressed her own imagination through my homemade prize-winning Halloween costumes; and who, if her fascination with horror movies and with the occult in general was any indication, was born one day later than she should have been.

Happy birthday, Mom. This one is just for you.

Veronica Mary Pinianski
November 1, 1923–March 29, 1984

ISBN 0-373-22250-5

HAUNTED

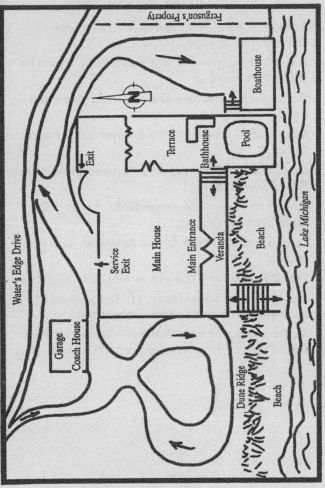

CAST OF CHARACTERS

Echo St. Clair—She always felt a presence at Dunescape Cottage.

Bram Vanmatre—He was haunted by a past he couldn't remember.

Donahue Vanmatre—The ghost of Halloween Past.

Miss Addy—Donahue's twin never left Dunescape Cottage.

Sibyl Wilde—Did Miss Addy's nurse know more than she was telling?

Uriah Hawkes—The groundkeeper was doing more than gardening.

Lena Rundle—What this housekeeper kept was secrets.

Travis Ferguson—The proverbial nosy neighbor.

Norbert Ferguson—Travis's father seemed *unusually* proprietary over Dunescape.

Katherine Vanmatre Quinlan—Bram's mother would do anything to keep the truth from her son.

Prologue

"What the hell are you doing down here?"

The deep-timbred response was equally strident, and the seven-year-old boy stirred against the snatches of argument that haunted him. A dream, that's all it was. A nightmare. Aunt Addy said nightmares couldn't hurt him. But he didn't like them anyhow.

"Make it go away, Aunt Addy," he mumbled.

"I know her as well as I know myself!"

But this nightmare wouldn't go. He squeezed his eyes tight, tried to close his ears from the inside so he couldn't hear, but nothing worked. He opened his eyes to another darkness, one that scared him because he didn't know where he was.

The voices continued. Faint. Hollow. Definitely spooky.

"Ghosts!" he breathed.

He tried to rise, but something held him fast to the spot where he lay. He couldn't move. His heart beat faster.

"I was desperate for a way out...."

So was he!

The thing enveloping him was soft and warm. Not a blanket. He wasn't snug in his own bed. Mind still fuzzy with sleep, he nearly panicked until he remembered: they'd made him wear a dopey velvet cape. When he'd come up here to get away from the yucky music and the painted ladies who'd pinched his cheeks—up to his hiding place secret even from Mother and Father—he'd wrapped the cape around himself against the chill.

Now he was sorry he'd ever left. He didn't like the scuffling and the cries that echoed around him. A sickening thud made him tremble. Checking every so often to see if the ghosts were gone yet, he began reciting a poem aloud, a verse Aunt Addy had read to him many times from one of his favorite books.

Finally, the dark space grew silent.

Except for his own breathing, which felt funny in his chest. He rose from the tattered cot and fought the sneeze the dust motes nearly teased from him. Blindly, he made his way around the boxes and the pieces of furniture in their shrouds. His hands found the wall. Then the shutter. He reached up to unfasten the latch and swing the slatted wood panel aside on its creaky old hinges. Through a grimy window, he looked out into a night cloaked by clouds and veiled by fog. Tentacles of gray mist curled up the building like fingers reaching for him....

With a sharp cry, he jumped back, unwilling to be taken.

Frozen to the spot, he watched the clouds jockey with the moon. A few seconds later, a blue glow led him back to the window. Tentatively, he peered down. The fog was parting. Another faint beam—this one a dull yellow—cut through the mist. Nose pressed against the glass, he watched, eyes widening at the activity below. His breath

umped in his throat at what he thought he saw, and he
needed to pee real bad.

Then he bolted.

He had to get down there. To see up close.

Suddenly, the moon switched off and he was running
blind. Something hit him across the shins and sent him
flying. His shoulder banged into a dull edge, his head into
a sharper one. He landed in a heap on the floor, stunned.

A warm thick liquid oozed down his nose and into one
eye.

He tried to stand, but his legs wobbled and he settled
on his knees, sobs racking his narrow chest. The pain in
his head made his whole body throb. He rocked back,
fear consuming him.

Through his tears, he saw a hazy shimmer. Close. Too
close.

No, no! Couldn't be . . .

"Go away!" he whimpered. One of the ghosts had
come to get him! "Leave me alone!"

The thoughts racing through his head were too much
for a small child to bear. The image wavered and weak-
ened even as the boy's lids fluttered closed. He collapsed
once more, his head landing on a rolled-up, moldy-
smelling old rug.

His mind shutting out what it couldn't acknowledge. . . .

Chapter One

Thirty years later

Through the slender fingers of mist rising from Lake Michigan, Dunescape Cottage loomed over the crest of a grassy, tree-covered dune like a preening vulture. *Cottage* was a misnomer for what was in reality a Victorian mansion, impressive in its heyday before it had fallen victim to the elements. The fierce wind never stopped blowing on this section of the lake. Storms were frequent and intense.

Rows of red brick, banded with crumbling black mortar, led up to the first-story windows. The full second story, partial third and attic were timber of similar colors...where nature had not yet worn the paint away. Cracked terra-cotta ridges trimmed the multileveled, sloped roof with its broken black slate tiles. Even the multitude of peaks and chimneys appeared crooked; and from different level peaks, two bent weather vanes challenged each other, as if to a duel.

Not at all what he remembered....

Then again, he didn't remember much that counted.

Bram Vanmatre stared at the impressive if decrepit monstrosity he had once called home, waiting for some feeling of recognition or welcome. Nothing. Not even rejection. Just the awful blank he'd learned to live with.

That had to change. He was here to do it. To find out. To remember. Whatever it took.

It was time he got on with his life.

Now he was an adult and he had returned to the place and the voices that had always haunted him. He'd come ostensibly to take care of Aunt Addy. To save her from herself. But, underlying this clear motive was the other....

He only wondered who would have the power to save *him* if he failed.

WONDERING IF SHE WOULD be able to save the situation, Echo St. Clair stood next to her car, which she'd parked back on the cul-de-sac at the beginning of the drive, and stared at Dunescape Cottage looming toward her through the dusk. Needing the walk across the grounds to relax her, the few extra minutes to gather her thoughts, she set off on foot.

Though she'd lived in Water's Edge for more than a decade, Echo had been inside its most famous edifice only twice before—both times in the past month. Her first visit to Dunescape Cottage had been to introduce herself to the reclusive lady of the manor, Adrienne Vanmatre, and to seek permission to use her home for the local youth group fund-raiser. Over her ritual afternoon tea, Miss Addy had agreed. The second time, Echo had toured the house with several of the teenagers who were eager to turn the place into their Haunted Mansion for Halloween.

And why not? The place was odd enough to give *her* a chill.

The beach residents of this small town on the Michigan coast already thought Dunescape Cottage was haunted, for they had seen mysterious lights and shadowy forms around the crumbling mansion on many a dark, moonless night. In fact, Miss Addy—or Crazy Addy, as some of the locals called her—claimed her twin brother's ghost hung around the place, and that, on occasion, she spoke to him. Donahue Vanmatre had met with an accidental death thirty years before.

On All Hallows' Eve, to be exact.

This year's holiday was less than a week away. The plans for the haunting had been drawn, the costumes made, the building materials purchased...and now it seemed that a fly named Bram Vanmatre had stuck himself squarely in the ointment!

Echo had been alarmed for more than one reason when she'd heard about the arrival of Donahue's son that morning. Rumor had it that Bram Vanmatre hadn't once returned to Dunescape Cottage in all the years since his father's death. Now, suddenly, the Chicago lawyer not only took it upon himself to visit his aunt, but to put himself in charge of her legal affairs, which—according to gossipy Mrs. Ahern, the town librarian—just might include preventing the youth group from using the mansion for the fund-raiser.

She forced herself to concentrate on that particular issue, not wanting to deal with the more serious implications of Vanmatre's presence.

An eerie wind blew from the lake over the grounds as she neared the crumbling mansion, whose base was now swathed in a light fog. Concentrating on how she was going to handle Miss Addy's nephew, Echo was startled silly when a bulky figure appeared out of nowhere to block her approach. She jumped back and swallowed a strangled cry.

"And where might you be going, miss?" the hulk demanded.

"You could give a person a heart attack, sneaking up like that." Her words had no effect on the groundskeeper, Uriah Hawkes, who always acted as if he owned the place. "I'm here to finalize plans about the fund-raiser, if you must know." She took a long, shaky breath.

Beneath the brimmed hat that covered most of his salt-and-pepper hair, Uriah's dark eyes bored into her. "Miss Addy expecting you?"

Echo held her temper and gave the beefy man a thorough once-over in return to let him know what she thought of his interference. As he had been on her last two visits, Uriah was wearing a cotton work shirt with sleeves rolled up—a light garment despite the fall chill—showing off his powerful forearms, one of which was tattooed with a skull and crossbones. Rubber boots caked with fresh mud appeared beneath the bottoms of baggy trousers held up by suspenders.

"No, I didn't call Miss Addy," she said, returning her gaze to his hostile expression. "I'm not here to visit her, anyway. I heard about her nephew's arrival and thought I ought to introduce myself."

"*He* know you're coming?"

"No!" As if it were any of his business!

Uriah barked a laugh. "Well, then, you both got a real treat in store, ain't you?"

Echo swallowed the lump that immediately formed at his words. So Bram Vanmatre could be difficult. So what? So could a lot of people, as she knew from personal experience.

And so could she, if necessary.

"If you don't mind, I'll be getting that *treat* now."

Uriah glanced back at a first-story window and moved out of her way.

Echo followed his gaze toward the house. Behind sheer curtains, she could make out the silhouette of a man. Her resolve strengthened, she set out to meet him.

As she approached the impressive, building-wide veranda that fronted the lake, fog licked at her ankles and slithered up the stairs before her, leading her to the front door, which stood open a crack.

About to knock, she poked her head in instead. "Hello?" she called, expecting Lena, the housekeeper, to be around. "Anyone there?" But no one answered.

Perhaps it was just as well. She wouldn't mind confronting Bram Vanmatre without anyone tuning in to her conversation. Inching open the door, she checked out the gloomy interior. The marble-floored foyer was empty, as were the open front parlors on either side. She guessed that the window where she'd spotted the man looking out at her would be in the second room to her left—the library, if she remembered correctly. She hadn't actually been inside it before, since the library was one of the few rooms that would not be available for the fund-raiser.

Straightening her spine as her grandmother had taught her, Echo crossed the foyer and hesitated only a second in front of the closed door before knocking. Her heartbeat was even as she waited for a response, but when none came, her pulse accelerated at the same rate as her annoyance. Surely he hadn't left the room in the short time it took her to enter the house. She tried again, but her knock either went unheard or fell on purposely deaf ears.

Either way, she had difficulty swallowing her irritation. She just *had* to talk to Miss Addy's nephew *now!*

That thought propelled her into grasping the knob and opening the door. A deep, seemingly empty gloom met her eyes. But as she stepped inside, her gaze penetrating the spooky atmosphere, touching on the walls of old books, she knew she wasn't alone.

Over in the farthest, deepest recess of the room, flames danced and crackled in a massive fireplace that was faced with green ceramic tiles. And before the hearth were two high-backed leather chairs, only one of which was empty. Settled along the wing of the other was a man's arm draped by a black silk sleeve of unusual fullness and caught tightly at the wrist.

Echo cleared her throat and stepped closer. "Mr. Vanmatre?"

At first she thought he planned to ignore her. Then, ever so slowly, he turned in the chair and peered at her. Deep-set eyes—haunted eyes—met her steady gaze. His angular face was intensely handsome and framed by thick black waves of hair. His expression was neither welcoming nor disapproving.

He seemed to be... waiting.

Thinking her best bet would be to appear business-like, she curved her lips in a confident smile, stepped forward, offered her hand and said, "Mr. Vanmatre, I've come expressly to see you, to find out what you intend to do about the Haunted Mansion."

What he intended to do? An odd way of putting it, when the mansion was already haunted.

He stared at the audacious woman who dared invade his sanctuary. As if realizing he wasn't about to take her hand, she settled it on the back of the chair opposite. Firelight made the long tangle of curls dancing over her shoulders gleam a red so brilliant that it almost hurt to look at her.

"Well?" she asked, both hands now gripping the chair back. Her polished nails were of moderate length, and she wore several unusual rings—more art pieces than traditional jewelry. "Mr. Vanmatre, I know you've taken over Miss Addy's affairs and that you have the power to deny us the use of Dunescape Cottage since we have no written contract," she said, "but I hope you'll see reason."

Everything about her was unusual. Her features were striking rather than classically beautiful. Not easily forgettable. Good bone structure. Full lips. Wide-spaced eyes a fathomless gray. A man could lose his soul in eyes such as those.

"We're talking about a fund-raiser for a good cause. The proceeds will be used to make what is now a deserted storefront into a real center for the Water's Edge Youth Group."

So entranced was he by the mobility of the woman's expression that he barely heard her words. As she continued her plea, a current emanated from her that held him fascinated.

"Until now, the kids have met in spaces meant for other activities—the church hall, the high school gym."

Her voice fairly throbbed with conviction and purpose.

"They need a place of their own, something they can be proud of, something that will keep them off the streets, out of trouble and away from drugs."

She was surrounded by a pulsing golden-red aura, all fire and light, the most exciting thing to enter this house in thirty years.

"Surely you can see that our young people need extra motivation to stay straight, considering the problems of this day and age, can't you?"

She was so... alive.

He couldn't think of a more appropriate description.

She was also losing patience.

Boldly arched eyebrows drew together as she frowned down at him. Color not of the fire's making flushed her prominent cheekbones. And her mouth, that mouth that could be so generous in a smile, tightened.

"Mr. Vanmatre, the least you could do is give me a civilized answer of some kind."

He stared. Silent. Fascinated by the pulse that beat in her throat.

An expulsion of breath punctuated her growing frustration. "All right, then. Since you don't want to be bothered, you give me no choice."

She drew herself together. Formidable. Tall and imposing beneath her multicolored coat. Enhanced by the firelight, flashes of purple and turquoise, rose and jade challenged the melancholy of the room.

"I suppose I shall have to find Miss Addy, although I had wanted to spare her... as I'm certain you've created enough disruption and stress in her life for one day."

With that, the fiery woman abruptly strode away and slammed the door behind her, leaving the library as empty and dull and lifeless as she'd found it.

ADMITTEDLY UNNERVED, Echo stalked the hall leading to the kitchen, hoping to find some sign of life there. "Hello?" Empty. "Anyone around?" Uneasiness grew inside her. "Miss Addy?"

Certain she heard low-throated laughter coming from above, a relieved Echo backtracked to the staircase that split the main house in two. She avoided so much as glancing at the library door as she passed it, but couldn't help murmuring, "Mean-spirited, aggravating man."

Halfway up the unlit stairway, she once more announced her presence. "Miss Addy? It's Echo St. Clair."

"Echo, hello." The mellifluous tones of Sibyl Wilde floated down to her. "We're in the upstairs sitting room."

Echo took that as an invitation and rushed right up to the second floor. A moment later, she stood in the doorway of the frontmost room, where she and Miss Addy had had tea on her first visit. Though the hour was not yet advanced, the lady of the manor was wearing a loose white satin nightgown and robe that might have been resurrected from the thirties. Miss Addy had a penchant for what she called "timeless" garments. Her hair—dark as a raven but for the white wings at her brow—spread over her shoulders and fell to her wrist. Thin and frail as she normally appeared, she now looked absolutely wraithlike.

"Come in, come in." She waved Echo over to a table that stood near a window with a view of the lake. "Forgive my state of undress—I'm afraid I didn't remember you were coming."

"I wasn't. I mean, you weren't expecting me. I'm sorry to bother you."

"No bother. Sit," she insisted.

Echo pulled up a chair.

"I always enjoy having company," Miss Addy said. "A body needs live people to talk to. Difficult having a good conversation with Donahue these days," she said of her late brother. "He's so out of touch with the real world." The loose skin around her faded blue eyes crinkled, and her laugh approached a cackle. "That's why I hired Sibyl here. To keep me entertained. Nothing wrong with me that some vitamins and attention can't cure."

Though Echo had heard otherwise, she didn't argue. She glanced down at the table of inlaid wood on which cards had been arranged in a Celtic cross pattern. Echo raised her brows. Sibyl had been reading Miss Addy's tarot. Owner of a New Age shop herself, she recognized the deck as one depicting goddesses from around the world in place of the more traditional images.

That Miss Addy's nurse-companion was into alternate paths really didn't surprise her. The woman played up her exotic looks—tawny-streaked dark brown hair, amber eyes and café au lait complexion—with ethnic touches in her dress and accessories that were reminiscent of the islands.

Noticing that she was wearing a beautiful shell-and-bone necklace that must have some metaphysical significance, Echo said, "That's a wonderful piece of jewelry." She'd never seen anything quite like it. Certain it was one of a kind, she asked, "Who's the designer? I would love to carry some of her work in my shop."

Sibyl fingered the necklace, and the mole at the corner of her mouth twitched. "This is a legacy of my mother's mother. Grandmama Tisa brought it with her when she emigrated from Haiti. I'm afraid the artist is long beyond your reach."

"A shame."

In addition to New Age books and recordings, Echo stocked her shop with art, both the kind to be admired on a wall or shelf and the kind to be worn. Everything she sold reflected the various spiritual avenues of their designers. Healing crystals, angel cards, dream catchers, pyramids... She would carry anything that represented the positive forces of man and nature and what lay beyond. Her shop was a bit unusual for a small town, but Water's Edge was part of a vacation area for Chicagoans and other city dwellers. Surrounding towns were rife with sophisticated galleries, shops and restaurants.

Turning back to Miss Addy, Echo said, "I came because I heard about your nephew's arrival."

A gleam entered the old eyes. "Bram is a good boy. He can be a bit annoying, but then, who isn't?"

Annoying was an understatement. "Yes, I tried speaking with him about the fund-raiser."

"You wanted him to be one of your ghouls, too?" Miss Addy had already insisted *she* be allowed to participate.

"I wanted to make sure he wasn't going to stop the fund-raiser," Echo explained. "Mrs. Ahern seemed to think he'd disapprove."

"That Nancy, always going on about other people's business." Miss Addy clucked. "Well, this time she's wrong. Bram can't disapprove of the Haunted Mansion because he doesn't know about it."

Echo winced. "He does now. I'm afraid I spilled the beans."

"Well, then."

"I'm afraid he wouldn't discuss the situation."

"Stuffed shirt!" Miss Addy grumbled. "Must come from Katherine's side of the family, not from ours."

Not wanting to rub any sore spots or distress the kindly if eccentric woman, Echo tried to be tactful. "So, you don't think there'll be a problem with your nephew, then?"

"Oh, just let him try to muddle things and he'll have me to deal with!" Miss Addy said. "Don't worry your pretty head. Nothing has changed, even if Bram *has* gotten some legal paper that gives him authority over me. Your youth group will have the use of Dunescape Cottage for Halloween. And if Bram tries to stop it . . . why, I'll send him to bed without his milk and cookies."

Echo had been heartened until Miss Addy got to the last bit. The elderly woman wasn't exactly on any plane of reality here.

"What's this about no milk and cookies?" came a deep growl from the doorway.

Miss Addy cackled again. "You know that's the rule if you misbehave, Bram!"

And Sibyl furtively gathered the tarot cards, slipped them into their silk pouch and hid the bundle in the pocket of her full skirt. It was obvious she didn't want Bram Vanmatre to see them. From her own brief experience with him, Echo didn't blame her.

"Excuse me," Sibyl said, rising, her eyes looking past Echo to the man behind her. They suddenly softened into pools of amber light. "But I need to use the telephone."

She moved away from the table in what Echo could only describe as a deliberately provocative slink.

"After I finish my call, I'm going to make Miss Addy her nightly hot chocolate," Sibyl said. "Would you like some, Mr. Vanmatre?"

While the nurse might not want him to know about the tarot cards, her tone of voice left no doubts in Echo that she was definitely interested in the man.

"I'll pass." He sounded amused. "That goes for the milk and cookies, too." He paused only a second before saying, "I see you have a visitor, Aunt Addy."

"Echo," the elderly woman volunteered.

"Pardon me?"

"Her name is Echo St. Clair. Didn't you bother to ask, you naughty boy?"

"Echo," he repeated.

Echo had no choice but to acknowledge him. She turned in her seat and aimed an assessing stare his way. "So, the cat didn't get your tongue, after all."

One eyebrow shot up at her sarcastic comment. "Bram Vanmatre." He held his hand out to her.

For a moment, she was tempted to ignore the overture, as he had done earlier. Telling herself she had better manners, she gave him a shake that was tepid, wholly unlike her normally healthy grip. Still, it felt too personal and she ripped her hand free.

She longed to tear her eyes away from his face as easily, but he was even more arresting than she'd discerned through the gloom of the library. He'd slicked back the black waves of his hair so his face appeared more angular, his features sharper. And now she could see a barely discernable fine scar that slashed his forehead, starting a bit above his right eyebrow and disappearing into his hairline.

He'd changed out of the black silk shirt. Now he was wearing a deep plum turtleneck and charcoal-gray trousers that accentuated his build. He was broad-shouldered and athletic-looking without being bulky. That he kept himself in such good shape annoyed Echo. She didn't want to find him attractive after her frustrating experience in their previous face-to-face.

Bram seemed equally fascinated with her. Eyes the deep blue of the sky at twilight assessed her inch by inch as if he'd never seen her before. She couldn't tell for certain what he thought of her, though she guessed that, in some peculiar way, he found her amusing.

"I would have thought you'd have tired of staring at me by now," she said with a stiff smile.

That's all he'd done earlier, after all—look—he hadn't said a word.

That eyebrow shot up again.

And Miss Addy suddenly rose. "I've got to say goodnight to Donahue. Put the girl at ease, would you,

Bram," his aunt commanded as she swept out of the room, her robe floating behind her.

And Echo realized Bram never took his eyes off her.

"Put you at ease about what?" he asked.

"The fund-raiser." Echo couldn't believe that, after all her talk, Miss Addy had abandoned her to fight it out alone. And to say good-night to her dead brother's ghost, no less. "The Haunted Mansion." And she could hardly believe that Bram's expression revealed no comprehension. "The reason I came to see you today!"

"You came especially for me." He grabbed a free chair, wheeled it around backward and straddled the seat. Folding his arms over the high back, he leaned closer. "How flattering."

She put on a positive face. "Then you won't interfere in our plans."

"Which?"

"To turn Dunescape Cottage into a Haunted Mansion for Halloween," she reminded him, quickly becoming as exasperated as she had when he'd refused to discuss the fund-raiser with her earlier.

Was he purposely being obtuse? But why? He seemed to be amusing himself at her expense. She'd misjudged him, then, for she hadn't thought he had a sense of humor.

"Tell me about it," he suggested, resting his chin on his arms.

"I just did," she said, referring to the scenario in the library.

"In detail."

Maybe he meant the actual plans for transforming the house. "Starting tomorrow, we're turning a bunch of rooms into horror chambers, like Dracula's Crypt and Dr. Frankenstein's Laboratory. We'll set up a specific path, ending with a maze on the lower level. We'll make certain no one strays into the parts of the house that are off-limits. And we're holding a Monster Bash in the ballroom."

"We?"

"The Water's Edge Youth Group," she reminded him. "The teenagers and their parents and sponsors. We're raising funds for the new center. Remember?"

"How could I?"

As if this were the first he'd heard of the plans. Echo gritted her teeth. "Look, I don't know what your game is. All I wanted was some reassurance that you wouldn't interfere with plans made and agreed to by Miss Addy weeks ago. We've already gone to a lot of trouble and expense. And the kids are hyped—"

"Your kids?" he asked, stopping her cold.

"I don't have kids of my own."

"Then what's your interest?"

"Other than having a responsibility to the community in which I live? A nephew. Jason. He's fourteen."

"So you're what? A teacher at the local high school? A counselor?"

"A shop owner. Echoes. You passed it when you came through town."

"Echoes. That New Age store?" Suddenly frowning at her, he pulled back and stood. "Now I get it."

"Get what?"

"The connection. The reason you want to be so chummy with Aunt Addy."

"I barely know your aunt."

"But you want to get to know her better, right?"

"Sure, I wouldn't mind. She's a sweet person." If a little kooky. But that certainly wouldn't prejudice Echo, not with *her* family background.

"And gullible."

She didn't like the way that sounded. "Excuse me?"

"I hope I can."

"Now look, Mr. Vanmatre, I don't know what you're accusing me of—"

"Nothing...yet. But I know all about the pap you sell in your store."

"How dare you!" she cried.

His eyes were like chips of flint. "Crystals with hidden powers. Cards that tell the future. Books on mystical healing. Well, there is no such thing as magic in this world, no inner superpowers to be harnessed. Only pathetic, trusting people who are willing to pay and pay and pay until they are bled dry, and all because they want to obtain something beyond their reach."

Insulted, furious and compelled to defend herself and her customers, Echo jumped up to face him. Though she was five-eight, she had to tilt her head to look him squarely in the eye.

"I sell things that make people feel good about themselves and this universe," she said, her heart pounding. "Things that give people hope when sometimes there is none. Ideas to better the world. I believe we humans have unlimited human potential to be tapped. What do you believe in, Mr. Vanmatre? Making big bucks in your Chicago law practice by overcharging people in desperate circumstances?" Wound up, she passionately demanded, "Don't you believe in the possibility that there might be something beyond what you can see and touch and prove?"

She could swear his face darkened further. He appeared almost apoplectic. The fine scar decorating his forehead that had seemed so faint now stood out in stark relief. And his hands were clenched into tight, threatening fists. She'd touched a nerve. A deep one.

"So help me," he warned her in a voice that throbbed with conviction, "if I hear one word about your scamming my aunt—one word about your reading her runes or channeling spirits for her—you'll have *me* to answer to!"

That he managed to frighten her made Echo as angry with herself as with him. "Mr. Vanmatre, I am an open-minded person with a predilection for the positive. I appreciate the spiritual tools people have created for themselves through the ages. And yes, I know how to use some of them. And I do. For my own enrichment and pleasure. I am not a professional spiritualist. Not a fake. Not a con artist. What you see is what you get."

She could tell that whatever he was seeing about her did not impress him. Echo's stomach sank, and she blamed herself for the loss of Dunescape Cottage as the youth group's Haunted Mansion. She should have handled this differently. She shouldn't have lost her temper.

Blast her temper!

Blast him for riling her like no one had in years!

What now? All the supplies and costumes. All the hopes the kids had. All lost. All because of her. Of who she was. About to storm out of the place and never come back, she was stopped cold when Bram grabbed her arm.

"I thought you came here to get an answer from me."

Her pulse was shooting through her like a bullet. "Didn't you already give it to me?"

"No. Just because I might not like who *you* are doesn't mean I would punish a bunch of kids who are trying to do something constructive."

She wasn't certain she understood him. "You're saying we can have the fund-raiser here?"

"On one condition."

"Which is?"

"That I supervise the transformation of Dunescape Cottage."

Echo's mouth dropped open. The last thing in the world she needed was some closed-minded stuffed shirt looking over her shoulder every step of the way. No, she amended, the last thing she needed was for him to cancel the whole event.

"All right," she agreed. "Expect a work party to arrive tomorrow after school."

She pulled her arm free and stalked toward the door, but was stopped again. "Miss St. Clair, I believe you forgot something."

"Now what?"

She whipped around to see him picking up an object from the floor. A tarot card, one Sibyl must have dropped.

Triumph darkened his expression once more as he held the card out to her, faceup. She glanced at it. The Lovers. How ludicrous!

"No thanks, I don't take what isn't mine." Tempted to tell him where he could stick the damn card, Echo instead said, "Put it under your pillow and maybe you'll have something to smile about in the morning."

Chapter Two

But Bram wasn't smiling the next morning. He'd dreamed not of the lovers on the tarot card, but of something much darker. Something he had to force himself to face.

Something he'd managed not to face for thirty years.

His father's death.

An accidental drowning was the cause of death listed in the official report. His mother, Katherine, had accepted the story. But not Bram. Deep in his heart he knew differently. Something terrible had happened that fateful Halloween night. He felt it in his soul—if he had one, which Echo St. Clair seemed to doubt.

No matter how hard he tried, he just couldn't make the pertinent memories surface.

Slipping into the library where a fire already crackled, Bram thought back....

He'd escaped the annual Vanmatre Fancy Dress Ball for his favorite hiding place. The attic. That memory was clear. Clear, too, was the pain he'd experienced when he'd awakened in Aunt Addy's arms.

She'd been holding him tight, sobbing, "Not you, too. Not Donahue *and* Bram. Please, God!"

And when she'd realized he was staring at her and at the blood on her flowing white costume—*his* blood—a smile so like his father's had wreathed her face and her piteous weeping had turned to tears of joy.

"Thank God," she'd whispered fervently, stroking his cheek. "Thank God. My precious Bram. At least I won't have *your* death on my conscience."

Her words, first of anguish and then of joy, had echoed through his head hundreds of times over the years.

Other words...muddled...confusing...had once echoed, too.

He'd heard voices that night. Only every time he tried to concentrate on them, to bring them into focus, his forehead pounded where he'd split it open on the attic dresser. And the scar would grow white and angry and throb until he stopped.

It was throbbing now. And the flesh across the back of his neck was crawling as if someone were staring at him. A glance around the library assured him he was alone. He swiped at the gooseflesh but didn't manage to make the sensation dissipate totally. Maybe he'd spooked himself thinking about the past.

Long ago, when he was still a child, he'd let his mother convince him it was best to avoid trying to remember.

But he'd never really forgotten.

And now it was time. He had to make it happen, no matter the consequences.

"YOU'RE GOING to make it happen," Isolde St. Clair Medlock insisted, straightening out a display of smudge sticks. "The Haunted Mansion is going to be the hottest, most successful fund-raiser this town has ever seen."

"Right." Leaning on the counter next to the cash register, Echo gave her sister a sardonic smile. "If Bram Vanmatre doesn't make me crazy first."

Izzy's eyes widened in shock. "He doesn't stand a chance. You are the most stubborn if lovable person I've ever known. Except maybe for Jason."

Jason was Izzy's oldest and the reason for Echo's involvement in the fund-raiser. He was also the reason Echo had run away from her grandparents' home only months before high school graduation. When they'd learned eighteen-year-old Izzy had become pregnant, they'd kicked her out. Only seventeen herself at the time, Echo had come flying after her sister without a thought for herself. All she'd known was that they had to stick together, for Mama's sake, as well as their own.

"You think we can talk Mama into coming out for Christmas this year?" Echo asked, thinking their mother had seen Jason and his younger sister, Gussy, only a few times.

Izzy's expression grew sad. "I... I think she's still afraid to leave Portland and come back."

Though their grandparents had been dead for several years, and their former home in South Bend, Indiana, was fifty miles from Water's Edge, Michigan, Mama insisted on staying in Oregon.

"Maybe she'll change her mind this year."

"Maybe." But Izzy didn't sound convinced.

While warm and understanding, Izzy was far more down-to-earth, practical and conservative in her opinions and actions than was Echo. Echo believed that anything was possible if you were willing to fight for what you wanted and believed in.

If she hadn't believed in herself and in the willingness of a small town to support an oddity of a business, she would never have opened Echoes. Not that she'd done it alone. Both Izzy and her husband, Roger, had spent numerous nights and weekends helping her convert a gloomy antique shop into a warm and inviting space filled with objects of optimism. But it had been her vision and her drive that had turned a dream into reality.

Wind chimes tinkled as the front door opened, and Jason came bounding inside, his best friend, Frankie, right behind him. "Ready to go, Auntie E.?"

"If your mom's ready to take over here."

"Ready."

"C'mon, brats."

"Hey!" Jason complained good-naturedly, wrinkling his freckled face. "We teenagers are sensitive, ya know."

"Okay. C'mon, darlings."

"I like 'brat' better," Frankie grumbled, pushing his glasses back up on his long nose.

"Save something for me to do," Izzy ordered. She'd already helped make several ghoul and monster costumes and was on the refreshment committee, as well.

"Don't worry." Echo set the wind chimes tinkling as she opened the shop door. "There's still plenty of work to go around."

She and the boys went out to her beat-up station wagon, which they'd helped her load with decorating materials that morning before school.

"Do we have to pick up anyone on the way?" Echo asked. More than a dozen kids were on the decorating committee.

"A couple of 'em can't come today. Mrs. Ahern said she and one of the other parents are driving the rest."

So the librarian was participating after predicting the event wouldn't come off. Echo wondered if Mrs. Ahern had volunteered to transport the kids, not only because

she was Mark's mother, but so she could get inside
Dunescape Cottage and see what it looked like before its
transformation. Something of the town historian, as well
as librarian, Mrs. Ahern had seemed intrigued by the
mansion's various incarnations. The private home built
with monies made in nineteenth-century Great Lakes
shipping had become the base for a bootlegging operation during prohibition and an exclusive small resort after World War II.

The Vanmatre twins had been responsible for the latter transformation, but after Donahue's death, Miss
Addy had literally closed the doors to outsiders.

Until now.

The town library's van arrived directly before they did.
Reminded of the private library that would be closed to
them, Echo glanced out at the house, which she fanci-
fully thought loomed over the area like a predatory animal, its power only heightened by the growing dusk.

Sure enough, as she had the day before, she spotted the
dark silhouette in the window. Maybe the lawyer would
have the good taste to stay put. She goosed the accelerator and smoothly took the curve toward the front of the
property. Mrs. Ahern and half a dozen kids were spilling
out of the official vehicle as Echo's station wagon lum-
bered up the drive to the front veranda . . . where Bram
Vanmatre stood waiting for them in the deepening shadows.

Echo started. He was certainly capable of moving fast
when the occasion suited him! She would have sworn he
hadn't had enough time to get from the library to the
front porch, but there he was, looking as if he'd been
waiting for a while.

Under his eagle-eyed gaze, Echo self-consciously or-
ganized the teenagers into unloading the boxes of deco-

ration materials from the back of her wagon and setting them in the west front parlor and dining room.

"You can take this," she said, shoving a heavy box into Bram's arms. "You are going to help, right?" She ignored the raised brow. "Not much sense in your standing around idly watching."

Score one for her. The stuffed shirt actually hid something of a smile as he turned to carry the box inside.

Pounding noises drew her attention across the west terrace and pool area, where workmen busy with repairs were being supervised by Uriah Hawkes.

Back at the station wagon, Echo dragged out brooms, dust pans and garbage bags. She'd brought the simple cleaning tools since most of the lower level had been long closed off from use. They would turn several rooms into a dark, spooky maze, so the cleanup didn't need to be intense.

By the time the station wagon was empty, a third vehicle pulled up with Mrs. Zankowski at the wheel and four more teenagers in tow. Waiting until the whole crew was reassembled, Echo divided the kids into three teams, with an adult in charge of each.

Obviously unhappy about being on cleanup detail, Jason complained, "Hey, how come I get stuck doing the gross stuff when I know the boss?"

Echo laughed and ruffled his hair, which was as red as her own. "That's why. You can't say no to me."

Echo watched as everyone disappeared into the house. Everyone but Bram, who was back at his post on the veranda. Leaning against a support, he didn't take his intent gaze off her as she headed up the stairs.

"Keeping an eye on everything at once should keep you busy," she told him. Nothing would make her happier, especially if he kept his attention on the kids rather than on her.

"I'll pace myself."

As would she. "Will Miss Addy be joining us?"

"Isn't it enough that my aunt gave you permission to use her home?"

Echo flushed. "I didn't mean I wanted her to roll up her sleeves and pitch in moving furniture. She was so enthusiastic, I thought she would enjoy watching the kids at work."

"I suggested she get some rest this afternoon."

And Miss Addy had undoubtedly complied rather than put herself under more stress. Echo clenched her jaw and walked by him, not uttering a word of what she was thinking: that his aunt was an adult who could make her own decisions. That Miss Addy didn't need someone taking over "for her own good." That she didn't need her nephew to decide she wasn't fit company for school kids. Miss Addy might be eccentric, but she was harmless.

As harmless as Echo's own mother had been. . . .

Echo's thoughts were interrupted by the activity inside. The two mothers were obviously having difficulty keeping a dozen energetic teens in line. Echo went inside.

"Mark, I told you not to touch anything," Mrs. Ahern insisted.

The librarian took a fancy silver picture frame from her son's hands, but stared at the photos herself before setting it down on the mantel. Then, with a strange expression on her face, she stared at something beyond Echo's shoulder.

Bram again.

Cautioning the teens to be extracareful with the mansion's furnishings, Echo instructed them to pack any

hing breakable into empty boxes that they would store
out of the way. Mrs. Ahern took over in the parlor, Mrs.
Zankowski in the dining room. Herding her own work-
rs to the lower floor, Echo was held up by Bram.

"So what's the theme to be in here?" he asked, glanc-
ng around the parlor.

The teens were disappearing around the back of the
taircase to a door that led to the lower level.

"We're not doing anything special in this room. Mostly
dding atmosphere. We'll sell tickets at the parlor door.
believe your aunt expects to be a ticket taker." Though
he waited for him to object, he didn't. "In costume."
Noting both of Bram's eyebrows shot up this time, she
dded, "It's for a good cause." Luckily for him, he
didn't argue the point. "We have a portrait of Edgar
Allan Poe with eyes that move, a trick mirror, a Dr.
ekyll/Mr. Hyde hologram and a cobra that weaves out
f a basket to spooky music. And mannequin body parts
vill be placed in creative places."

Bram crossed his arms in front of his chest. "It doesn't
ound all that scary to me . . . unless you're about five."

What a spoiler! Or maybe he was trying to get her
oat. From the challenge in his eyes, Echo could believe
he latter. Why in the world was he being so difficult? He
eemed to be holding the tarot card he'd found the night
efore against her, even though she'd denied it was hers.

"Everything about a Haunted Mansion doesn't have
o be real scary. It can just be fun." Laughter drifting
rom the parlor told her the teens in there were having a
reat time now. "You know what fun is, don't you, Mr.
Vanmatre?" she asked deliberately, taking delight in the
ightening of his mouth. "We're starting with the small
tuff and working up to the truly terrifying on the sec-

ond floor. Then visitors will be led back down to th
lower level and the maze.''

"Sounds like an accident waiting to happen," Brar
said, his gaze narrowing. "The stairs, especially. Yo
have bought extra insurance for the event, haven't you
In case someone gets hurt and sues?''

A lawyer *would* think of that. And no, they hadn't
They probably couldn't afford it, either. Why hadn't i
occurred to her before? Not knowing how she was goin
to handle this situation now that she was aware of it, sh
avoided answering directly.

"The stairs will be well lit with red light. Besides whicl
a costumed adult will supervise all stairwells and halls i
addition to each room on the tour.''

"Are you certain you'll have anyone left to *pay* for
tour? This is a fund-raiser. Isn't the object to *mak*
money?''

If Bram Vanmatre said one more negative thing, Ech
would be tempted to punch him!

"Look, I know you're used to a big city where activi
ties get numbers because of the huge population. Bu
small towns can make events like this one work, espe
cially when the word is out to all the other surroundin
towns from Lakeside to Michigan City." She expected th
nearby Indiana residents to be as plentiful as those fror
Michigan state. "The tour is designed to appeal to sma
children as well as adults. The maze is an idea suggeste
by our teens, and the bash in the ballroom will be a hoc
for anyone who can dance or just likes to watch. Wh
wouldn't people take the opportunity to do somethin
that sounds like such fun?''

For the first time, Bram nodded agreeably. "Local
probably wouldn't pass up the opportunity to se
Dunescape Cottage after all these years.''

Something about the way he said that put her on guard. "If you're through..."

About to leave, she halted in her tracks once more when he said, "You didn't tell me about the dining room."

"An unfinished feast. The kids are really enthusiastic about this one." Though she doubted he would be. "Dead rubber bugs. Fake splashes of blood. A sound-activated roasted chicken whose legs wiggle. A pumping heart on a plate."

"Appetizing."

"Exactly." She was out of patience and certain he could hear it in her voice. "I should get downstairs to supervise." Time was flying. Dusk had fallen, casting deep shadows throughout the first floor. "Coming?"

"I'll be along."

Relieved that she'd be free of him for a while at least, she rushed off before he could think of another reason to detain her. Hopefully he wouldn't do his best to discourage the kids who were having such a good time transforming the parlor and dining room.

The stairwell to the basement was dark and naturally spooky. She'd have to see about installing a safety light here. A third of the way down, an errant breeze as seductive as a man's breath ruffled the hair on the back of her neck. A chill crawled down her spine and her flesh pebbled. Though she was the only one on the staircase, she would swear she was not alone. Something about the old mansion got to her every once in a while, made her uneasy, as if something were about to happen. She was disturbed by an internal pressure she didn't understand and therefore couldn't put into words. She'd felt this way the day before, when she'd first approached Bram in the library.

It was eerie.

As if the place really were haunted.

Then the murmur of strained voices ahead connecte
her with the real world again. But her mood swiftl
darkened when she heard one of the girls calling, in
worried voice, "Jason. Jason, can you hear me?"

Heart jumping into her throat, Echo flew down the las
few steps and along the corridor.

Now it was Frankie's voice pleading, "Hey, buddy, it'
me. Say something."

Following the light spilling from an open room, sh
paused in the doorway to catch her breath and assess th
situation. A knot of teenagers crowded around he
nephew, who lay on the floor, seemingly unconsciou:
Blood trickled from his forehead to his cheek.

"Oh, my God, Jason!" she cried, rushing toward him
"I told you guys to be careful. What happened?"

Parting to let her through, the kids avoided answe
ing . . . or looking at her.

But no sooner was she on her knees bending over him
than Jason opened his eyes and gave her a goofy smile
"Gotcha, Auntie E.!"

"Jason Medlock!"

Her nephew whooped and the other kids snickerec
She glared at them as she rose to her feet. "This is n
funny," Echo stated in her most authoritarian voice.

Which made the kids laugh with glee.

"Fake blood looks pretty real, huh?" Jason askec
launching himself to his feet and wiping the stuff from h
forehead with a tissue.

"You're lucky I'm young and tough and have a stron
heart. We'll talk about this later, brat," she promised.

Even while she tried to sound stern, Echo had to swa
low a smile. If she hadn't been so scared, she might b

laughing herself. Her nephew was an inveterate practical joker.

"Now let's all get serious and get to work," she ordered.

More than a half-dozen rooms, some connected by inner doors, were available for their use. From the occasional piece of furniture and shelving that still remained, Echo guessed they'd been mostly servants' quarters or storage rooms. She split the teenagers into two teams and set them working at different ends of the basement, while she took another look around. First they had to make certain the place was free of debris, moving any obstacles out of the way.

They certainly didn't need any *real* accidents.

The question of insurance was preying on her mind when the lights suddenly went out. Thinking her nephew wasn't done with his pranks, she sweetly called, "Oh, Jason, you can turn on those lights now."

"Okay," came his reply. "Where's the switch?"

"How would I know?"

Switch? The whole lower level was shrouded in darkness. A single wall switch wouldn't have turned all the lights off. Of course, the teenagers could be playing a more elaborate joke on her, each of them taking a different room . . . only she hadn't noticed anyone sneaking around. Nervous laughter from a couple of the kids sounded too real to be faked. Maybe the workmen outside had overloaded the electric lines or something.

"Hey, Auntie E., cut it out," Jason called, his voice a bit shaky. "You got me back, okay? Now turn on the lights. This isn't funny."

"She's not trying to be funny" came Cheryl's protest from the other direction. "She's an adult, for heaven's sake."

Amused by that observation, Echo nevertheless realized *no one* was trying to be funny.

"C'mon," complained Yvette. "I don't like this Whoever turned off the lights better turn them back on."

A chorus of "It wasn't me" made Echo think they were experiencing an honest-to-God power failure.

"Maybe a fuse blew," she said in her most reassuring voice. "Has anyone seen the box?"

"Nope."

"Not me."

"Somebody get the lights on!" Yvette cried.

Great! She'd have to stumble around looking for it in the dark. For some reason, the very idea put her on edge.

"Everyone stay where you are," she called. Then she felt a little relieved when she remembered, "I've got a flashlight." Sort of. One of those miniature jobs on her key ring. "Give me a few minutes to find the fuse box."

Rummaging through her jacket pocket, Echo retrieved her keys. A second later, she snapped on the tiny flashlight. When her first sweep of the beam caught a dark figure near the back stairs, she jumped.

Hoping Bram didn't notice, she got a firm grip on her nerves. "You made it down here just in time to save the day. So where's the fuse box?"

He was staring at her intently, making her skin prickle. The same sensation she'd had on the stairs a while ago.

"Or do you even know, considering how long you've been gone?"

His gaze drove into her like a living thing. With flutters threatening to turn her stomach upside down, she laughed nervously. What in the world was wrong with her?

"Hey, what's going on?" Jason called.

"Patience," she replied, sending the light over the nearby walls and into the closest room. Nothing. "The fuse box has got to be around here somewhere."

But where? The lower level was cut up into something of a maze itself, with several twists and turns.

Bram moved off toward the right. Feeling insecure because she wasn't able to see where she was setting down her feet, Echo didn't dare follow as quickly. As she moved, she constantly swept the beam before her. Suddenly she realized Bram was taking her into a part of the basement she hadn't explored before.

Noticing the distance between them had widened considerably, she called after him, "Wait for me, will you?"

Though he glanced over his shoulder, he didn't even hesitate. She sped up, but a second later he vanished, as if he'd been sucked into the very dark. She stopped dead in her tracks, a chill having nothing to do with temperature creeping through her.

"Bram?" Her pulse was crashing through her like waves against the beach during a storm.

"Did you find anything?" came a plaintive cry from the other end of the basement.

"No, but I'm still looking," she called back in the most reassuring voice she could muster.

Cautiously, she inched forward and noticed a half-open door. Is that where Bram had gone? Why the devil hadn't he said something?

Echo stepped inside the room and fought a feeling of alarm when she realized he wasn't there. Trying not to think about how he could have so neatly disappeared on her, she inspected what she could of the interior. An old coal-storage room, from the looks of it. Three bins occupied the opposite wall, looking every bit like primitive jail cells. The thought of being locked in one of them made her shudder. About to leave, she turned smack into something soft.

Another body.

Heart pounding, she gasped aloud. "Bram?"

"Sorry to disappoint you, Miss St. Clair," came a vaguely Eastern European accent.

A second later, the lights went on and Echo heard youthful cheers. Lena Rundle closed the fuse box.

"Why didn't you say something to let me know you were behind me?" Echo asked the housekeeper, who was dressed in a dowdy colorless garment that blended well with their surroundings.

"Why... I did. Perhaps you were so absorbed in your search that you did not hear me."

Though Echo found that hard to believe, she had no reason to distrust the housekeeper, even if she didn't care for the woman. Lena's comfortable-looking, matronly figure was at odds with the continually tight-lipped expression that was accentuated by graying hair scraped firmly back from her face. And this hadn't been the first time the woman had appeared seemingly out of nowhere to startle her, either. On her first visit to the mansion, Lena had almost given Echo a heart attack. She seemed to come and go as mysteriously as Bram just had.

Jamming her key ring back into her pocket, Echo realized something else was odd. "You don't have a flashlight." The housekeeper had been proceeding blindly through the pitch-black basement.

"I do not need one." Lena smiled, her dark eyes remaining flat. "I have lived here since I was a young girl. I know every nook and cranny of this house as if it were my own."

Echo had the distinct impression that Lena Rundle was possessive about Dunescape Cottage, as if it *were* her own...and that she disapproved of its being used for the fund-raiser and considered them all intruders.

"Well, thanks for coming to our rescue."

Lena nodded and Echo set off with a quick check to see if Bram were around somewhere, then flew down the twisting corridor. In her haste, she took the wrong turn and found herself in yet another unfamiliar area. She could hear the kids' voices to the right and behind her. She'd somehow passed them and had landed in another murky area with several paths to choose from. Which way?

Taking a step in the direction from which she'd come, she hesitated. Instinct stopped her. Or something stronger. The atmosphere around her changed subtly, and she felt as if the house were *breathing*. She backed up. It wasn't the house. It was *her*. It was all in her own head.

"Aah!"

A wall forced her to a stop and she accidentally kicked some containers piled against it. A metallic ping whipped her attention to the left. Some small object had rolled to the floor, probably loosened by her clumsiness. She was picking it up when Jason found her.

"There you are. What's that?"

"I don't know. I can't quite see."

Jason led her back in the correct direction. All the while, Echo held on to the object gingerly. Then, in the light, she let it roll into the center of her palm. At first look she thought it was a piece of costume jewelry—an earring or small brooch. But upon closer inspection, Echo identified the object as a fancy button. Something about the way it felt in her hand disturbed her. The metal was too cold. Her palm crawled and she had an urge to drop the thing. Realizing all the kids were watching, however, she got a grip on herself and moved closer to a bare bulb hanging from the low ceiling. There she examined the piece more carefully.

"Awesome, isn't it!" Yvette exclaimed.

"It's something, all right."

While she wasn't an expert on fine jewelry, Echo would swear the gold was real, not plate. The green-and-white stones encrusting the button looked like tiny emeralds and diamonds—a half-dozen finely cut and polished stones of a quarter carat or so. One of the emeralds was loose in its setting.

Although oddly repulsed by its stunning beauty, she murmured, "This really looks valuable."

"What does?"

Echo looked up to see Miss Addy descending the stairs, her expression curious. And movement from the corner of her eye assured her that Lena had not left. The housekeeper remained buried in the shadows.

Watching.

As if she were spying on them.

"I found this button," Echo said, the metal still cold and repellent against her palm.

Wearing a faded party dress that swirled around her too-thin calves, her dark hair coifed in soft, old-fashioned rolls and decorated with a fresh flower, Miss Addy stepped closer. Her gaze on the button Echo held out, she stopped short. Froze. Her lashes fluttered and the breath she took sounded like a gasp of dismay.

"Miss Addy?" Echo stepped closer.

The elderly woman seemed to panic and almost tripped in her haste to back up. Mark caught and steadied her, but she ripped free of his grasp and fluttered her hands at Echo. "No. I don't want it. Get it away from me!"

Realizing Miss Addy was truly frightened, Echo slipped the button out of sight into her jacket pocket, then was uncomfortably aware of its presence on her person. Before she could say something reassuring, Lena flew out of the shadows to put an arm around the frail old shoulders.

"Miss Adrienne, let me take you upstairs."

"It's a bad omen." Miss Addy gripped the housekeeper's free hand. "From the last party. Maybe I shouldn't have opened the house. Maybe Donahue is angry with me."

Lena was nodding as if in agreement, and the teenagers were staring at the scenario in silent fascination.

"I don't understand," Echo said before the housekeeper could take Miss Addy away.

"Mr. Donahue died on All Hallows' Eve thirty years ago," Lena said. "After the last fancy-dress ball held here."

A collective gasp issued from the kids.

"Then how can he be angry?" demanded a practical Jason.

"People think he's long gone, but he's not," Miss Addy said. A wild glint appeared in her faded eyes as she looked around as if expecting to see him. "He's here with us, waiting for justice. That's why I can't ever leave this place. Bram can't make me. Donahue was my twin, you know. I must stay until his spirit is at rest."

Echo tried to calm her. "But his death was an accident—"

"Lies! Donahue's drowning was no accident!" Miss Addy shrieked. "My brother was murdered!"

Chapter Three

Murdered.

She hadn't pried that out of the old lady before. Then again, she hadn't seen Adrienne Vanmatre so distraught, not since she'd finally found the opportunity to insinuate herself into life at the crumbling manor. She'd waited for so long. Too long. But she had learned to be a patient woman.

"You been having those dreams again, Miss Addy?" Sibyl Wilde asked her charge as she tucked the frail bones into a chaise near the fire, which, with the help of one small lamp, cast eerie shadows throughout the otherwise dark room.

"Dreams . . . reality . . . Where does one end, the other begin?"

"Sometimes it's hard to say," Sibyl agreed, staring into the greedy flames.

She'd been haunted by dreams all her life, and they weren't reality yet. Soon, though. She could feel it in her bones. Soon all the plotting and waiting would end and she would have the reward that was her due.

Her inheritance.

"Grandmama Tisa used to do the dreaming when she was awake. She taught me that spirits are all around us."

Miss Addy's face brightened. "You believe me, then? About Donahue?"

"Of course."

"Well, good. I wasn't certain. Most people think I'm a loony old bird."

Yes, Sibyl thought, though she'd never seen him herself, if Donahue Vanmatre had been murdered, she did believe his soul still wandered about Dunescape Cottage seeking release. Of course, she would say so even if she didn't believe it—she wasn't about to let this great opportunity slip by. While Miss Addy was always talkative, she normally rambled in circles or went off on tangents, never quite getting to the subject Sibyl most longed to discuss.

"Could your grandmother call up those spirits when she wanted to?"

Sibyl nodded and fed another log to the hungry flames. "Grandmama Tisa was a powerful obeah woman." Even if she *had* left Haiti as a very young woman.

"What about you?"

Heartbeat growing stronger, she gave her patient a slanted look. "I have some talent in this area, yes."

"Teach *me.*"

"Why?"

"So I can talk to Donahue."

"But you said you had."

"Yes, yes," Miss Addy said impatiently. "Being that we were twins, we have a special connection. I feel his presence here always, but he doesn't necessarily appear to me when I want him to, and he leaves whenever the heck he feels like it. I never have enough time to settle some things between us. If only he would actually talk to me." She cackled. "Even dead, Donahue has a mind of his own. I want to be able to find him!"

Sibyl considered this and came up with a plan. "Not everyone has the power."

"How can you tell if I do or not?"

"You must be able to go into a trance easily. Perhaps if you let me hypnotize you..."

She let the suggestion hang, not wanting to sound too eager and thereby take the chance of souring the deal before she could take advantage of the situation.

A cunning expression crossed the old lady's face. "Hypnotize me, huh? Why would you need to do that?"

Sibyl thought quickly. "I can lead you back into the past, to the events that led to tragedy, to the time when your brother hung between life and death. Perhaps if you can connect with him there, you'll be able to call him back yourself whenever you want."

And she would be able to find out what she wanted to know. Nearly four months had gone by with her rotting just like this old mansion, and with nothing to show for it. But if the old lady agreed to this...

"When do we start?"

Sibyl smiled.

THINKING THEY'D MADE a good start despite the disruption, Echo waved to Jason as he and Frankie squeezed into the library's van. She reentered the house and walked toward the library door, fingering the mysterious button she'd stuck in her pocket nearly an hour ago. After getting Miss Addy calmed and taken care of by the nurse, she'd made sure her team had finished cleaning the lower level before joining their friends on the first floor. All in all, everyone was satisfied with what they'd accomplished in such a short time and they were raring to come back for more the next afternoon.

Not necessarily expecting an answer—he'd chosen to ignore her interruption the day before, after all—she knocked at the library door.

Bram's immediate "Come in" surprised her somewhat.

Again, the fire was blazing, but this time he sat behind a mahogany desk. The green glass shades of its twin brass lamps glowed, the lights themselves casting a golden sheen over the man and giving the room a different, softer feel. Less claustrophobic.

Still, she couldn't quite relax. There was something about this room . . . that unsettled her. A sense of gloom and doom, of emotions suppressed and ready to explode.

"The kids are gone," she said.

"That time already?" Bram checked his watch. "I got tied up with a long-distance call." He indicated the papers strewn across the desk. "Just because I take some time off doesn't mean my work won't follow me."

"After we got the lights back on, I found this." Noting his puzzled expression, she held out her hand.

Taking the button from her, he said, "Sit," indicating the chair facing him next to the desk. His brows shot up when he took a good look at the jeweled piece. "Wonder where this came from."

Following his lead, Echo sat. She couldn't help looking around, giving the room a once-over, expecting to see someone else. . . . Of course, there was no one. The reputation of the house just wouldn't leave her alone.

"Your aunt mentioned the last fancy-dress ball held here."

He sank against his high-backed chair and stared at her. "That was thirty years ago. Hard to believe something this valuable could go unnoticed for so many years, though as far as I know, Aunt Addy hasn't been throwing any parties lately.''

⌃ Though she hated to do it, Echo said, ''Miss Addy thinks our finding it now is an omen.'' He would, after all, hear about the outburst soon enough, perhaps from his aunt herself. ''She thinks Donahue's angry that she's reopened the mansion to outsiders.''

''My father is *dead*.''

''Yes.''

''If you already know that, why bother me with this pap?''

Because she felt as if they might be back to square one. ''What if Miss Addy changes her mind—''

''Still worried about the fund-raiser? Don't.'' Though his words might have been meant to be reassuring, his expression certainly wasn't.

''Even if she doesn't want us here?''

''My aunt's not making sound judgments these days. Actually, it's been a very long time since she has.''

Feeling edgy about the implications of Bram making judgments *for* Miss Addy, Echo asked, ''How would you know? You haven't been around. From what I hear, you haven't been back—''

''Since my father died? True. That doesn't mean I don't know everything that's going on here. I've made it my business to know.'' In reaction to her skeptical expression, he said, ''I engaged the law firm that has seen to Aunt Addy's monetary affairs for the last dozen or so years. And I'm the one who hired Sibyl Wilde to take care of her when it became clear that she wasn't properly seeing to her own health.''

Echo couldn't help herself. ''So why did you come back now?''

"My aunt is losing it, not that it's any of your business. As you've heard for yourself, she believes my father is still here, among the living."

He gestured with his hands as if Donahue Vanmatre might be with them at this very moment. As if in response, a draft swept through the room, making the fire flare and the hair on the back of Echo's neck bristle. She caught her breath. That feeling again, stronger than ever. She stared at Bram. For a moment, he, too, seemed aware of the disturbance in the atmosphere. But he quickly closed himself off from it.

Getting hold of herself, she said, "From what I've been told, Miss Addy has always believed that your father's ghost walks here—as, I might add, do many of the residents of Water's Edge."

Bram glared. "Does that include *you?*"

The back of her neck still tingled. "I believe it's possible that someone's spirit might linger, yes." She smoothed the hair at her collar. "But even if your father has been at rest all these years, even if there's no ghost, Miss Addy isn't harming anyone by believing otherwise."

"She's harming herself."

"That's ridiculous!"

"Is it? Look around . . . or are you blind? This place is a mess. Crumbling from the inside out."

A fact that was impossible to miss, but Echo was certain the reason had little to do with Miss Addy's superstitious nature. "Many elderly people don't have the money to keep up their homes. And this property would be tremendously expensive to maintain. No doubt she's run out of funds."

"It wasn't Dunescape Cottage that broke her financially."

The way he said it made her ask, "What then?"

"Her obsession with her dead twin."

"I don't understand."

"Over the years, Adrienne Vanmatre has been the tar get of every con artist that has come along." Bram sa forward and his eyes reflected his derision. "She's con sulted palmists and tarot readers, she's sought out peo ple claiming to have ESP. She's even held séances an hired a team of ghostbusters—not to get rid of my fa ther's ghost, mind you, but to call him out so she coul talk to him."

He did make Miss Addy sound more than mildly ec centric. "I—I didn't know."

"Why do you think the locals call her Crazy Addy?" Bram asked, his angular features darkening. "She's bee taken advantage of, fed a lot of hooey, ripped off in major way so that she's in danger of losing Dunescap Cottage to back taxes. The original portion of this hous was built by my family before the turn of the century. can't let it slide into the dumper if I can prevent that fron happening."

Which was his greater concern—his aunt or Dunescap Cottage? Miss Addy hadn't had children, and Bram wa the only child of her only brother. He stood to inherit th place. Was that his interest? Protecting an investment fo the future?

"So why wait so long?" She couldn't hide her ow censure. "Why didn't you help your aunt out years ago maybe involve yourself personally in her life before thing got to this desperate point?"

"I don't need to explain myself to you," he said coldly "Suffice it to say that I'm in charge now."

Realizing she'd hit another nerve, she pressed her advantage. "What does that mean? That you're moving in?"

"I hadn't seriously considered that option."

At least, not for the present. "That you're moving Miss Addy out, then?"

"I'll decide what's *best* for her. As for me—"

"Surely you don't mean to institutionalize her."

A vision flashed through Echo's mind, the image so strong it nearly brought tears to her eyes. Her mother sitting silently, rocking, not recognizing her own daughters. The electric shocks that had forever erased parts of Mama's memory had supposedly been for her own good.

"Please, *please* tell me you're not going to institutionalize her," Echo begged.

Appalled at her own heartfelt outburst, Echo held a shaking hand to her mouth. She struggled for the breath that came too shallow and only with great difficulty. The room went dead silent but for the sputtering of a log in the fire.

Bram was staring at her as if he'd never seen her before.

"I haven't decided what my aunt needs yet," he finally said. "At the moment, I'm concerned with making certain the place is safe. That's why I've brought in workmen."

"Y-yes." Her fingers dug into the arms of her chair. "I saw them earlier doing something out by the pool."

"They're repairing the retaining structure that's keeping the pool and terrace from sliding into the lake. The terrace is built so far out, the high tide nearly floods it."

He was watching her carefully, as if looking for signs that she was ready to lose control again. Echo forced away the feeling of humiliation that was all too familiar

and that she thought she'd successfully overcome year
ago.

"First thing next week, a contractor will give me a
estimate of what it'll cost to bring the building up t
code," Bram went on. "Until I have a clear picture of th
financial situation, I won't be making any permanen
plans."

For himself or his aunt? "Start with the electrica
work," Echo said, calm and in control once more.

"Electrical work?" he repeated.

"More power, for a start. And a breaker box some
place where you can get to it easily, instead of the ar
chaic fuse box in the coat bin."

Bram started. "What were you doing in the coal bin
Surely Aunt Addy didn't give you permission to use tha
area."

"I thought *you* went in there."

"Why would I be in the coal bin?" he asked, as if h
didn't remember her following him in that direction.

"I don't know. You just disappeared and..."

Bram was giving her that weird look again, making he
sink into silence. What was going on here? Was he a
loony as his aunt? Echo didn't want to consider the a
ternative—that *she* had something to worry about.

Gathering herself together, she rose. "I really ought t
be leaving."

"I'll see you to the door."

Was he afraid she might not make it all the way out
Realizing the conversation, and especially the blast fror
the past, had left her feeling overly sensitive, she didn
object as he followed her from the room.

BRAM STUCK TO ECHO like glue across the foyer. The
stopped near the front door. He almost thought to apo

ogize for having been so rude earlier. But he'd had reason to suspect Echo St. Clair of being a fraud. He still did, though he'd softened to her some. Anyone who could convince him that she was honestly concerned about Miss Addy couldn't be all bad. Of course, he'd gotten the distinct impression that she'd had to dig deep for that outburst of emotion. Whatever the reason, he'd responded to her.

He was responding to her now. He was attracted to Echo despite his good sense.

"So is everyone coming back tomorrow?" he asked.

"As far as I know. Same time, same place, same faces."

"Including yours?"

She was staring at him at the scar on his forehead. She seemed perplexed. "Uh, right. I'll be here, too."

"Good." Then he would be able to spend more time with her, maybe psyche her out a bit.

Bram wasn't going to fool himself—there was still the tarot card he'd found in Aunt Addy's sitting room. If Echo hadn't dropped it, who had? He simply wasn't certain if he could take Echo at face value or if she had ulterior motives for wanting to get to his aunt. That was the reason he'd been so straight with her about his aunt's finances.

No, he couldn't be certain of Echo St. Clair's ethics. Yet.

But something told him he would find out exactly what kind of woman she was, and he'd enjoy doing so. And why wait? Why not now? "So what are your plans for the rest of the evening?"

Before Echo could answer, loud voices coming from outside startled them both.

"Don't be disturbing people, Ferguson!" Uriah Hawkes ordered.

But from the *bam, bam, bam* at the front door, Aunt Addy's neighbor was ignoring the groundskeeper.

"Vanmatre, you in there?" a deep voice demanded.

"Sounds like someone really wants to see you," Echo said.

Bram merely grunted and jerked open the door. A sandy-haired man immediately filled the doorway. He was slightly taller than Bram—probably six-one or so—and powerfully built.

"Travis, isn't it?" Bram recognized him, though he hadn't seen Travis Ferguson since they were kids.

The man nodded. "Been a long time, Vanmatre."

Not long enough for Bram, unless Travis had changed from the obnoxious thug he'd been as a kid.

"Let's get down to business." Travis didn't mince words. "Keep your workmen off my property."

Immediately irritated by the man's high-handed approach, Bram pushed past him onto the veranda where Uriah Hawkes waited, hat in hand, his face thunderous. "I tried dealing with Ferguson myself, but—"

"No problem, Uriah. Go on home. I'll take care of this."

The groundskeeper gave Travis an especially black look before retreating to the coach house over the garage. Bram peered out to the west and the Ferguson property—not that he could see much in the dark. He did make out a white-haired old man staring back at him from the distant porch. The only illumination on the beach in any direction came from the homes lining the dune.

"I didn't know the workmen were on your property," Bram admitted. "You say they did some kind of damage?" He couldn't help but sound disbelieving.

"They screwed up my beach."

Of course. He hadn't forgotten how impossible the shore residents could be. Most posted signs that threatened strangers with a royal fine if they so much as walked on the sand of a private beach.

"Define 'screwed up.'"

"Your workers left chunks of old concrete from the retaining wall strewn all over!" Travis said heatedly.

"And they spent the better part of their lunch hour sprawled down near the waterline!" came a familiar voice from the next porch. "Don't forget that!"

Bram realized he was hearing from Norbert, Travis's father, another unpleasant sort, from what he remembered.

"I'll take care of it, Dad!" Travis shouted to the white-haired man in return.

"When the workmen arrive in the morning," Bram said, "I'll tell them to clean up the debris immediately and instruct them to lounge on the Dunescape beach if they're so inclined. Will that satisfy you?"

"Yeah, I guess."

Travis's attention shifted away from Bram and back to the doorway of the house. Bram followed his gaze to see Echo standing there, silently taking in the altercation. The light from the foyer surrounded her with a golden glow, an appealing aura of sorts. Once again, he realized he was a bit taken with her.

"I know you," the big, sandy-haired man said as he stepped toward her. "You're the owner of that New Age shop in town, right?"

Nodding, she smiled and identified herself. "Echo St. Clair."

And she held out her hand. Bram didn't like the way she connected firmly with Travis—she'd been lukewarm about greeting *him* the night before—and he didn't like the way Aunt Addy's rude neighbor lingered over the touch before letting her hand go.

"I didn't realize you had company, Vanmatre." Travis was staring down at Echo with a provocative expression. "You know, I've been meaning to come into your shop just so I could meet you."

"How flattering. Well, now that we've met, don't be a stranger. Actually, I was just leaving." Her smile faded as her gaze shifted to Bram. "I'll see you tomorrow afternoon. And it was nice meeting you at last, Mr. Ferguson."

"Travis."

"Travis," she repeated.

Both men watched her race down the stairs and climb into her station wagon.

Echo was barely starting the engine before Travis said, "She's a real looker. Back in town for a day and you've already got a beautiful lady visiting. Fast worker."

No matter what he did or said, Travis seemed to know how to push Bram's buttons. "Echo is transforming Dunescape Cottage for the Haunted Mansion fundraiser," he said, his voice tight.

"Oh, yeah, I got a beef about that, too. I told Crazy Addy to put a stop to the idea as soon as I heard about it, but she wouldn't listen to me."

Hardly believing the man was mouthy enough to insult his aunt in his presence, Bram took pleasure in reminding him, "This is Vanmatre property. She doesn't need your permission to do as she sees fit."

"But we've got to put up with noise we don't want. And not only will people be parking illegally along Water's Edge Drive, their kids will be swarming all over our shoreline."

The damned beach again. "We'll do our best to see that doesn't happen. Why don't you do your best to remember it's for a good cause."

Bram surprised himself. He was talking as if he had a personal stake in the fund-raiser. Maybe it was just that he didn't like the adult Travis Ferguson any more than he had liked the boy. He definitely was taking pleasure in thwarting him.

"Any damages and I'm holding *you* responsible," the sandy-haired man threatened.

"I wouldn't have expected any better from you."

With a growl of frustration, Travis whipped around and stalked away from Bram, who waited until his aunt's neighbor was back on his own property. Still out on the porch, Norbert was muttering something to him in a low tone, and Travis barked an answer, but Bram couldn't make out more than the discontent both men must be feeling at having been foiled.

Shaking his head at the unexpected and unpleasant invasion, he was about to enter the house when he noticed car lights sweeping across the grounds.

"Now who?"

Wondering if Echo might have forgotten something and was returning put him in a better frame of mind. The woman certainly was growing on him. But it wasn't her station wagon that pulled up the drive. Recognizing the silver BMW Bram stepped off the veranda with mixed emotions. The driver exited the car reluctantly, then stood staring at the house as if in shock at its condition.

Moonlight made her pale hair, artfully pinned into a French twist, glow silver. Whatever the light, she still looked closer to his own age than fifty-seven. Holding out his hands in welcome, he approached her.

"Hello, Mother."

"Bram, darling."

They kissed cheeks. No messy hugs. He might wrinkle her perfectly tailored suit that showed off her well-kept, youthful figure.

"What are you doing here?"

"I might ask the same of you," she said, sounding wounded. "When I got back from London and heard what you were about, I couldn't allow you to go through it alone."

A smile slid through Bram's defenses. "Go through it?"

"The trauma you must be experiencing coming back here after all these years."

"I hadn't thought of my returning in quite that way." Leave it to his mother to dramatize the situation. While his visit might spark unpleasant memories, he certainly wouldn't be traumatized by them. In fact, he welcomed the truth he couldn't remember. "Did you bring bags?"

"In the trunk." She held out her keys. "You didn't even hint at your plans before Joel swept me away from Chicago on business," she said of her fourth and youngest husband, who was only a dozen years older than Bram. "Has something untoward happened? What are you up to, exactly? And how long do you plan on staying in this...place?"

He grinned at the rapid-fire questions. "I'm here to see to the well-being of both the property and Aunt Addy. However long that takes," he said firmly, removing the three suitcases she'd packed.

It looked as if she, too, was planning to stay indefinitely, undoubtedly as long as he. But why?

"You could have let the local lawyers handle it."

"No, Mother, it was time." Time to face the past.

"You're not thinking of moving here?"

The second person to ask him that. He hadn't come with that intention, but...

"I don't know," he finally answered. "Anything is possible."

He led the way up the stairs. His mother's heels clacked after him in a way that let him know she was annoyed. Katherine Anderson Vanmatre Bodreaux Whitney Quinlan took charge whenever the whim suited her and she was clearly displeased that she had no control over this particular situation. Knowing from experience her efforts would be useless, she hadn't bothered trying to take charge of him in years. And it had been even longer since she'd acted truly "motherly"—not since he was a kid.

So why now? What scheme was fomenting in that beautiful head of hers?

Why would she choose to install herself indefinitely in a former residence that she'd never liked and had wasted no time leaving after his father's death?

"My goodness, Adrienne has let this place rot," she murmured as she followed him inside. "Your father must be spinning in his grave."

Bram set the bags down in the foyer and, with a straight face, said, "Perhaps you'll have the opportunity to ask him yourself."

Her individually glued-on lashes fluttered alarmingly. "Pardon me?"

"Aunt Addy talks to him, though she says he's not exactly chatty himself. Maybe you'll have better luck."

"Don't be ghoulish."

As if on cue, Lena appeared at the head of the stairs and gasped, "Miss Katherine?"

The housekeeper looked as if *she'd* seen a ghost. Undoubtedly the former Katherine Vanmatre was the last person she'd expected. Bram remembered the day his mother had taken him away to her parents' home in Chicago. She had vowed never to set foot in Dunescape Cottage again.

"Lena," he said, snapping the tension that hung among them all, "do we have a suitable room available for my mother's use?"

"Bram darling, don't be ridiculous." His mother's voice was unnaturally tight. "This used to be a resort. There must be a dozen available rooms."

He quirked a brow at her. "If you don't mind sharing them with a monster or two."

He quickly caught her up on the fund-raiser activities. While her features pulled into a frown, she didn't voice disapproval as he'd expected.

Still at the head of the stairs, Lena volunteered, "Miss Adrienne did not give the townspeople permission to use your old quarters, Miss Katherine. And they are cleaned once a week as is the rest of the main house."

Bram would swear his mother blanched.

"Adrienne might object to *my* using them, as well."

"Nonsense," he said. "Aunt Addy put me right back into my old rooms." Although he had insisted on having a larger bed moved in from the guest wing. "I'm sure she would be fine with your staying there. Unless *you* object."

"No. No. Why should I?"

Though he had the distinct feeling his mother was lying, he wasn't about to say so. Instead, he played the dutiful son and carried her bags upstairs. His parents' suite—sitting room, bedroom and bath—was exactly as he'd remembered. Only now the papered walls and furnishings seemed shabby, even though no one had used the suite in thirty years. As she paced the sitting room, his mother seemed nervous.

Lena pulled the heavy drapes closed over the windows. "Quite a coincidence. First the button turns up...then you arrive...and both in the same night."

"What button?" his mother asked.

Bram explained. "One torn from a ball costume."

"Miss Adrienne believes someone lost it the night Mr. Donahue died." Lena stared right through his window. "I shall tell Miss Adrienne you have arrived," she said, then left without looking back.

Bram hadn't a clue as to why the housekeeper thought his mother would be interested in a lost button, but he realized his mother seemed even more agitated than she had a few minutes ago. Her fingers were plucking at the stray hairs around her neck.

"Mother, are you all right?"

"It's this house. It feels...odd" was all she would say. She just missed meeting his eyes. "Give me time to unpack and freshen up. I'll meet you downstairs."

"All right. You'll find me in the library. I have some work to finish up that I need to fax to Chicago tomorrow, but it won't take long. Then we can have tea in front of the fire and you can tell me all about London and Joel."

"That sounds marvelous."

Bram rushed back downstairs, but upon reentering the library, his mind wasn't on his work. The talk of the button reminded him he hadn't yet secured the valuable object, which he'd left in full view on his desk.

Sinking into his chair, he held the gem-studded gold disk to one of the lamps. Odd that the button had been secreted on the lower level. Now that he thought back, he realized guests at Vanmatre family balls had normally been confined to the main floor—the ballroom and parlors. He couldn't imagine what one of the guests had been doing wandering around below, or how the button could have gotten torn from his or her costume.

A log popped and Bram started. As usual, the library felt alive. Filled with another presence. Ghosts? A nonbeliever in specters, Bram grimaced. His own ghosts, perhaps, the kind that lived inside a man, were getting to him. He was trying to make a connection with the past, with his father's death, and this had been Donahue Vanmatre's favorite room.

The things he felt in here had to come from his own imagination. His own sense of frustration. His own sense of loss.

His own growing belief that, even if Aunt Addy were deluded in her fantasies about his father's ghost roaming the house, she might have been correct about his death.

For years he'd put his inner life on hold. He had a brilliant law career, escorted beautiful, smart women to exclusive social events. But it was all surface, and he was sick of it. Something kept him from making the life for himself that he really wanted. He longed for a sense of community. Friends. Family. People he deeply cared about. Things he didn't even know how to go about getting.

Things his father had before he'd died.

Perhaps been murdered.

He stared at the button. Unbidden, the sound of a struggle echoed through his mind.

Heavy breathing . . .
. . . muffled curses . . .
. . . knuckles against flesh . . .

Startled by the sudden shift to the past, Bram tried concentrating. Nothing more would come but a throbbing at his temple. He focused on the bauble in his hand and fingered an emerald that was loose in its setting. The tiny gems glowed back at him like a half-dozen miniature eyes.

He waited in vain.

Finally setting the button in the top right-hand drawer of the desk and securing the lock, he couldn't stop wondering . . .

What might those lifeless eyes have seen that fateful night thirty years before?

FOR THIRTY YEARS, dark secrets and lies had smothered all the life out of Dunescape Cottage.

Staring out into the darkness, perhaps for the first time he considered that things could be different. He had been trapped in a timeless warp of the everlasting present. One day had followed the other, all the same. No past. No future. No reason to feel. No reason to hope.

The lake was restless tonight, and so was he.

The urge to roam was strong. The house had been upended by all the activity. He had been upended, too.

Suddenly the past was catching up to the present. And with the realization had come anger. Outrage.

And a belated need for justice.

Chapter Four

I know her as well as I know myself!

The familiar declaration invaded Bram's sleep. He was aware of this being a dream ... and yet not. A memory was surfacing.

Even that she's my mistress?

Mistress? Whose mistress?

She wouldn't do that, not take up with someone like you!

He fought to tarry in the early morning world of half sleep, where imaginings based on reality danced through the mind ...

Shall I tell you the details?

... but, as always, he was unsuccessful.

Fully awake whether he would or no, Bram sat straight up in bed, skin damp with sweat. The words in his dream had been as clear as any he might have heard. He *had* heard them, long ago. He rubbed the throbbing scar at his temple to still the pain.

His mother's arrival had sparked the dream.

His mother. Here. Why had she come after vowing never to set foot in Dunescape Cottage again? After a lifetime of discouraging him from confronting his past?

Bram struggled out of bed and into the bathroom. In the shower, he considered the implications of voices.

His mother was on her fourth marriage. There had been other men between. Maybe during. He was an adult. He could deal with the reality of a woman being unfaithful to her husband.

If that's all it was. . . .

For years, his mother had tried to convince him the voices hadn't been real, and believing he'd had a nightmare had been easier for a seven-year-old to accept. But part of him had always known the voices *had* been real and they had come from *somewhere*. The old mansion was studded with hidden crannies and tunnels and even a few secret rooms dating back to its days as an alcohol distribution point during prohibition.

Out of the shower, Bram toweled off, threw on black trousers and shirt, and scraped at his hair with his fingers.

Grabbing a flashlight, he made a foray into the lower level using one of the hidden interior staircases, this one accessed through a second-floor linen closet. Someone else had been there before him—dust on the bannister had been disturbed and footprints made a path into the coal bin.

Echo had been in the coal bin, he mused.

Once on the lower level, he looked for the hidden rooms, but the basement—practically a maze—confused him after so many years. Aunt Addy had to know every inch of the place. Thinking of her strong reaction to the button, Bram climbed the main stairs and headed for the library to fetch the bauble.

Wood burning in the fireplace surprised him, and he wondered who had set the logs so early. Perhaps thinking he wanted to get to work first thing, Lena had decided to take the chill off the room for him.

Once again, though, he felt as if he weren't alone. It was as if someone were standing behind him, looking over his shoulder. His gaze swept the room. Empty. But he couldn't shake the odd feeling, nor the frame of mind that left him speculating. He would swear he sensed . . . emotions. A grab bag of happiness and regret . . . and, above all, frustration.

Ridiculous. He was merely in touch with his own anxiety.

Still, a slithering sensation disturbed the back of his neck as he pulled the key from its not-so-hidden resting place—a fancy stamp box at the edge of the desk. Unlocking the drawer, he frowned when he didn't immediately see the button. Perhaps it had rolled between sheets of stationery. He riffled the contents and finally pulled the drawer free and dumped everything on top of the desk.

The button was gone!

But who would have taken it?

Probably everyone on the estate knew about the recovered button and had access to the desk. The key wouldn't have been difficult to find.

Still, he'd thought a locked drawer was safe enough. . . .

"Donahue, there you are!"

Startled by his aunt's voice, Bram spun around, half expecting to see some shadow in a corner that could be taken for his late father. But she was staring directly at *him,* as if he were a ghost. Dressed in an old-fashioned flowing garment at least a size too big, she looked otherworldly herself.

"Sorry to disappoint you—"

"I can't believe it worked!" Her frail body trembled with excitement. "She said it would, but I doubted her—"

"Doubted who?" Echo?

"You're speaking to me!" She swept forward, her eyes wide, her hands fluttering around her wrinkled face, which was wreathed in a triumphant smile. "Say something else, Donahue, please, so that I know I'm not dreaming!"

"Aunt Addy, it's Bram."

Her happy expression puckered, communicating her sudden confusion. "Not Donahue?" A bony hand darted forward to lift the hair from his brow, and her faded eyes reflected a deep disappointment as they took in the scar. "Bram."

Aware he looked much like his father—Donahue Vanmatre had died at thirty-seven, his age now—Bram accepted that his aunt might mistake him for her twin. What he couldn't accept was her thinking she was speaking to a ghost. Not when he couldn't quite shake the sensations that were starting to make him edgy.

"My father is dead, Aunt Addy."

"Dead but not forgotten."

Noting the quick tears that spilled onto hollow cheeks, he said, "No one expects you to forget."

"They do. They all do. But I won't. Never. That's why I stay here. To be with him."

Concerned that she was becoming overagitated, Bram backed off. "I know the two of you had many happy times in this house."

"And we will again," she insisted, moving toward the fire. "It's only a matter of time." She sat in one of the high-backed chairs and stared into the flames. "Once

Donahue's murderer is brought to justice, we can all be happy again.''

Bram gave his aunt a decidedly *un*happy look. Aunt Addy had always been a bit eccentric. And, yes, she'd taken his father's death hard. They'd kept up with each other via letters and telephone calls and the many visits she'd made to Chicago to see him during his youth. But now too often she strayed past eccentric and became totally out of touch with reality. That worried him. If it were a matter of her physical health only, he would entrust her care to Sibyl Wilde indefinitely. But her mental health was another matter.

He wasn't certain he could turn his back on Aunt Addy by leaving her virtually alone when he returned to Chicago. Who knew what straits she might get herself into? What harm she might cause? Though he had tried his best to stop her, she had already managed to run through her considerable fortune and was nearly destitute.

He supposed he ought to start looking into care facilities for the elderly. If one would take her. He didn't want to think about having her "institutionalized," as Echo St. Clair had feared.

Remembering he'd meant to talk to his aunt about the house's secret rooms, Bram took the vacant chair in front of the fireplace and gave her a long searching look. She seemed calm. More composed than he, certainly. Sitting here...in his father's chair... His pulse raced and he was aware of his own growing expectancy. Ruthlessly, he shut down what he chose not to address and got back to the task he'd meant to accomplish.

"Aunt Addy, are there blueprints for Dunescape Cottage?"

"Of course. Somewhere. Donahue would know. Ask him.''

Avoiding feeding into her fantasy, he asked, "Do you remember if they detailed everything? The passageways and hidden rooms?"

His aunt wagged a finger at him. "You're not supposed to go there. You know your father told you not to." She was going off into her own world again.

Bram took her hand to ground her. She felt so fragile, unlike the woman who'd held him so fiercely after finding him unconscious in the attic. "That's when I was a child. Father wouldn't mind anymore."

Her gaze refocused. "Yes. You are grown-up." She cackled. "You wouldn't get lost now."

Bram grinned. He had gotten lost once. Locked in one of the hidden rooms. It had been Addy who'd found him then, too. So she did remember things.

"If you don't know where the blueprints are, maybe you could show me the hidden rooms yourself." Bram wasn't even certain why he needed to see them, he only knew he did.

"And give up the house's secrets?" She shook her head vehemently. "No. Not that again. A mistake."

"What do you mean, not *again?* Who did you show before?" One of the supposed psychics who had ripped her off? Echo?

But she had shifted gears and was off on another tangent. "All Hallows' Eve is almost upon us. Have you chosen your costume?"

Bram doubted she was referring to the Halloween fund-raiser. "For the ball? Not yet," he said, figuring it wouldn't hurt to indulge her. He also saw his opportunity to get to the other subject on his mind. "Didn't someone lose a button at the last ball?"

"Do you remember the costume you wore then? Katherine picked it out without asking you, of course."

She shook her head. "How you hated that cape. Called it 'dopey.'"

"Aunt Addy, about the button. Your friend Echo found it downstairs yesterday."

He squeezed her hand, but she shook it free and popped out of the chair. "I don't know anything about buttons!"

But he could tell she did know something. He rose and pressed the issue. "Yes. You saw it. You said it was an omen."

Her mouth opened and silently closed again. And in her eyes, he read what could only be fear. Of him?

"I'm sorry, but I promised. It's for a good cause, Donahue. It's for the children. They'll take it all away. In a week, you won't even know anyone has been here."

There she went, mentally off kilter, mixing him up with his father's ghost.

"I'm Bram, not Donahue," he reminded her. "And the button was here in this room last night. In the desk drawer." His gaze flicked over the contents still splayed across the desk top. "I know, because I locked it away myself. Now the button's gone. Did you take it?"

She shook her head. "No, I swear!"

"Then who? Who would have been poking around in here?" he asked more of himself than of her. "And in the hidden staircase that goes to the coal bin? Someone has been in there, too, and just recently." He directed the next question to his aunt. "Do you use those stairs?"

Her eyes went round. Head still shaking, she backed away from him toward the open door.

"If it wasn't you, Aunt Addy, then who could have been sneaking around this house?" Bram followed as she backed into the foyer. "Prying where they shouldn't."

Wild-eyed, she suddenly turned and fled up the stairs.

And Bram cursed himself for frightening her. He
dn't meant to. He just wasn't a particularly patient
rson. Meaning to apologize and settle her down, he
nt after her, taking the stairs two at a time.

"Aunt Addy, wait, please."

But she scooted into her bedroom and slammed the
or in his face. Bram took a deep breath and counted to
n. Maybe she was spooked after letting slip her "mis-
ke" in sharing the house's secrets with someone.

Echo St. Clair had been in the coal bin. Checking out
e hidden staircase? And what else? Had she been pok-
g around, looking for the secret rooms, as well? He also
ondered if she knew anything about the missing but-
n. He didn't really think she'd stolen it, but he needed
be sure. He was attracted to her, wanted to see her
,ain, wanted to trust her. He had to trust someone.

Once he calmed Aunt Addy down, Bram decided,
ocking softly, he would make it his business to pay a
sit to Echoes and find out how intimately the owner of
e New Age shop had gotten to know his ancestral
ome.

NGRY AT YET ANOTHER disturbance in *her* home, Lena
undle stepped out of the shadows of the staircase.

She'd heard everything that had gone on in the li-
ary. She didn't like it. She liked none of what was go-
g on these days. Not the invasion of the townspeople.
ot Bram Vanmatre's return. Certainly not his moth-
's....

"Lena, where are you?"

On her way to her quarters next to the kitchen, Lena
as stopped by that imperious voice she'd learned to hate
arly forty years before, when Mr. Donahue had first
ought his new bride to Dunescape Cottage.

"I'm here, Miss Katherine." Playing her role of th[e] dutiful servant to that woman made her burn with fur[y.] As if the witch had rights!

Bram's mother stepped around the back of the stai[r]case, making Lena wonder where she'd been and ho[w] much she'd heard. "I would like my breakfast now."

"Already made. Scrambled eggs, French toast an[d] bacon are in warmers on the kitchen counter."

"You may serve me in the conservatory."

Normally she didn't serve anyone but Miss Adrienn[e.] But under the steely green-eyed gaze, she found herse[lf] saying, "Yes, Miss Katherine."

Lena's eyes narrowed in hate as the other woman r[e]treated. She'd known *this one* was going to be troub[le] from the first. And she hadn't been wrong. Muttering [to] herself in her own language, she scurried to the kitche[n] where she put together a tray with the breakfast item[s] plus coffee and juice. She crossed to the oval conserv[a]tory and found Mr. Donahue's widow sitting at one [of] the small tables situated amidst the tallest of the plant[s.] The silver-haired witch was taking it easy as she alwa[ys] had, reading a newspaper.

Katherine looked up when Lena entered. "So what[']s this I hear about Dunescape Cottage being turned in[to] some kind of haunted house?"

"The local high school teenagers are holding a fun[d] raiser," Lena grumbled with a sniff.

"My son gave them permission?"

"Miss Adrienne gave them *her* word."

"I see."

A wealth of disapproval was conveyed to Lena. Wh[o] did this one think she was, passing judgment? And wh[y] had she returned after vowing not to?

Lena's uneasiness grew. All was as it should have been
or nearly three decades. Now Mr. Donahue's widow had
eturned and would stir things up. Make trouble like she
ad before, all those years ago.

Lena knew all the secrets of Dunescape Cottage.

And she intended to keep them.

No matter how.

"So, WHAT'S YOUR SECRET?" Echo asked the moment
er sister entered the shop to relieve her for lunch. "How
o you work part-time, run a household, volunteer for
ivic and school committees, deal with two kids and have
nough energy left over to be creative?"

She indicated the new display using incense burners
rom the Southwest. Izzy had taken the clay pueblo
uildings, beehive ovens and tepees, and turned them
nto a smoking city on a snowy hillside.

Hanging her jacket on a tree near the front counter,
zzy laughed. "They wore you out in one day, huh?"

"Actually, it was more the situation and Bram Van-
natre than the kids," Echo admitted, stifling a yawn.

"Ah, the ogre of Dunescape Cottage."

"He's not really an ogre."

Or so Echo hoped. He hadn't promised anything when
came to his aunt's care.

"I hear he doesn't *look* like an ogre, either."

"He's...interesting." When Izzy's brows shot up,
cho cut her off before she could comment. "Don't
tart."

"What?"

Before they could get into it, the wind chimes signaled
n arrival. Echo turned to see a customer step through the
oorway.

"Travis Ferguson," she murmured.

Passing her on the way to the stockroom, Izzy whis
pered, "You didn't tell me about *him*."

Echo ignored Izzy and greeted Travis. "I didn't ex
pect to see you quite so soon."

"A visit was long overdue."

To her or the shop? "Looking for anything in partic
ular?"

"That I am." The way his hazel eyes assessed her mad
Echo think she was the reason he was there, until he said
"A present for a young lady. My niece's birthday is nex
week. What would a fifteen-year-old like?"

"Young women usually like jewelry." She pulled ou
a tray of pendants.

"I hear you're in charge of the Halloween fund
raiser."

"One of the organizers. I'm helping the kids tur
Dunescape Cottage into a Haunted Mansion."

He laughed. "It doesn't have far to go to make th
grade, does it?"

Echo didn't comment. Aware of Miss Addy's finan
cial circumstances, she didn't want to criticize the place

"What about this pink crystal with the unicorn?" sh
suggested.

"Hmm, I'll keep that one in mind," he said as he mad
a cursory study of the other pieces on the velvet-covere
tray. "So, you have the run of the place, right?"

"Most of it. The rooms that aren't being used by th
residents."

"Even the *lower* level?" he asked. "I remember hov
spooky I thought the cellar was as a kid. I imagined par
of it was an old dungeon."

"The coal bin."

"So you *have* been in there." His lips quirked, but n
smile lit his eyes. "What about the secret rooms?"

Echo narrowed her gaze. What was Travis's purpose in visiting the shop? Had he really wanted to see her, or buy something... or drill her for information about Runescape Cottage? Before she could come to any conclusion, the front door opened again.

"Can I help you?" Izzy volunteered as she breezed back into the shop.

"I'm here to see the owner."

At the sound of Bram's voice, Echo whipped around, vaguely registering Travis's growl of frustration.

"Wait your turn, Vanmatre," the sandy-haired man said.

Bram ignored him, fixing his intense gaze on Echo. Adrenaline shot through her. "We need to talk. Now."

Though she felt like showing Mr. Bram Vanmatre who was in charge in *her* shop, she figured he wouldn't have bothered making a special trip to see her unless it was important. It had to be about the fund-raiser. Her adrenaline dropped along with her stomach.

She flashed Travis a conciliatory smile. "Would you mind if Izzy finished taking care of you?"

"Vanmatre hasn't left either one of us a choice, has he?" Travis's jaw muscles clenched. Hard. Making him look less attractive. "I really was enjoying our chat. Maybe we can continue it later. Over dinner?"

"I'll be busy with the youth group."

At least, she hoped so. Bram's scowl was anything but reassuring. What now? Had Miss Addy put up a big enough fuss to throw a wrench in the works, after all?

"You've got to eat," Travis insisted. "A late supper?"

For some reason, Echo wasn't certain she wanted to dine with the man at all. He was attractive, she couldn't deny that, but she didn't feel totally comfortable with

him. And she suspected he had an ulterior motive i
seeking out her company.

Just in case her objectivity was being colored b
Bram's presence, she suggested, "How about a rai
check?" Now both men were scowling, making Ech
wonder if they were merely annoyed with each other—o
with her, too. "Izzy, would you take over?"

Her sister gave her a "you'll have to tell me everythin
later" look as she moved to help Travis. Echo rounde
the counter and stopped a safe distance from Bram. H
was a potent male presence, and her physical respons
was automatic, her pulse suddenly zinging without h
permission. She hadn't had this decidedly disturbing r
action to Travis. Or any other man, for that matter.

"So what's up?" she asked.

"We need to talk in private. You have an office?"

She did, but Echo stubbornly refused to give him tot
control. "I was planning on running home for a break.
Having left some bills she'd meant to mail on the kitch
table, she'd thought to fetch them while catching a qui
lunch. "We can talk there."

A couple of steady customers arrived, and she to
them to see Izzy when they'd picked out their purchase
She noticed that Travis didn't seem to be finding an
thing he wanted to buy.

Pulling on the sweater jacket with an abstract orang
yellow and magenta design, she went straight to her st
tion wagon. Bram eyed the well-used vehicle warily, b
eased into the passenger side without comment. Hon
was two blocks from the lake, about three minutes awa
from the shop...enough time for Echo's nerves to stret
taut, especially when Bram tried to give her advice.

"I'd stay away from Ferguson, if I were you."

Though she wouldn't necessarily follow up on the rain
heck, she didn't care for Bram's interference. "You're
ot me."

"He's volatile. Had a nasty temper even as a kid."

"Are you saying Travis abuses women?"

"I wouldn't know. I just don't like him."

Echo figured the feeling was mutual. She pulled into
er gravel drive, wondering if Bram could be jealous of
Miss Addy's neighbor.

"We wouldn't have the same perspective on that one,
ow would we?" she asked.

"We may not have the same perspective on lots of
hings."

"Such as?"

"Honesty. You told me what I see is what I get. So why
were you in the coal bin?"

They climbed out of the vehicle. Glaring at him over
he roof of the wagon, she said, "I told you."

"Did it take you long to find the hidden staircase? Or
did Aunt Addy show it to you?"

First Travis questioning her about secret rooms, now
Bram about hidden staircases—what was going on?

"I don't know what you're talking about."

All kinds of rumors had shadowed the old mansion,
nd Mrs. Ahern *had* mentioned an escape route for pro-
ibition-era bootleggers.

She took the wood-chip path to the front door of what
ooked like a *real* cottage set in a clearing among a small
tand of trees and bushes. The modest two-bedroom
lapboard had handcrafted trim that was painted muted
reens and reds. She'd bought the land shortly after
noving to Water's Edge, but hadn't been able to secure
loan to build the place until two years ago. Maybe in
nother couple of years, when she got one-up on her

mortgage, she would be able to afford a new vehicle, four-wheel drive that would look right at home parked i the naturally wild-looking landscape.

She had the door open before Bram started in on he again.

"And you don't know about the button, either right?"

She glanced over her shoulder to flash him a look o annoyance. "I gave it to you, remember?"

"Then took it back?"

"No, of course not." She resented the implication. " may not be wealthy like you are, Bram Vanmatre, but have enough—everything I really want." She stepped int her home's big, open-space living area, which wa sparsely appointed with natural wood furniture and col orful accent pieces. To her eyes, it was simple but beau tiful. "I don't steal."

Bram's gaze locked with hers, as if he were trying t read her very soul. He nodded, accepting her statement "You seem to have an attachment to my aunt."

"I like her, yes, and I sympathize with her. But we'r hardly close."

"Not close enough that she would share the house' secrets with you?"

Throwing her sweater jacket on the textured buck wheat couch near the fireplace, she asked, "Good grie what secrets?"

"Hidden rooms and stairwells, for a start."

"The only thing Miss Addy shared with me was a po of tea. I know you have problems where your aunt i concerned, Bram Vanmatre, but stop assuming I hav anything to do with them."

He finally seemed satisfied and backed off. "Al right."

That was it? She was off the hook so easily, and after he'd made a special trip to confront her? Suspicious, Echo wasn't able to forget the interrogation. But it wasn't in her nature to hold a grudge. And it did seem Bram was concerned for his aunt. He'd confronted her for a reason. She told herself to relax. To give the man a chance. To find out what he *really* wanted.

"Would you like some coffee?" she asked. "Kenyan?"

"Great. Black."

"How about starting the fire and I'll put the coffee on."

She moved to the open kitchen area where she switched on the coffeemaker and put together a couple of sandwiches—thick-sliced whole-wheat bread, turkey, Swiss cheese and a range of vegetables. A good, wholesome lunch to which she added some definitely unwholesome salty potato chips.

Carrying a handcrafted tray with their meal, she joined Bram, who'd made himself comfortable on the couch. She set the tray on the coffee table and sat cross-legged on the area rug opposite him. The warmth of the nearby flames soothed her, as did her first sip of coffee.

"You didn't have to go through all that trouble. But thanks." He held his mug under his nose and inhaled the strong aroma of the coffee. He eyed her appreciatively when he said, "Gets the juices flowing," making her wonder if he meant the coffee or her.

Flushing, she said, "So the button is missing." That still had to be on his mind. "Could you have misplaced it?"

"I locked it in the library desk after you left last night. This morning, the drawer was still secured, but the button was gone. Aunt Addy insists she didn't take it."

"One of the servants... Do you think Uriah or Lena or Sibyl needs money badly?"

"Something so distinctive would be hard to hawk without word getting out. Besides, there are other, more valuable things in the house to steal."

Echo was thoughtful as she swallowed a mouthful of sandwich.

"It must have something to do with the button itself," Bram continued. "There was a theft at the last costume ball held at Dunescape Cottage, you know."

"I heard something about stolen jewels that never surfaced."

She took a long, satisfying swallow of coffee and almost choked when he said, "And a possible murder."

"What? You mean your father? But the police report—"

"I don't believe his drowning was an accident. It might have had something to do with the jewels. And maybe that button."

His father murdered as Miss Addy had suggested? She was beginning to understand why the button's disappearance was so important to him. "Could the button have been part of the cache?"

"I don't know. I was too young to remember much about what happened that night," he admitted. "Unfortunately, I can't count on lucid answers from Aunt Addy, either."

"I know who you can ask—Mrs. Ahern, the woman who was supervising in the parlor yesterday. She's the librarian and takes pride in being the town historian. I'll bet she knows all the details."

He hesitated only a second before asking, "Do you have time to come with me before getting back to work?"

Why should she help this man who had been nothing if not rude to her from their very first meeting? She tried telling herself she wouldn't mind keeping an eye on him for Miss Addy's sake, but that didn't wash.

And yet . . .

"Why?" she wanted to know. "Me, I mean."

For a moment, she thought he might not answer. A myriad of emotions played over his features, and she had the distinct feeling that he wasn't comfortable explaining himself.

"You couldn't have been involved thirty years ago," he finally said. "And you seem to be a caring person. And as much as I hate to admit it, I could use some help. I know it's a lot to ask, especially since I've been so—"

"I'll make time," she interrupted, realizing he was trying to apologize, but uncertain of her own motivations. She could see the sincerity of his need, how he might be haunted by the past just as she was. "My sister can take care of business since she's scheduled to work all afternoon, anyway."

"Thank you. This means a lot to me."

Bram wolfed down his sandwich as though he'd been starving. Echo ate at a more leisurely pace, watching him surreptitiously. She studied his angular features, which at the moment were relaxed, the scar on his forehead so faint she could hardly see it. Bram Vanmatre fascinated her. He might be insular, acerbic and judgmental at times, but he had another side to him—the equitable side that approved of a good cause even though he hadn't approved of her.

Echo considered herself an astute judge of human nature—a result of her unusual upbringing, no doubt. Though not infallible, most often she was able to read between the lines of what a person said. And experience told her Bram Vanmatre was a man of considerable depth. She only hoped his compassionate side was far stronger than his pragmatic side...for Miss Addy's sake.

What might happen to the elderly woman in the immediate future worried her, for she feared Bram's commitment to his aunt was limited, that he acted more out of duty than personal concern. Her grandparents had had the same kind of attitude toward her mother, their own daughter.

She tried not to shudder with the memories.

"If you're finished, we can get going," she said, appetite suddenly deserting her. She hadn't started on the second half of her sandwich. "I'm not as hungry as I thought. I'll wrap this and take it with me for later."

He helped her stack the tray, which she self-consciously whisked back to the kitchen area. Aware of his close scrutiny, she set the mugs and plates in the sink and bagged the leftover sandwich. With it and the unmailed bills in her possession, she was ready.

To help solve a mystery? she asked herself.

Or to get to know Bram better, for some reason she did not yet care to consider?

Chapter Five

Addy paced before the library fireplace, her hands twisting the deep blue crepe of her flowing skirts. Donahue had always loved this dress. He'd bought it for her because he'd said it matched her eyes. *Their* eyes, really—the only identical thing about them. She'd worn the garment especially for him, but he hadn't told her how nice she looked.

He wouldn't even appear today, though maybe she ought not take it so personally. After all, it wasn't yet dusk.

"Donahue, I must speak with you."

She knew he was here. Always knew when he was around. They were like two sides of a coin—both were needed for it to be worth something. Without him, she was a shell of the woman she had once been. Thirty years had passed since his death, much of it as in a dream.

Rather, a nightmare.

But she'd managed to deal with the past in her own way. They said she was crazy. Maybe she was. All she knew was she needed to talk to him.

"Your son...Katherine...they're both here. But you know that."

She felt his warring emotions. Love. Sadness. Anger. She wanted to make him feel better. She really did.

But how could she when she had to admit, "I'm afraid, Donahue. The boy loves me, but he doesn't understand. And Katherine... I'm afraid they're going to separate us. You don't want that to happen, do you?"

Why wouldn't he answer her? Make her feel better?

"Why can't you tell them you don't want me to go away?"

Maybe if they *believed* the house was haunted...

She stopped and thought a minute.

If Donahue wouldn't cooperate, she would have to figure out a way herself.

"WELL, IT'S QUITE a mystery what happened that night," Mrs. Ahern said, happily falling into the role of town historian. Her eyes shone behind her thick rose-tinted trifocals. "The case remains unsolved to this very day—the Courtland jewels have never been recovered."

The three of them sat in the library office, which also served as a sorting and indexing space for new and returned books. Everywhere Echo looked, stacks piled around them on shelves and carts threatened to teeter and fall.

"What can you tell us about that fateful night?" Bram asked the librarian.

"Quite a bit, actually. I wasn't there, of course—not enough clout. But I've talked about it to people who were present, including the victim." Mrs. Ahern was in her storytelling mode, her voice rich and throbbing, her hands waving about theatrically. "From what I've been told, the ball was absolutely spectacular. No gross monster costumes like the ones young people prefer now, you understand. The annual All Hallows' Eve Ball at

Dunescape Cottage was the kind most people only dream of attending. But I'm certain you already know that," she said to Bram. "Guests not only drove in from Chicago and Grosse Pointe, but a handful even flew in from New York and Palm Beach. As you can imagine, the costumes were elaborate confections—either historical or high fantasy. And the women wore incredible displays of jewels."

"I thought wealthy women wore paste in public while the real thing is safely locked away," Echo said.

"I'm certain that's true in most cases," the librarian agreed. "But, alas, not in Priscilla Courtland's. Her husband had recently bought her an entire matching collection and hadn't had time to have it duplicated. She insisted on wearing the real thing." Mrs. Ahern ticked off the items on her fingers. "An elaborate choker, double bracelets, a ring, hair ornament, earrings and a brooch. Some said Mr. Courtland paid several hundred thousand for the collection, and that was thirty years ago."

So its worth would have multiplied, Echo realized. "What kinds of stones?"

"Canary diamonds studded with sapphires and emeralds."

"What about buttons? Did Priscilla Courtland's costume have large jeweled buttons, also, like the one I found yesterday?" Echo had shown the find to the librarian before turning it over to Bram.

"I don't believe so. At least, I never heard anything about buttons being missing. Mrs. Courtland wore a beaded flapper costume, so it's doubtful. Anyway, at the stroke of midnight, the lights went out and everyone assumed that was a planned part of the festivities. Several minutes went by before someone thought to find a torch and go see to the fuse box. When the lights came back on, poor Mrs. Courtland was passed out on the ballroom floor... sans jewels.''

"So she had no idea of what happened?" Echo murmured.

"How could she? The thief chloroformed her."

But that's where Mrs. Ahern's ready knowledge stopped. She could give them no further information about the investigation itself.

"If the stones ever did resurface, they would have been in different settings, of course," she said, "and that would have decreased their value, wouldn't it have?"

Echo was well aware that much of the value of the collection had been due to the design. "But no one could hope to sell obviously hot pieces. The thief must have planned to have the stones reset from the first. So, of course, it would seem as if they'd never resurfaced."

"Only one thing wrong with that theory," the librarian said. "The Tiger Canary—the central stone of the choker. Hard to disguise twenty-five carats of yellow diamond."

"Unless it was recut," corrected Bram. "True, all of the stones could have been reset. But what if they weren't? Any speculations on what else might have happened to them?"

Now Mrs. Ahern seemed uncomfortable. "Well, the pieces could be in some private collection... or they might never have left the house... or..."

"Or...?" Bram urged.

The librarian swallowed and tilted her head, the trifocals catching the fluorescent light so Echo couldn't see her eyes. "There was a theory that they went into the lake with your father."

His features immediately darkened. "Pardon me?"

"Not that *I'm* making accusations, you understand," Mrs. Ahern said nervously.

"Someone intimated my father stole the jewels and what?" he asked, rising from the chair to tower over the librarian. "Did the person think he was trying to swim them to a fence and just happened to drown on the way?"

"Mr. Vanmatre, please, this is a library. You must keep your voice down."

"I'll go one better." The scar stood out against his flushed forehead. "I'll leave."

Echo made a face and commiserated with the librarian. "Sorry. He didn't mean to burden you with this, really."

Bram wasn't the only one sensitive to what people said about his parent. Echo could definitely relate. Assured that Mrs. Ahern hadn't taken offense, she went after Bram. Already outside, he strode down the street as if ghosts from the past were on his tail. Echo practically broke into a jog to catch up with him, and while she was certain Bram knew she was there, half a pace behind him, he made no effort to slow down.

"Do you believe the nerve of that woman, implying my father might have stolen the jewels?"

Not certain if he was talking to himself or to her, she agreed. "Rumors can be vicious."

"Especially when they're about a dead man."

He stopped short. Echo almost ran into him before putting on the brakes. He seemed to be lost somewhere deep inside himself, as if he were in a different dimension.

When she touched his arm, he started. "What's going on?" she asked.

He shook his head, appearing vague. "Something I remembered hearing."

"When?"

"The night of the theft," he said, looking inward again, as if he were forcing himself to hear. The scar on his forehead seemed to pulse. "Someone saying he was desperate and needed the money."

"Who?"

"I don't know. The voices in my head . . ." He looked directly at her and yet through her. "They're never clear enough. . . ."

Either Miss Addy wasn't the only one who needed stabilizing, or Bram was fighting the past. Maybe he didn't want to remember.

"You think you heard something having to do with the theft?" she prompted.

He folded back into his cocoon for a moment, then said, "The night of the theft. The jewels were stolen at midnight. My father disappeared . . . but at what time?"

"Mrs. Ahern might—"

He snapped to. "She won't be wanting to talk to me again."

Echo didn't believe a woman who loved trading juicy gossip would be so easily put off. "Come back inside. If you won't talk to her personally, surely you don't object to seeing what the local paper had to say?"

In the end, Bram acquiesced. He allowed Echo to turn him around.

In doing so, she spotted a familiar figure in a four-wheel drive parked across the street from the library. A newspaper quickly hid the man in the driver's seat, but not before she got a glimpse of his face. She couldn't fail to recognize Travis Ferguson.

But why was he hiding?

Because she was with Bram, a man Travis disliked—or because he was spying on her?

Though she was tempted to pose the question to Bram himself, Echo didn't want to upset him more than he already was. She hurriedly opened the glass-and-steel door and pushed him inside, giving the bulky vehicle a last worried look before disappearing into the library herself.

While Mrs. Ahern was far less chatty this time around, she didn't seem to hold Bram's outburst against him. The librarian was all business, setting them up at a station where they could check out accounts of the robbery on microfilm. And if the few patrons had heard the loud interchange, they didn't seem to be interested in Bram's return.

Bram himself seemed contrite. "Thank you, Mrs. Ahern. You've been very gracious."

A smile fluttered about her lips. "Mr. Vanmatre." And off she went, leaving Bram and Echo to their research.

The *Water's Edge* was published on Wednesday and Sunday. Since excitement in a small town was minimal, the All Hallows' Eve incident took first-page coverage in both editions each week until Thanksgiving, at which time the theft was relegated to an inside page, and after a few more weeks, it disappeared altogether.

Donahue Vanmatre's death had been an open-and-shut case. Echo flipped back to the initial story and the picture of Bram's father. She caught her breath. Staring at her from the front page was a replica of the man next to her. "If I didn't know better, I would think you had posed for this picture." The only discernable difference between father and son was that Donahue's hair waved over his forehead while Bram's was slicked back.

"I've been told I look like my father," he agreed.

Echo had the spookiest feeling, one she was determined to ignore.

Bram scanned the article. "A few contusions on the head attributed to a drunken fall off the terrace wasn't enough to warrant a full-fledged investigation by the local police," he said. "Father was never available for questioning, either, which meant he'd disappeared about the time of the theft."

Bram didn't look happy and the crawly feeling along Echo's spine wouldn't go away until they left the place, Bram both thanking Mrs. Ahern and offering her yet another apology.

Settling into the station wagon, Echo glanced across the street as she started the engine. Travis Ferguson was gone.

"Your father dying the night the jewels were stolen," she murmured. "Odd that the newspaper articles never made much of a connection."

Perhaps there *not* having been such speculation was for the best. Perhaps the connection would have been the same one that had made Bram so angry at Mrs. Ahern. Echo couldn't help but wonder how many others suspected Donahue of thievery.

"'What do you propose to do about it?'" Bram muttered to himself.

"What?" she asked, pulling the wagon away from the curb.

"A direct quote from one of the voices...." She felt his intent gaze on her as he said, "Aunt Addy isn't so crazy, after all. My father *was* murdered, Echo. I'm convinced of it. Now, if only I could figure out why."

FIGURING SHE'D FIND her sister-in-law in the conservatory, Katherine Quinlan readied herself for a confrontaon. *Eureka!* At last she'd found Adrienne alone, uttering with some plants set along the counter next to the sink.

Entering the oval sunlit room, Katherine raised her rows at the other woman's peculiar outfit. A deep blue ress, low-cut and calf length, hung loosely about the old ones, and a pale blue ribbon tied beneath the wrinkled hin held a big picture hat in place. The outfit was undoubtedly circa early 1950s. But what else did one expect from someone living in the past?

A woman very much of the present in a designer outfit meant to set off her silver-blond beauty, Katherine leared her throat; When the other woman glanced her way, she said, "Adrienne, I've been meaning to speak with you since I arrived."

"To me... or *at* me?"

"That was always *your* specialty. Or perhaps it was *through* me," Katherine murmured.

She remembered the first time she'd set foot in this ouse. And all the years she'd lived here. As far as Adrienne had been concerned, her brother's wife had had no ore value than a stick of furniture—an object to be alked about and moved around with no regard for its eelings. Now she felt pure hatred washing over her, ouring from those faded blue eyes.

The feeling was mutual.

Without preamble, she demanded, "Why is Bram ere?"

A secretive smile curled those thin lips before Adrienne turned her attention back to the plant she was repotting. "He's your son."

Not that that meant he shared his every thought with er. "And your brother's."

Adrienne's expression softened for a moment, the turned crafty as she slid Katherine a glance. "Donahu wants to know why *you've* returned."

Though she'd have liked nothing more than to lash ou at the other woman, Katherine held on to her tempe "To protect our son."

"Should've thought of that thirty years ago."

"I always had Bram's welfare at heart."

"By keeping the truth from him?"

"He didn't need to know then!" Katherine insisted "Not after what happened. He doesn't need to know now, either. Do I make myself clear?"

Adrienne shrugged. "What if Donahue tells him ev erything?"

"*Donahue* had best not," Katherine stated clearly "After all, he wouldn't want to see his dear twin locke away with the other lunatics, would he?" She waited fo the threat to sink in, to see the pale cheeks color unnat urally, before adding, "Don't try me, Adrienne. Yo know I can arrange it."

With that threat hanging between them, Katherin stormed off, a teeny part of her hoping that Adrienn would defy her and damn the consequences. Then, a last, she could get the revenge she'd once yearned for s very long ago.

THE KIDS RACED THROUGH the shop then out to load th station wagon. Echo's small storeroom was still stacke with boxes of decorations and props. The larger item were spread about town in various garages and base ments. Some of the other parents would be deliverin those later that evening or the next day.

Sighing, Echo shook her head. She really was down. Bram's father murdered....

Crazy Addy was not so crazy, after all. That was the only good part.

Maybe Bram would be better off in ignorance. After all, how could anyone solve a thirty-year-old murder? Instinct told her Bram was about to try, and in the process he would become even more frustrated. She tried concentrating on the day's mail stacked next to the register.

Miss Addy's fate was somehow tied up in the past...and so was Bram's. Despite their rocky start, she was drawn to him like no other man she'd known.

"So, ready to give me the scoop?" Izzy asked, buzzing around her. She nudged Echo and, her tone teasing, said, "You and Bram Vanmatre were together an awfully long time."

"We were doing some research at the library." She felt weird saying anything to Izzy when she didn't even know if Bram returned her interest.

Her sister gripped her arm and shot her a disbelieving look. "You spend your time with an outrageously sexy man in a stuffy old library?"

"Sorry to disappoint you."

Izzy huffed. "Well, Travis Ferguson is interested, too—"

"I'll just bet he is." Echo slapped a bill against the counter. "The question is, in what? He was spying on me for Bram. I'm not certain which. He was parked across from the library watching us."

"Maybe he wanted to borrow a book?"

Echo raised her brows.

Izzy looked worried. "Maybe you'd better be careful around *both* of them."

"Mmm," she murmured noncommittally.

She'd be happy to stay away from Travis. She knew she couldn't stay away from Bram. She only wished she knew how far she could trust him, not only with Aunt Addy's fate, but with her own....

"YOU'RE SUPPOSED TO STAY away from my property!" As Bram crossed the terrace, he heard Norbert Ferguson yelling at the men who were working on patching up the retaining wall.

Bram recognized the voice of the foreman of the group. "Listen, sir, we were told to keep off your property, and we have," he responded in a far more patient tone than Bram himself would have used.

Through the rapidly falling dusk, he could just make out an overly excited Norbert waving at the work area. "You shouldn't be here at all, not at all, digging around where you don't belong."

Arriving at the edge of the terrace, Bram looked down on his aunt's neighbor, who stood between the wall and the Dunescape boathouse. "That's my decision to make," he called. He'd never liked Norbert any more than he liked his son Travis, and Bram doubted he would change his mind now.

Norbert's bushy white hair bristled. "*Your* decision? You don't own this land." The frayed collar of his starched white shirt quivered, and he nervously wiped his palms on his already shiny navy suit jacket as he plunged up the steps. "We'll just see what Addy has to say about this."

Bram put out an arm to hold him back. "No need to bother my aunt, since I have control of all of her affairs, including this estate."

"You?" Norbert appeared shocked, as if he had a personal stake in the property himself. "You're not planning to sell, are you?"

"Why? Are you interested in buying?"

"Buying? Buying? I don't have that kind of money. Not yet," he muttered. The man's hazel eyes bulged as he became more agitated. "You can't sell this place! You'll have to wait a while longer!"

"I didn't know you were a lawyer," Bram said wryly.

"I'll get a restraining order." Norbert was mumbling to himself now. "That's what I'll do—get a restraining order." He shuffled back down the steps and off toward his own property. "No one's going to cheat me of what's rightfully mine."

Bram waved at the workmen. "Sorry about the hassle, guys."

"Mr. Vanmatre," the foreman said, "unloading the supply truck would take a lot of time, and then we might have to move some of the materials Monday, anyway. I thought we might leave it here over the weekend, if you don't mind."

The Lakeside Construction pickup parked in front of the boathouse was stacked with bags of concrete. "No problem."

Bram was wondering about Norbert's last statement. What made him think Dunescape Cottage was rightfully his? Or did he merely fear new developers moving in and razing the old manor so that they could build lakeside town houses? The thought of the estate being destroyed gave Bram pause. A century old and part of his heritage, it deserved better. But as it was now, Dunescape Cottage was a decrepit and very expensive albatross.

His gaze swept over the building and locked on the library window where a slight movement made his pulse accelerate. He had an odd feeling . . . a feeling that came and went ever since he'd arrived at the house. Almost as if he were never alone. Not a man subject to whimsy, he grimaced when the word *ghost* popped into his mind. Surely his father couldn't really haunt the old estate, Bram told himself even while fighting a crawly sensation that was becoming all too familiar.

Approaching the veranda, he realized his mother stood there in the semidark, waiting for him. "Mother."

"Hello, darling. Where have you been off to for hours and hours?" she asked.

"Town." He climbed the stairs and stopped on the porch. "I was trying to find out exactly what happened here thirty years ago."

She had never talked about it. Even now, she appeared uncomfortable. Evening shadows accentuated her strained expression. "You mean your father's accident?"

"Among other things. *If* his drowning *was* an accident."

She wet her lips. "Of course it was. What else could it have been?"

"Murder?"

"You've been listening to Adrienne's prattle. You know she's senile. You can't believe anything she says."

"I'm not so certain," he said. "If we look hard enough, we might find a few truths buried among her imaginings."

That's when he became aware of a movement around the side of the house, as if someone were listening. Chances were this was Aunt Addy herself, and Bram didn't want another confrontation, especially not with a woman who wasn't responsible for herself, so he let it go.

"Bram darling, this is exactly what I was afraid of," his mother said in her most motherly tone. "That you would get yourself all worked up for nothing."

"I'm not particularly worked up... and my father's death wasn't *nothing*."

"No, of course not. Donahue was a fine man, and his death a great personal loss to us both. It took me many years and a couple of mistakes in my other marriages before I was able to let go," she admitted. "I wish you would do that, too. Get on with your life."

"I have gotten on."

"With a career, perhaps. But your personal life, my dear son, stinks. You are thirty-seven years old, remember, and not getting any younger."

"You would hardly let me forget." For this wasn't the first time she'd bugged him about his advancing age and his prospects for the future. "Mother, you would detest being called 'Grandma.'"

She gave him one of those looks intended to quell the faint of heart. "There are other titles more suitable to a woman of my youthful vibrancy."

"Nana?"

Her expression turned horrified. "*Grand-mère* would do nicely."

"I'll see what I can manage," he said wryly.

Echo's clunky station wagon pulled up the drive, as if on cue.

Startled by the idea, he didn't know if he should be amused or aggravated. The owner of a New Age shop should have been the last person in the world he would want to get involved with. Then he'd gone and asked for her help. Some unspoken covenant existed between them that he couldn't explain. For an hour or so, he'd felt an unexpected bond with a woman he hardly knew and had from the first been determined to dislike.

Only he couldn't.

She wouldn't let him.

He didn't know what it was about her.... Maybe something in her own past that reached out to him...something that made her feel protective about a relative he cared about. He was drawn to her in a more real, down-to-earth way than he'd been with any of the women he'd had so-called relationships with.

"We're being invaded again" came dry tones from behind him.

"Mother, behave yourself. I realize you don't normally get hands-on involved with your charities, but you can make an exception this one time. For me," he coaxed. "Use your creativity for a good cause."

As Echo popped out of the station wagon and began issuing orders to her nephew and his friend, Bram was once more struck by her looks. She wasn't drop-dead beautiful. She was better, as unique as the colorful clothing that accentuated her flame-red hair and her equally vibrant personality.

No cover model, Echo was real. Earthy.

Touchable.

Bram narrowed his gaze. Though no stranger to women, he was unfamiliar with the gut-wrenching feelings shooting through him at the thought of touching her, exploring every inch of her more closely. Uncomfortable—that's what she made him, he realized. He'd found something he didn't want to let slip through his fingers. Something that further complicated his life, even though he'd come to Dunescape Cottage not only to set Aunt Addy's affairs in order, but to find himself.

Bram was determined to penetrate the voids and half-truths he'd lived with all his life, no matter the consequences. He would work on breaking through the mental barriers he himself had set up as a child. Only then, only when he recognized and banished the ghosts of the past, would he be able to get on with his life.

The future beckoned, closer than it had ever been.

For the moment, however, he would focus on the present. On the fathomless gray eyes staring into his own. Echo was coming up the steps, her complete attention centered on him.

"We're ready to get started," she said. "You okay with that?"

"I'm terrific with that."

Thinking he should introduce her to his mother, he glanced over his shoulder only to find her gone. Without his knowing it, his mother had slipped away into the shelter of a house of secrets.

SECRETS.

How many did Dunescape Cottage harbor?

Echo was somewhat surprised that Bram could so easily put the speculation of the afternoon behind him. But here he was, helping to fabricate a maze more complex than the cellar already provided. The lower floor was almost finished.

"If you want to spook your customers," he was telling a group of enthralled teenagers, "try hanging black threads in every doorway. The people going through won't be able to see anything, but the threads will brush their faces as they go from room to room."

"Creepy," Yvette said.

"Yeah," Mark agreed. "Let's do it!"

Cheryl seemed equally enthusiastic. "So where's the thread?"

"I'll see if I can find some," Bram promised.

From across the room, Echo saw him glance her way. A thrill shot through her, a decidedly uncomfortable sensation. Izzy had been right on about the man's sex appeal—even if he was wrong for her in every other way, he did make her pulse dance. But he was a danger she did not need.

Moving to the opposite doorway, Echo murmured, "And I'll just check on things in general."

Aware that he was headed for the main stairs, she moved in the other direction, wandering along the corridors, following the pattern set up for the customers. Everything seemed in order until she saw a movement down a darkened hall roped off from the path.

"Hey, you're not supposed to be there," she called. "C'mon back."

No response. No further movement. But she knew she hadn't imagined it. The skin on her arms crawled. Someone stood in the dark. Watching. She could feel the eyes staring out at her. Irritated that one of the teenagers was defying her authority, defying the common courtesy due Miss Addy, who had generously given them free run of three-quarters of the manor, Echo slipped under the rope and away from what she could see toward what she could not.

"Hey, it's almost time to go home and get dinner. Surely you're hungry." She forced herself to be reasonable and was not really surprised when there was no response.

Jason.

The name came unbidden. She didn't remember seeing her nephew for a while. It had to be him.

Another "gotcha."

It was past six and dark had fallen, so no light came through the ground-level windows to relieve the inky blackness. And this time, Echo had no flashlight. Her key chain was in her jacket, which she'd left in one of the rooms they'd been setting up. Only the muted glow behind her kept her from feeling as if she were blind. She cautiously advanced, waiting for her eyes to adjust.

After a minute, though she couldn't actually see clearly, Echo had the vague impression of doors just ahead on either side. One of the doors creaked slightly.

Her heart beat jaggedly. She whipped her head to the right and squinted. The door appeared to be open a tad. Finding the wall with her hand, she continued forward, aware of her pulse coursing through her fingertips. Silent now, she drew closer. That was it. Nothing to get excited about. No reason to feel this lump in her throat.

Just wait until she got hold of Jason!

On tiptoe, she slid through the opening without making the door swing and creak. But if the hall had been dark, this space was without so much as a hint of light.

Truly blind, she fought panic.

Though she tried to breathe normally, the air rushing slowly through her parted lips sounded as loud as the wind blowing across the lake. Or so she imagined. She held her breath and listened, but had no clue as to where Jason could be hiding. Turning her head, she froze when a draft of air caressed the left side of her face and neck.

As if another door had been opened further ahead, she thought.

She slowly turned her head from one side to the other. The draft remained constant. Hands stretched out in front of her, she felt her way to its source. Fingers bumped wood and hinges squealed in response.

"Aah!" Unable to help herself, she jumped. Blood rushed to her head, warmth following. Enough. "Jason!" she hissed. "Where are you?"

A shuffle behind her alerted Echo. She started to turn. Her body was in that awkward position—half twisted this way, the other half that—when strong hands contacted her upper body. Jerked off balance, she went sprawling sideways.

She tried to right herself.

The person pushed again, toppling her forward onto her hands and knees. Not Jason. Jason would never do such a mean-spirited thing. He would never hurt anyone.

"Wait, whoever you are!"

Her cry was muffled by the door slamming shut, followed by a metallic sound indicating a lock had been slipped into place.

Echo began to hyperventilate.

She was trapped!

Chapter Six

No, please! Don't l-leave me here, p-please!''

Echo nearly choked getting out the words. She'd always been terrified of closed spaces, ever since she saw Mama locked in that room, the straitjacket strapping her hands to her sides. Mama had thrown her body at the padded walls and screamed piteously for release, but she'd received no mercy. Not from the attendants.

Not from her own loved ones, either.

Eleven at the time, Echo had screamed, too. They'd had to drag her away from the exclusive private institution. Her grandmother had lectured her on appropriate behavior all the way back to the big cold house that she lived in for the next six years. Miserable years but for the comfort she and Izzy had found in each other.

For months afterward she'd had nightmares about the padded room. Sometimes it was *she* rather than Mama that was locked up.

And now she *was*.

Panic bubbled up in her chest and she gagged trying to scream for help. All that came out was a piteous sound that she didn't recognize as belonging to her.

She wasn't to be pitied, Echo told herself furiously. She was the one who had taken control at seventeen. She had

run away with Izzy and had seen her sister through he
pregnancy. To help support them, she had worked at job
she'd hated. She'd done what she had to. She wasn
weak.

She wasn't Mama.

For that's what she feared most.

Pushing the fear to the back of her mind, Echo tol
herself there was no need to panic. Her hands were fre
not strapped to her sides. She took comfort in being ab
to move them. Now if only she could breathe normall
If only she could think rather than huddle on the col
concrete floor, bathed in her own tears, swept away t
her old terror.

She slashed her palm across her face, removed the w
proof of her weakness. She closed her eyes and forced
deep, deep breath down into her lungs. She concen
trated. Imagined the lock releasing, the door opening, h
walking out of this space, whatever it was, of her ow
accord.

Subtly, her mood shifted, and the horror subsided. Sh
almost imagined a kind hand touched her cheek, as if
assure her she was in no real danger, that she would be a
right. Her lids flashed open.

She wasn't alone.

She sensed another presence.

"Is anyone there?" she whispered.

No answer. Rather, no words spoken. But sh
felt ... comforted. She imagined a warm breath rufflir
her hair, a kind hand on the underside of her arm urgir
her to get up off the floor. She followed this curious i
stinct, and once on her feet, reached out in front of he
Solid material met her palms. Not the normal wood o
door or paneling, but something that felt thick and sof

Anxiety returned for a moment, and once more she saw the padded walls of the institution that had been her grandparents' solution for Mama's grief.

But the presence soothed her, and the alarm subsided. She ran her hands over the material more carefully. This wasn't the padding used to keep a patient from hurting herself, but the kind meant to muffle noise.

"One of the secret rooms," she whispered, feeling the wall until she found what had to be the door.

As she'd expected, there was no handle, no easy way out. Neither could she find a hidden release. There had to be one, but where? She followed the wall to the left with her hands. Then suddenly there was nothing, and she pitched forward, banging a shin and catching herself on what felt like a stair.

"A hidden staircase!"

Hands exploring, she realized the steps were very narrow, barely wide enough for a person to use, and very, very steep. Dangerous. But the size made sense if one wanted to keep the hidden staircase secret. Wondering where the stairs led, she started to climb them, feeling as if she were being urged to do so.

Crazy. That's what they'd call her if she told anyone how she felt as if she weren't alone. At least she wasn't *hearing* someone she couldn't see or touch.

Mama had heard voices.

Ignoring her racing pulse and the myriad questions demanding answers she could not give, Echo concentrated on putting one foot in front of the other, on feeling her way up, searching the walls on either side for some indication of another door.

Eventually, she reached a tiny landing where the stairs turned and continued upward.

Pausing, she explored the walls and eventually was able to trace the outline of another door. This must be the main floor. As before, the opening was tightly sealed, and she could find no handle, no trick release.

Trapped. But why? And by whom? Who was this presence she felt but could not see?

She stilled herself for a moment, trying to make sense of the situation. The high school students would hardly know the house's secrets, and so she didn't believe any of them had played a nasty trick on her. And if she had been following one of the house's occupants, why hadn't that person reassured her? It would take a warped mind to trap another person in this endless dark for no apparent reason.

The presence pushed at her, urging her on.

Stalling, she whispered, "Who are you?" not really expecting an answer.

And of course there was none except for a reassuring feeling and an invisible pressure propelling her upward.

She continued her climb, managing to stay the awful feeling that she was indulging in an exercise in futility, that there was no way out. As she groped toward yet another turn in the stairs, she wondered if Dunescape Cottage really was haunted, whether Donahue Vanmatre was playing guardian angel. She reached another landing. The second floor.

This time she felt a slight irregularity in the outline of the door. Her heart pumped with excitement. Enough room to force her fingertips through. Enough hope to make her feel light-headed. She pulled and the panel whispered open to yet another dark space. Heart thumping, she waited. Waited to hear a noise or see a light.

Waited for the presence to join her.

But she knew she was alone. Whoever or whatever had ided her was gone. She was on her own.

Blindly, she reached out, her hand immediately tan-ing in something soft and giving. Material.

Clothing?

She inched forward, both hands coming into contact ith other fabrics. Giddy from the excitement of know-g she must be in a bedroom closet, she laughed. Be-nd her, she heard the panel swing closed with a soft ush, as if the hinges had been oiled lately, unlike those ' the lower-level door. Shouldering through the gar-ents, she smacked into what had to be the closet door. c slid her palm down the wood to waist level and found e knob. As her fingers curled around the metal, her eath came shallow and furious.

Thank goodness the knob gave easily. Freedom! With gasp of relief, Echo stumbled into a large space a shade s dark than the closet. A night-light on a dresser lamp owed softly against the opposite wall of the bedroom.

But *whose* bedroom?

Her eyes adjusting quickly, she made her way to the nopied bed. A brass-and-stained-glass lamp perched on e antique, hand-carved rosewood chest. Gazing at the ntents on the surface, she realized she was in Sibyl ilde's quarters.

The bone-and-shell necklace she had so admired lay fore a framed photograph of a much younger Sibyl and older woman whose strong mahogany features were mplemented by the brilliantly patterned caftan and ad covering she wore. The resemblance between the o was unmistakable. They were posed, arms linked, in nt of a long table covered with an embroidered cloth which sat burning candles, small pots—one of which

held a dark red substance—and a plate of what looke
like bones.

Though she had a liberal view of spirituality and othe
people's beliefs, Echo couldn't help but shudder as sh
stared at the ritual altar in the photo.

Then her gaze hit upon a small turquoise pouch em
broidered with strange yet familiar symbols. Its draw
strings loose, the cloth bag lay open. Unable to stay he
curiosity, Echo put out a finger to lift the material....

"Something I can help you with?"

Startled, she whipped around to face Sibyl Wilde, wh
stood in the doorway. Not having expected to meet th
nurse face-to-face, she had no ready explanation as 1
why she was in her room. She only knew she didn't wai
to share the truth, not until she figured it out.

"Sorry." Echo apologized with the appropria
amount of embarrassment. "I wanted to talk to yc
about Miss Addy. I didn't mean to invade your pi
vacy."

Sibyl's look said they both knew this was a lie, but th
nurse didn't challenge Echo. Her mouth was tight, a
centuating the mole at the corner. Her amber gaze shift
to the chest and the objects that lay there. "I see you'
met Grandmama Tisa."

"I thought so. And isn't that an altar?"

Sibyl inclined her head and came closer. "Though sl
was brought to the United States from Haiti as a ve
young woman, she already had developed her gifts."

"What kind of gifts?"

"As an obeah woman, she had visions...and cou
make many powerful spells. Good fortune. Love. Cur
for illnesses."

"And this?" Echo asked, indicating the pouch. "D
your grandmother make it for you?"

"That's to keep me in good health. Somehow I went off and left it today."

Sibyl quickly rectified the situation, picking up the pouch and slipping it in her skirt pocket before Echo could get a closer look. And she hadn't confirmed that Grandmama Tisa had made the pouch for her, either. Odd enough that an educated nurse would use an old superstition to keep her well...but might *she* have made the pouch herself?

"I hope your forgetting it doesn't mean you're in for the flu or something," Echo joked.

"I don't think so." Sibyl flashed her a sly expression. She hesitated a moment, her amber gaze penetrating as if she were trying to see into Echo's very soul. "Now, about Miss Addy?"

Echo's excuse for being in the room. "I was wondering how she was taking our being here. Her reaction to my finding the button worried me a bit, and I haven't seen Miss Addy since." Without thinking, she added, "And now I understand the button has vanished again."

A curious expression flashed across Sibyl's features, one Echo couldn't read. "While Miss Addy is prone to excitement one moment, she might forget what was bothering her the next. She seems resigned that the fundraiser will go on as planned."

"Is there anything I can do?"

"Attend to your young charges. Miss Addy is *my* responsibility."

Echo was startled by what sounded like a warning, and from a nurse who'd only been in the Vanmatre employ for a short time.

"Of course. I'd better see what they're up to," she said, grabbing the opportunity to get out of a sticky situation. "It's probably about time to get them headed for home."

She felt Sibyl's eyes on her back all the way out of the room. Surely Sibyl herself hadn't had anything to do with trapping her in the hidden staircase, though Echo was certain the nurse must know about the passage, considering the entrance to her closet had been left open. It was as though Echo had been meant to find the way out.

Or to find Sibyl's room.

But by whom? Sibyl or someone else? Someone who didn't like the nurse?

Thinking about Sibyl possibly following in Grandmama Tisa's footsteps filled Echo with a sense of unease. Considering the way Bram felt about people who'd taken advantage of his aunt in the past, she couldn't believe he knew about Sibyl's background. Should she tell him? Then she'd have to explain everything, and she wasn't prepared to share her evening's experience with anyone yet.

The information about the nurse could wait a while longer, she decided, as she checked the progress on the second floor before descending into the dark, uninviting bowels of the manor once more. And Bram was the first person she saw halfway down the stairs. When his deep blue gaze lit on her, his expression changed subtly. Softened.

"Where have you been?" he asked.

"Wandering around, checking things out." A half truth.

"You've been gone so long, I was nearly ready to send out a search party."

Something she would have appreciated. "How flattering."

"The question is, would you have wanted to be found . . . by me?"

Something invisible and unexpected surged between them, rooting her to the bottom stair. Attraction, pure and simple. And, she realized, it went both ways. Her stomach did a tumble and she had to remind herself to breathe. Echo hadn't expected Bram to reciprocate her feelings. But there he was, staring at her as if he wanted to drag her off somewhere. . . .

"Hey, Auntie E., come check this out!" Jason's voice snapped her out of her musing.

"What?" she asked, frustration evident in her tone.

He put on a hurt expression. "We're almost finished down here. It's way cool. I just wanted you to check out what a great job we've done."

"Coming?" she asked Bram.

He shook his head. "I was going to find Lena about dinner. See you shortly."

Concealing her disappointment, Echo trailed Jason through the maze and tested out some of the special effects, most of which had been made possible by the expertise of several parents.

Mirrors and strobe lights in one room gave everything an eerie, surreal feel, which Jason assured her would scare the stuffing out of the customers when "monsters" came after them. The "victims" would feel as if they were only able to move in slow motion. The subtle hanging threads made her swipe the itchy feeling from her face. And she was impressed with the wind-tunnel effect in a darkened room—those wearing skirts or loose clothing would certainly be busy keeping their attire together.

Throughout the tour, Echo made certain she didn't venture alone into any part of the maze—one bad turn was all she could tolerate right now. The house seemed to be taking on a life of its own.

And while she might be willing to chance losing her heart in this place, Echo wasn't willing to chance losing her mind.

"I HAVE NOT LOST my mind, Donahue."

Bram froze at the library door when he heard his aunt's voice, then started when he realized he was straining to hear a reply—as if there would actually be one.

"Please, don't look at me like that," his aunt went on, her voice shrill. "Don't be angry with me anymore. You know I *had* to do it!"

Bram quietly opened the door and entered the room to watch her, expression intense, shout at one of the empty high-backed chairs that faced the blazing fire.

"They *have* to believe in you, or—"

She stopped in midsentence, her head snapping up, her shocked gaze locking with Bram's. She blinked. Her expression grew confused.

"It's Bram, Aunt Addy," he said, stepping closer. "What is it you had to do?"

"Nothing." She shook her head, and her body trembled as if she were frightened of him. "I didn't do anything wrong. I swear!"

"It's all right. Everything is going to be all right."

But his calm reassurance made her more frantic. "No! It isn't!" She edged around him. "It won't be unless—" With a gasp, she ran out of the room.

Bram thought to go after her, then changed his mind, fearing he'd only make it worse. He shook his head. Aunt Addy thought he was her enemy, when all he wanted was to make certain she was all right. Troubled thoughts about her fate running through his mind, he wandered over to the ever-present fire and stared into the flames. He knew she talked to the supposed ghost of his father, but finding her actually doing so was very disturbing.

An ember popped and a draft caught Bram where he stood. The shift in air pressure made him start, for immediately he grew physically uncomfortable, hot and cold at the same time and filled with unease...as if...as if someone else were inside his skin with him.

What the hell was going on? He wasn't susceptible to suggestion!

He was a lawyer, for God's sake, a man who dealt in facts, in tangibles. So why did he have this overwhelming feeling that a presence was trying to make itself known?

What the hell are you doing down here?

He stood frozen, his eyes widening, as the voice from the past haunted him. Down where? Here? The library?

I know her as well as I know myself!

His father's voice.

This man's a liar....

Feeling icy sweat dribble down the center of his back, Bram stared down into the empty chair Aunt Addy had been addressing. Still empty.

Could he possibly be feeling his father's presence?

No sooner had he considered the idea than the discomfort diminished, as if, in guessing the correct answer, he had been rewarded.

Within moments, his physical being went through another transformation, returning to normal. The room was comfortable once more. All was as it should be.

All but him.

THE MANSION'S transformation was coming along according to schedule, so by the time Bram rejoined her, Echo suggested they pack up and break for the evening.

"How about staying for a while?" he suggested.

"I'm pretty pooped." Drained from her experience was more like it, but she wasn't about to play true confessions yet.

"You do look tired. But you'll feel better with something in your stomach. I'll bet you never even finished your sandwich."

Odd, but he was on edge, and not because of her, Echo realized. He wanted her company.

"I forgot all about the sandwich," she admitted, wondering where she'd left it.

"Then let me feed you." Bram's smile was strained. "It'll give us a chance to talk."

"All right."

He looked genuinely pleased. "Great."

Remembering their encounter at the bottom of the stairs, she saw the kids off, and with a growing sense of expectancy, followed Bram into the kitchen where Lena was stirring a pot of stew.

She breathed in the rich, spicy fragrance. "Mmm, smells wonderful."

"Lena is a wonderful cook. Ethnic European dishes are her specialty."

"Shall I serve you in the conservatory, since the dining room is no longer available?" Lena asked Bram while giving Echo a pointed look that said the unavailability of the dining room was all her fault.

"Don't trouble yourself, Lena." Bram took the ladle from her to taste the stew. "Delicious. You've had a long day. I can take it from here."

"Of course, Mr. Bram."

She flashed a smile at her employer's nephew, the first Echo had seen cross those stern lips. Then the housekeeper inclined her head and silently departed the room.

"*You* certainly have a fan."

"Lena? Don't mind her. She comes off like a dragon lady, but she is loyal to the Vanmatres and has a real heart beneath the starched surface." He filled a bowl with stew. "She took turns with Aunt Addy drying my tears and bandaging my wounds when I was a kid."

"I thought that was a mother's prerogative."

He set the first bowl down and filled a second. "My mother loves me in her own way, but she was never into the nuts and bolts of child care."

"How sad for her."

They ate in the kitchen at the worn and scarred table that also served as a work area. The stove and sink could be classified as antiques, Echo thought. The heart of the old house probably hadn't been modernized since the late forties, when the estate had been turned into an exclusive resort.

"It was my father's idea," Bram told her, seeming to unwind totally in her company. "Of course, Aunt Addy went along with whatever he wanted. She was so devoted to him. They ran the place together."

"Until your father married your mother?"

"I told you, Mother is not a nuts—"

"—and bolts person," she finished, wondering what Katherine Vanmatre had done to keep herself occupied if she hadn't had a hand either in running the resort or raising her own child. "So you lived here—how long?"

"Until I was seven."

The year his father had died by fair means or foul, Echo realized. "I was told you never came back, not until a few days ago."

"Correct."

"Odd. I guess I would have been a bit more curious about my childhood home."

If that home had been a happy place. She'd revisited the farm that had once been the commune her family had belonged to. So many good memories there. But she had avoided the cold, forbidding Indiana house like the plague, even though she and Izzy had been the sole inheritors of their grandparents' estate. They'd given away everything to a progressive outpatient-counseling facility in Lafayette.

Even such a generous use of their grandparents' money could not make up for what the righteous couple had done to Mama.

"At first, Mother discouraged me from coming back," Bram was saying. "She didn't think it would be healthy for me. Then I guess I managed to avoid the situation for years, what with college and law school and building a practice. Eventually, Aunt Addy started needing more guidance, however, and she only had me to look out for her. I hired a respectable law firm to manage things here and kept promising myself I would get personally involved once I had a break in my schedule."

"Only that never happened," she guessed, picking at the last of her food.

"Something always came up."

Echo recognized genuine regret when she heard it. She started to question the harsh assumptions she'd made about Bram's sudden return.

"Why didn't your Mother want you to visit?" she asked curiously.

"The nightmares. She thought they would get worse."

"You were having nightmares about Dunescape Cottage?"

He took his time chewing a last chunk of meat before saying, "Something happened to me that last night.... I must have fallen. I managed to split my head open like a ripe melon." He worried the scar on his forehead with his free hand; then, as if realizing he was doing it, he threw his fist to the table. The plates and flatware jumped with the smack. "Something happened that I can't quite remember."

Instinctually, she said, "The voices."

He nodded. "An argument. Accusation. And then..."

His forehead pulled into a frown of concentration and the scar stood out in relief. Echo sensed that he was desperately trying to remember. What? Something to do with the theft? Or with his father's death? Feeling his pain, his frustration, she reached out and covered his hand with her own.

"Maybe you're trying too hard."

He stared at her so intently, she had difficulty remaining still in her seat. She wanted to squirm when his hand clasped hers, taking command. As his fingers gripped her tightly and his thumb ran along the length of her palm, her pulse sped up in alarming fashion. Her mouth went dry and she fought the temptation to lick her lips.

"I'm afraid I haven't tried hard enough," Bram was saying. "I put off facing my past for too long...and now I'm afraid it may have slipped away forever."

She was staring at the scar. Curious how she hadn't even noticed it the first time they'd met in the library. "Where did you have this accident?"

"Up in the attic. It was my secret hiding place away from the adults. Or so I thought. Aunt Addy knew. She's the one who found me lying there on the floor, unconscious."

Again emotion surfaced in his voice when he spoke of his aunt. Surely he cared enough deep down that he would never really have her institutionalized.

"How do you feel when you go into the attic?" she asked. "Does anything new come to you? Do any memories surface?"

He was shaking his head. "I wouldn't know. Haven't been up there yet."

He'd been back several days, and he'd managed to avoid the scene of his accident. And the source of the "voices." Echo didn't put words to her thoughts—that he sounded as if he were reluctant to enter the attic. Reluctant to learn the truth. Still.

"If you want company..." she offered.

"No. It's something I have to do myself." He freed her hand and pointed to her empty bowl. "Want more?"

"I've had too much already. I'm stuffed."

He pushed his chair away from the table and stood. "What you need is a walk. I'll get your jacket and we'll go down to the beach."

Echo gave over readily. Bram's confiding in her made her feel closer to him. She considered that fact. She'd never allowed anything serious to develop with a man, but she knew this was different. For the first time in her life, Echo wanted to take the chance.

But as they descended the board steps that eased the steep incline down to the lake, she wasn't thinking about anything but giving herself over to the whispers of a mild October wind and the soothing sound of water rushing to shore. The moon was full, though the sky was crowded with clouds. A portent of the bad weather that had been predicted for the next few days. They had just enough light to see where they stepped.

When Bram wrapped an arm around her shoulders, she found herself leaning into him. As they dared cold, damp sand to invade their shoes, a sense of expectation filled her, and she yearned for something that had always seemed out of reach—complete trust in someone other than Izzy.

She wanted to trust Bram.

"There's something about the lake that's therapeutic, don't you think?" he asked.

"Chicago is on the lake, too," she reminded him.

"Not the same. Too many reminders of civilization. High-rises. Traffic on Lake Shore Drive. Bicyclists and people on Rollerblades."

"At this time of year?"

"Hmm, you may be right. I guess I don't take full advantage of the lakefront in any season. Here, though, the lake is unavoidable."

"If you're lucky enough to have beach rights," she said wryly, aware of the main tourist complaint—the difficulty in getting down to the water, except for the few and far between public areas.

"You can use the Dunescape beach whenever you want," Bram offered. "And Aunt Addy has agreements with most of her neighbors."

She noted they were heading east, away from the Fergusons' property. "Actually, I'm a member of a cooperative that owns a half-mile strip of shoreline, but thanks."

"Thank you. For listening like you cared back there in the kitchen."

"We all need someone to talk to at times." And she was glad that he'd opened up to her. "My mother taught us that every human being has something worthwhile to give, if only we allow ourselves the privilege of finding it."

"Sounds like quite a woman."

Echo forced herself to keep her voice light. "She is."

"Though she might have changed her mind if she had met me under the same circumstances."

"Oh, I don't know. Her temper is much more even than mine. Besides, you're not such a tough nut to crack."

"Hundreds of people would tell you otherwise—people who *aren't* my clients."

She laughed. "That's better. I was beginning to think that you were modest and self-effacing. That would have totally blown my perception of you."

"If I was modest and self-effacing, we wouldn't have this chemistry building between us."

So he was willing to admit it. Smiling happily, she teased, "My, aren't you smug."

"Perceptive," he corrected.

"Plus, you have an inflated ego."

"So you're telling me I'm wrong? Then it won't bother you at all if I do this."

Before Echo knew what Bram was about, he whipped her around in his arms and kissed her. Not a light, tentative kiss, the kind two people shared when they weren't sure of each other, but a thrilling, no-holds-barred exploration that swept away any doubts that she might have had about his interest. As his tongue invaded her mouth in a boldly sexual assault, Echo's restraints broke free. She didn't want to think, to consider the consequences. She wanted to feel, to lose herself in the now.

To lose herself to Bram Vanmatre...what should be a very scary thought.

But Echo wasn't afraid. She was elated. She returned his unexpected passion, her own having been held in tight check for so very long. She couldn't get enough of him, of the feelings he stirred in her. Desire. Hope.

One of Bram's hands firmly cradled her head, while the other pressed into the small of her back, keeping her snug against him.

If they weren't both wearing jackets...

No matter the extra layers of clothing, she was melting, from the tips of her toes to the tips of her breasts pressed into his chest. She couldn't remember the last time she felt so alive.

Subtle sounds nearby broke through the haze of desire enveloping her. She pulled back from the kiss enough to register the noises issuing from the bluff above. She heard a rustling, as if someone were disturbing the tall dune grass. Then furtive footfalls. An object kicked. A stumble?

She wrenched herself out of Bram's tight embrace and stared upward. "Did you hear that?"

"What?"

Her heart was pounding, and not merely from the personal contact with him. Her earlier experience was too fresh to be ignored. Could the person who'd pushed her into the stairwell be following her now? Thinking she saw a clandestine movement, she narrowed her gaze; but the moon was jockeying behind the clouds and not enough light shone on the area.

Maybe her mind was playing games with her.

She swallowed hard at the thought, let her insecurities surface for a moment. Then she heard it again. The rustling sound seemed magnified to her ears.

"Someone's creeping around up there," she whispered to Bram. "Spying on us."

"Could be a loose dog."

Could be, but she was certain the culprit was all too human. Though tempted to climb the dune and meet the stalker face-to-face, she couldn't make her legs move in that direction. She sucked in a lungful of fresh air and told herself to calm down.

"Let's go back," she said, her voice hoarse with renewed fear.

There's nothing to be afraid of, she told herself. She wasn't in some closed space this time. And she wasn't alone.

"I swear, there's no one," Bram said, still staring at the ridge.

But his calm reassurance didn't sit well. "Then I'll go alone."

Echo strode away, but a second later Bram grabbed her arm and spun her around to face him. Her heart raced even faster. Enough moon shone through the clouds that she could see he was frowning down at her. But when he spoke, his tone convinced her he was concerned rather than angry.

"I really don't think anyone has reason to spy on us, but I'll be glad to take you back."

She nodded and fixed her gaze on the dune ridge as he took her arm and guided her.

He didn't believe her. He knew of no reason for someone to be spying on them. And now he probably thought she was a high-strung nervous Nelly... or a fool!

No FOOL HE, Uriah Hawkes slipped into the house through one of the tunnels. From the cellar, he came up into the kitchen using a hidden staircase. Miss Addy disliked him entering the house unannounced, so he had to watch himself. Stepping out of the pantry, he checked to

ee that Lena was alone. She was cleaning up at the sink.
Ie wanted to talk to her, to find out what exactly the
ousekeeper knew.

Lena gave him an annoyed look as he poured himself
cup of coffee and said, "I suppose you don't like what's
oing on any more'n I do."

"Turning a great estate into a freak show?" Lena's
oice rose. "Sacrilege, that's what it is."

Not exactly what he'd meant. He took a sip of coffee.
Ĵreat estate, his Aunt Fanny. The place *was* a haunted
ouse, complete with a couple of old bats running it.

He tried again. "That St. Clair dame, she's some-
hing else, ain't she?"

"She reminds me of *that one.*"

Uriah got her drift. Katherine. Lena had never liked
Bram's mother. He took advantage of that fact. "They're
oth trouble, huh?"

"The young one is nosing around, digging into the
ast. Mr. Bram's past," she clarified with a sniff. "I
eard her."

He'd heard and seen some things, too. They were get-
ing close! If Vanmatre sniffed himself out a honey, he'd
e staying on longer or making regular trips from the city.
ỏon they'd both be sticking their noses where they
houldn't be.

He didn't like the possibility, not at all. If he had his
ay, neither one of 'em would ever set foot in Dunescape
Ĵottage again!

Lena could help him. She used to have a thing for him.
Maybe still did. She wasn't as dry as she looked.

"Lena, I think you and me, we gotta talk. In private."
Ie was thinking of his quarters and his big bed. Maybe
would make Lena nostalgic. More amenable.

Turning from the sink, Lena dried her hands on her apron. "The coach house?"

She gave him a sly smile that put him off for a minute. Who was using whom?

Chapter Seven

By the time they reached Dunescape property again, Echo was keeping a good foot of space between them. Bram wondered what was bothering her. He hadn't seen anyone, but he had been undeniably preoccupied.

What reason would anyone have to be sneaking around the dunes after them in the dark?

Determined not to let Echo get away so soon, he said, "By the way, I let my fingers do the walking earlier," as they neared her station wagon.

"You *what?*"

"Went through the local telephone directory and found Priscilla Courtland's number and address. She happens to be in town. Whoever answered said she'd be around by eight or so." It was almost eight-thirty. "Thought you might be interested in meeting the woman whose jewels were stolen. I thought we could surprise her."

"I don't know—"

"Say yes. Indulge me . . . or your own curiosity," he baited her.

Curiosity got the better of who. "A short visit couldn't hurt."

When she turned to the door of her station wagon
Bram took her arm. "My car this time, if you don'
mind."

She acquiesced with a shrug, and Bram swept her to
ward the garage, where his late model sedan, an infi
nitely more comfortable vehicle, awaited. Glancing up a
the darkened coach house, he briefly wondered wher
Uriah Hawkes had gotten himself to. He'd wanted to tel
the groundskeeper about the supply truck left parked a
the boathouse, but he hadn't been able to run the mar
down all day. Bram wondered if Uriah was pulling hi
weight—or the wool over Aunt Addy's eyes.

"Do you really think Priscilla Courtland will be abl
to tell you anything the newspaper accounts didn't?'
Echo asked when they arrived at his car. "Especially af
ter thirty years. She's not a young woman, and wh
knows what her memory is like."

"True." Her mind could be Swiss cheese, like Aun
Addy's. "I'd say it's worth a shot."

The hairs on the back of his neck prickled, and now
Bram had the distinct feeling they weren't alone—a dif
ferent sensation, however, than the one he'd felt in th
library. Maybe Echo had been right. Opening the pas
senger door and holding it as Echo slipped into her seat
he casually glanced around. His penetrating gaze fer
reted out no sign of life nearby. Still, he couldn't shak
the feeling as he got inside and started the engine. H
inched away from the coach house, using his rear- an
side-view mirrors for as long as he could see. No move
ment. No doubt Echo had stirred his subconscious an
now he was imagining things.

In less than five minutes they arrived at the Courtlan
beach house. The side entrance to the mansion glowe
pink in the dark. The Floridian-style building was dis

tinctly out of place on the shores of a midwestern lake. Priscilla Courtland's residence added to her having worn showy, expensive jewels to a large party made Bram quickly conclude she was one of those people who enjoyed being noticed and talked about.

Leaving the car in the drive, Echo and Bram approached the house together. He rang the bell.

"This place is looking a little run-down, too," Echo said in a hushed voice.

He had noticed a bit of peeling paint and some cracked flagstones along the garden path. "I'd say it's in prime condition compared to Dunescape, though. Takes a lot of money to keep up a place this size, especially one so overly exposed to the elements."

His head was still reeling with the number of things that had to be taken care of to get Aunt Addy's place back in good enough shape to find a buyer...if that's what he chose to do. On the other hand, staying and making a new start in a town that he'd avoided for thirty years held an appeal that surprised him.

A moment later, a young woman answered and led them into the dated, painfully pristine living room. It was done up in mostly eggshell-white but for touches of pale pink, mauve and rose. Priscilla Courtland sat before the fire working with a skein of yarn and a crochet hook, what looked to be the start of an afghan in her lap. Her rose-and-cream dress was designer, but also dated, and her silver hair was swept away from her fine-boned face. With skin nearly as smooth as a young girl's, she hardly looked her age, which had to be about sixty.

Eyes wide on Bram, she indicated a sofa opposite. "Please sit. Excuse me for staring," she said in a cultured, well-modulated voice, "but the resemblance to your father is remarkable."

Bram placed a hand at Echo's back and guided her to the sofa. "So I've been told. This is Echo St. Clair. She owns Echoes in Water's Edge. And she's helping to turn Dunescape Cottage into the Halloween Haunted Mansion."

Bright blue eyes taking stock of Echo now, Priscilla regally inclined her head. "I've heard of your shop. And of your worthy project for the young people. Very admirable, since you are not a parent yourself."

"Close enough," Echo said as they sat. "I'm an aunt."

Priscilla asked if either wanted tea, then waved her young maid off. "So what can I do for you?"

"Share some memories, if you would," Bram said.

"Of your father?"

He nodded. "More to the point, of the night your jewels were stolen."

"Ah, the jewels." She shook her head sadly. "The start of all our bad luck."

"There were other thefts?" Echo asked.

"More like business failures. Within months of the theft, poor Grover lost the company his father had started. Then we had to sell our Palm Beach estate and New York City apartment and move into this house full-time within two years." She clucked and shook her head harder. "Forgive me. I am rambling on about myself. You wanted to know about the jewel theft. May I ask why?"

Bram hadn't been prepared to answer that particular question. He didn't want to suggest that he thought the theft and his father's death might be connected.

As if sensing his hesitancy, Echo piped in, "While we were cleaning up yesterday, I found a gold, gem-studded button that reminded Bram of the last ball and your loss."

"My costume didn't have buttons of any worth."

"So we've been told."

Priscilla sighed. "Thirty years is a long time. If only you could recover the jewels.... The economy has been terrible for everyone, hasn't it? And without Grover... I'm lucky that I haven't been forced to sell this house and move into something even more modest. As it is, I live on the first floor and leave the second closed so I don't have to heat and light it." Her laugh was troubled. "It's almost as if someone put a curse on us."

Bram didn't believe in such nonsense, but he nodded sympathetically and pointed the conversation back to the theft. "The jewels never surfaced. Could someone have stolen them out of spite? An enemy of yours or of your husband, perhaps?"

"Enemy? Oh, dear, how dramatic. Anyone with wealth has those who are envious of their good fortune. But Grover was a dear man, amiable and generous to a fault. He never made an enemy in his life. If the fault lies anywhere, then it must be with me."

Her eyes shone with unshed tears as she gazed at the portrait hanging over the fireplace. The middle-aged man was classically handsome, with a full mouth, a tiny mole at the corner, a straight nose and broad forehead. His light brown eyes held a sly expression, as if he were laughing at a private joke.

"So you had no indication that anything was wrong that day before coming to the party," Bram went on.

She frowned as if remembering something, but said, "Not really."

Perhaps she'd had a disagreement with her husband. Bram didn't want to pry.

"So what exactly did happen at the ball?" Echo asked.

"We alternated dancing and speaking to friends—those we could recognize in their costumes. Then, just before midnight, the buffet was put out. Grover was hungry, of course. He was a man with very healthy appetites of all sorts." She grew silent for a moment, her face softening as if she were recounting pleasurable memories. "We were about to get in line when he was called away to the telephone."

"Who would try to contact your husband at a social event?" Bram asked.

"We never found out. By the time he got to the phone, the caller had hung up."

If there had been anyone on the other end in the first place. "Who notified him of the call?"

Priscilla's forehead puckered. "What *is* her name. Age you know." She waved her smooth hand around her head. "Tends to scramble the brain a bit. She worked for your family. A severe looking young woman. I believe she may still be in Adrienne's employ."

"Lena?"

"I believe so."

Bram chewed on that one for a minute. The newspaper accounts hadn't mentioned Lena—he would have remembered. Or a mysterious telephone call for that matter. All the stories had revealed was that Grover Courtland had been out of his wife's company when the robbery took place....

If only his mother would be more forthcoming. He'd asked her about that night more than once, but she always avoided the topic with a vehemence he hadn't understood.

"Go on," Echo urged.

"Well, I was alone, staring out the terrace windows toward the lake when the lights went out. People were frightened. I remember hearing a scream." Her fingers fiddled with the crochet hook in her lap. "And then...nothing. Next thing I knew, I woke up in my dear Grover's arms and was told I had been robbed. What a tragedy, considering he'd only bought the collection for me a few weeks before."

"Not enough time to have paste duplicates made," Bram commented.

Priscilla shrugged. "Fate was not kind. Who would have thought thieves of any sophistication would be afoot in a backwater Michigan town?"

"Do you have any pictures of the jewels?" Echo asked.

"We had a shot taken of us that evening in full dress, of course. I believe it's packed away with our costumes. Would you like me to check?"

Five minutes later, they were in one of the closed-off bedrooms, at a closet neatly stacked with clearly marked storage cartons. It only took Priscilla a moment to find the correct one. Lifting the cardboard lid, she removed clothing an article at a time—an old-fashioned tux and shirt, a gold-beaded flapper dress and a matching purse, among other items. From the bottom of the carton, she pulled out a smaller box in which she'd placed the invitation, her formal dance card and a pack of photographs.

She gave them to Echo, who took a quick look at the top shot, then passed the pack on to Bram.

While he was busy studying the photographed jewels, Echo seemed to be taken by the garments on the bed, no doubt attracted to the glitz. She picked up the beaded bag and turned it over carefully.

"What's this?" she asked, as something slipped from the bag's mouth.

Bram noted the smaller silk pouch was embroidered with some strange symbols.

"My personal maid insisted I carry it for good luck. She was very superstitious. Her upbringing, I suppose."

Echo fingered open the pouch and her eyes widened as she peered inside. "Your maid? Where was she from?"

"Oh, somewhere in the Caribbean. She was very young when we hired her to work in our Palm Beach home, but she became so indispensable we quickly began taking her to all our residences. We were together through some *difficult* times for both of us." Priscilla shook her head. "I was sorry to let her go after our turn in fortune. Of course, I had no choice. I gave her excellent references, but she didn't take with her new employers. One day, she just up and disappeared."

"Her name," Echo said. "What was it?"

"Letitia," Priscilla said. "You haven't met her, have you?"

Bram frowned. What was Echo's interest in the maid?

"No, I haven't," Echo said. "Did Letitia come along to the ball?" she asked, making him even more curious.

"Why, yes. Adrienne asked if she could prepare some of her exotic dishes for the buffet, and Letitia agreed."

"Interesting."

But Echo was obviously not about to be forthcoming about her line of questioning at the moment, and Bram chose not to press her until they were alone.

He indicated the photos. "Could I borrow these for a while?"

Priscilla waved a hand. "You may keep them. I have no desire to dredge up old memories. Not bad ones, at any rate. I doubt that I would ever have removed anything from this box if you hadn't asked."

Bram stuffed the pack of photos in his jacket pocket while Priscilla quickly repacked and replaced the storage carton. Then she led them back downstairs to the living room.

Sitting at the edge of the couch, Bram asked, "At the ball, did anyone seem overly interested in your jewels?"

"Everyone." Priscilla's laugh was still a girlish trill. "They were worth a fortune."

"Who knew you would be wearing them?" Echo queried.

"Everyone," Priscilla said again. "I must admit I am not the most discreet woman. My husband bought me objects of beauty and I enjoyed bragging."

"What about my father?" Bram asked. "Did he—"

"No!" Priscilla stared at him for a moment. "I was wondering how long it would take you to get around to that. My jewels and your father disappeared at the same time, but as I assured the police, he had nothing to do with the theft."

Though relieved, Bram kept pressing. "How can you be so certain?"

"He was such an honorable man . . . and far too preoccupied to be planning some nefarious scheme."

"Preoccupied with the guests?"

"Katherine had . . ." Priscilla's eyes widened and she seemed to be biting back what she was about to say.

"What about my mother?"

Flustered, she quickly said, "I merely supposed they were both completely involved with the nuances of hosting a memorable ball."

Though Bram didn't challenge her, he had an odd and unwelcome feeling about what she refused to say.

"The button." Echo pulled a small pad and pen from her pocket. "I wonder if you might remember it? It was solid gold with tiny faceted diamonds and emeralds." She made a quick sketch.

Priscilla looked it over and did not hesitate. "That came from a vest. I remember admiring it and wondering if the materials could be real. He assured me they were."

"Who?"

The older woman concentrated. "It was... No, I'm afraid I don't remember."

"Are you certain?" Bram asked, disappointed.

"I remember admiring them...commenting on how grand they were...." She shook her head.

Figuring that was all they were going to learn, Bram rose. "We've taken enough of your time."

"Yes, thank you." Echo joined him. "You've been very cooperative."

"But not particularly helpful," Priscilla said with a sigh. "What difference does the truth make now after thirty years, anyway?"

All the difference in the world to him, Bram thought.

There had to be a connection between the jewel theft and his father's death. He wouldn't have a moment's peace until he figured out why someone had felt it necessary to kill Donahue Vanmatre.

WHAT MADE ONE HUMAN BEING kill another?

The age-old question haunted him.

He stood a lonely sentinel in the window of the library, which was dark but for the embers that glowed and sparked in the fireplace. If only flames could warm him. He'd been cold and empty and devoid of emotion for so very long.

Until *she* came.

Staring out into the night, he watched the sedan snake along the drive and turn off toward the coach house. Watched them alight in silence.

Watched *her.*

Echo St. Clair. A beautiful name for a beautiful woman with an even more beautiful psyche.

The aura surrounding her vibrated and danced invitingly as she drew closer to the house. That she might enter this very room quickened his spirit. He was drawn to her by some strange and wondrous bond that transcended time and circumstance, a bond that even he could not explain.

After an eternity of nothingness, she had wakened his very soul, and for that he would be ever grateful.

He knew the moment she stepped foot in the house, for the structure wakened from its deathly slumber and sighed with contentment. Her voice floated on the very air. Soft. Earthy. Filled with concern for Bram.

Concentrating, he sensed something else that made him uneasy. An evil that lurked in the shadows... growing... waiting to be fed.

An evil that, if not stopped, would cast Echo in the same hell that was his curse.

NOT KNOWING WHY Echo lingered to delve into his private hell rather than escape to the quiet isolation of her own home, Bram opened the door for her and let her inside.

"Lena," he said aloud to himself. She would know.

"What?"

Preoccupied, Bram didn't bother answering, but went straight to the back of the house and through the kitchen to the housekeeper's quarters. He knocked at the door. Waited a moment. Rapped harder.

"Surely she's not asleep yet," Echo said. "Maybe she's out for the evening."

"Something I can do for you, Mr. Bram?"

He whirled around, noting the housekeeper had given Echo a start, too. Lena had appeared out of nowhere. Or out of the butler's pantry, he thought, seeing that the door was cracked open. Staring for a second, he visualized another door. A hidden door. Leading to a hidden staircase.

"I need to talk to you."

Her expression was inscrutable. "A problem with the house?"

"With the past, Lena."

She seemed instantly on the alert. Bram took a better look at her. The top button of her Mother Hubbard dress was undone. And her normally tidy hair was awry. A few strands dangled along her neck as if someone had mussed it.

"My father . . . was he preoccupied with something the night of his death?"

"Mr. Donahue had many things on his mind."

"Anything out of the ordinary? Anything to do with my mother?"

Lena took her time answering. Bram couldn't miss the glint in her eyes. Knowing. Smug? As though she'd been waiting for this opportunity, he thought.

"It had to do with the divorce."

She dropped the bomb without preamble and Bram could only stare. He couldn't have been more surprised if Lena had slapped him across the face.

"The divorce," he echoed. He was stunned, really, hardly felt the comforting hand Echo immediately placed on his arm.

"Miss Katherine only told Mr. Donahue that she planned to leave him that very morning."

"Mother asked Father for a divorce *that* morning?"

He said it as if he'd known of the impending split, if not the details, when in fact, he'd never had a clue. He felt as if he were seven again...and as if his world would never be the same.

"Such terrible timing," the housekeeper continued, her eyes reflecting her elation. "Poor Mr. Donahue. *That woman* was unusually cruel to him. She should have waited until after the weekend, when the guests were gone."

Though he wanted to walk away from this, go somewhere to think it through alone, he stuck it out. "My father told you about my mother wanting a divorce?"

She hesitated only a second before admitting, "Miss Adrienne did, afterward."

Bram couldn't help but wonder if Aunt Addy could have been making up such a story to account for her twin's distraction—to cover the fact that he might have been involved in the theft.

"I don't think she meant to," Lena was going on. "But he was so distraught. We both were."

He could believe that. Lena's devotion to his father had been very clear, just as had her antagonism toward his mother.

"So the intended divorce came as a complete surprise to everyone?" Echo asked.

Lena turned a hostile expression on Echo. "*Everyone* knew Mr. Donahue never should have married Miss Catherine in the first place."

Bram wondered if Lena's relationship with his father had gone deeper than mere devotion. An affair? He'd

already mentally accused his mother of the perfidy. Bu
what if his father had been the one... ?

Head suddenly aching as it did when he concentrate
on lost memories, Bram refused to chew on the situatior
further.

"That's all—"

"One more thing," Echo interrupted. "Before th
jewel theft, you found Grover Courtland and brough
him to the telephone."

"Yes, I remember."

"Who called?"

"A woman." While she addressed Echo when sh
added, "She did not leave her name, miss," she wa
staring at Bram, her expression enigmatic once more. "I
that is all, may I be excused?"

Bram nodded and waved her away. "Thank you
Lena."

He stood there frozen, still trying to digest this newes
twist in a decades-old story. How could his mother hav
kept an intended divorce from him? How could she hav
kept up the charade that she loved his father and grieve
for him?

Echo stared at Bram, who looked as if he were carve
out of granite. He seemed to have forgotten her pres
ence. She only wished she could say something to mak
him feel better. He wore an expression she could onl
describe as *betrayed*.

"You look like you could use a drink."

He started and focused on her. "Have one with me?"

A moment later they were in the library and she wa
wandering toward the fireplace. "Mmm, the blaze feel
good." She stopped suddenly when she grew uncomfort
able. She spun around, checked the corners and th
shadows. All seemingly empty. Her heart beat swiftly.

"Are there any secret panels in here leading to one of your infamous hidden rooms or staircases?"

"I wish I remembered. If I ever knew," Bram said. His voice was tight. "My father discouraged my explorations, especially after I got myself in trouble."

Echo noted his visage darkened at the mention of his father.

Donahue Vanmatre. Murdered. His spirit destined to wander through the darkened recesses of Dunescape Cottage, unable to find rest because his killer hadn't been brought to justice. Despite her determination to remain clear-headed and as unlike Mama as she could be about this particular issue, part of her believed. Something had gotten her out of that stairwell whole and sane. And now she was experiencing that same sensation. She could almost feel a comforting hand touching her.

Unafraid, she leaned against the high back of a leather chair, closed her eyes and concentrated....

"Maybe this brandy isn't such a good idea," came Bram's voice.

Her eyes flashed open. "Why not?"

"I don't want you falling asleep at the wheel."

"I'm not that tired." Echo took the bulbous glass splashed with amber liquid, flushing when Bram's fingers touched hers. She couldn't forget his kiss. "I was merely soaking up the atmosphere." With all its nuances.

"Do it properly, then." He indicated a chair and took the other himself. Once settled, he lifted his drink. "To the truth," he said, his tone ironic.

Echo touched her glass to his and wondered if the truth might not destroy him. His reaction to the news about the divorce had been intense. He hadn't known. Her heart had gone out to him then.

"So what *is* the truth, Echo, about what went on at Priscilla Courtland's?"

Having known he would get back to the maid issue, Echo chose to tell a half-truth, omitting the part about being trapped in the stairwell. "I saw a pouch like the one that slipped out of her beaded bag earlier today. It belonged to Sibyl . . . whose Grandmama Tisa was born in Haiti."

His expression was surprised yet skeptical. "Coincidence?"

"If you believe in that sort of thing."

"Are you suggesting Sibyl has some ulterior motive in taking care of Aunt Addy?"

"I don't know. I'm only speculating. How did you hire her? A recommendation from a service?"

He frowned. "Come to think of it, she approached me when the nurse I originally hired took sick suddenly."

"Took sick—or was made sick?" Echo remembered Priscilla's statement about being cursed. The pouch given to her by her maid had contained shards of bone—and certainly had not looked like a good-luck charm. "What if Letitia and Tisa are one and the same. What if she had something to do with the robbery?"

"I was wondering about Grover myself," Bram said. "First the jewels stolen, then his father's company lost. The theft could have been an insurance scam. And he could have hoped to save the company with the payoff."

"He would have needed an accomplice," Echo said, thinking Grover had looked familiar. "Letitia was here that night."

"And what if this is all a clever fabrication? What's Sibyl's interest? What if Tisa and Letitia *aren't* the same woman?"

More questions than answers. But Echo's instincts told her that the two women were one and the same, and that Sibyl hadn't shown up by pure luck.

Bram said, "Let's not forget Lena found Grover and told him about the supposed phone call."

"And it looks like Norbert Ferguson was someplace he shouldn't have been." She remembered the son spying on them. "Travis. He knows something. Maybe I should find out what."

"Stay away from that man. He's bad news."

"I consider myself warned." Though Echo made no promises.

But Bram seemed satisfied. "I'd certainly rather believe that any of *them* were responsible for the theft than my own father."

Bram stared into the fire, suddenly seeming lost in his thoughts. Dark thoughts. His angular face appeared hard. Unapproachable. The flicker of firelight licked his clenched jaw and furrowed brow. The throbbing scar was a dead giveaway. He was ready to explode with emotion. Her body stirred, responding to the very darkness that she feared.

Echo strangled her glass with two hands; then, realizing this, she loosened her grip. Despite her better judgment—she was afraid of getting too close to a man with such strength, so used to controlling people and events—she reached across the gulf between their chairs and slipped her hand over his clenched fist.

"Sometimes our families aren't everything we want them to be," she said. "That doesn't mean they don't love us or that we shouldn't love them."

His hand still balled tight beneath her fingers, he stared at her. "How do you know where the lies stop?" he demanded. "What someone you love might be hiding?"

"You can never be sure. No one is guaranteed happiness. You have to have faith."

"Who taught you that? Your mother?"

"Life. My mother was a very unusual person. She believed in things other people don't choose to face. She was ... spiritual."

"You mean religious."

"No. I mean a little removed from reality." A lump in her throat made it difficult to continue. But the fist softening under her hand urged her on. "Her own parents didn't understand her innocent, open view of life. When she joined a commune with her boyfriend, my grandparents threatened to disown her."

"Your parents were hippies?"

Echo hated such easy labels. "My parents were the kindest, most well-intentioned people I knew. We were all so happy—Mama and Daddy and Izzy and me. Our parents taught my sister and me to be worthwhile human beings by example."

A sigh whispered through her lips, and she could feel his eyes on her face. Caressing her. Making her uncomfortable. As if he had already discovered the anguish she always kept tucked away in a secret part of herself, he softened, turned her hand and wove his fingers through hers.

"So what went wrong with this paradise?" he asked softly.

Bram was perceptive. She would have to give him that. Echo had never told another soul about the horror she had lived through, but suddenly the story came pouring out.

"Mama always swore she was connected to another world beyond this earth." As a child, Echo had accepted this without thought. "Mama might have heard voices, but she wasn't crazy. She was happy with the simple things. And then Daddy died. His appendix burst, and he didn't get medical treatment in time. Mama couldn't bear his loss. She went over the edge a little more, swore Daddy wasn't gone, that she saw and spoke to him.''

Bram squeezed her fingers comfortingly. ''She needed professional help.''

A wave of warmth swept over her. From Bram? The fire? Or something less tangible?

''She needed loving and understanding from someone who could get through her grief. Izzy and I were scared and confused. We didn't know what to do... and someone mistakenly called my grandparents.'' Her laugh was bitter. ''I think they actually rejoiced in our loss. They saw Daddy's death as a way to get back something they never had in the first place—a daughter who fit into their conventional idea of what a perfect child should be.''

''Echo, you don't have to—''

''They had her committed to a private sanitarium and got legal custody of Izzy and me,'' she said before she could change her mind.

She expected a reaction, not the silence that forced her to look at Bram. If she had seen pity, she would have run from the room. Instead, she read anger. *For* her. She was inordinately pleased.

''Your mother,'' he said, squeezing her hand, ''she's still institutionalized?''

Echo shook her head. ''She was released eventually. After the drugs and the padded rooms and the electric shocks, she didn't hear voices and talk to Daddy anymore. She didn't say much. She was never the same. Ironic, but my grandparents still weren't satisfied. They wouldn't even let her see her own daughters unsupervised. As if Mama would ever hurt us.''

Bram swore under his breath. "What misguided fools."

"She was harmless then, just as she had always been." She deliberately added, "Just as Miss Addy is." When he didn't respond, she forced the issue. "You do agree your aunt is harmless?"

"For the most part."

His careful answer made her uneasy. "You can see how wrong it would be to take her away from here and lock her away from what she knows and loves."

"I live in Chicago," Bram pointed out. "She doesn't have anyone else. She's alone here. She can't take care of herself anymore."

"She has a nurse." Remembering the conclusions she'd drawn about Sibyl Wilde, she added, "And you can hire someone else, someone you trust."

"I'm afraid that wouldn't be enough."

Bram's words pierced her heart. Echo twisted her hand from his grasp. "You're going to do it, aren't you?" she accused.

"I haven't decided anything."

She didn't believe him. "How could you think about locking Miss Addy away after what I just told you?"

"If I were to find a...a home for Aunt Addy, she would be treated kindly. No padded rooms. No electric shocks. Their situations are different."

Only on the surface. "You'll kill her," Echo choked out.

His tight voice and expression distanced him. "She would be well taken care of."

"You'll kill her spirit. You'll strip her of who she is, and there won't be anything left." Popping out of her chair, she felt an invisible aura trying to smother her.

"You're overwrought."

"Maybe I am. I have every reason to be."

Blindly, she ran from the room, fighting off the presence that, rather than comforting her this time, frightened her. Mama had been connected to another world, too, and look what had happened to her.

"Echo, wait. Please."

No, she would be all right, Echo assured herself.

Even if she *was* like Mama, no one could do anything to her. No one could lock *her* away. Izzy never would, and she'd made certain no one else had that kind of control.

"Echo!"

Emotions flooded her as she grabbed her jacket from the hall chair and struggled into it while racing out to the night and the sanctuary of her station wagon. She had to get away from Dunescape Cottage. Fast.

If only she never had to come back....

But getting out wasn't as easy as she had hoped. The engine wouldn't start. Frustrated, she slapped the steering wheel with the flat of her hand over and over, as if that would make the old wagon behave. She tried again. The engine still refused to turn over. Her battery was dead!

What now?

She couldn't go back into that house and face Bram. Not when her emotions were so out of kilter. Not ever, if she had her choice. While spilling her guts, she'd imagined a real connection between her and Bram. Now she simply felt humiliated. Resolving to walk the mile or so home, she grabbed her flashlight from the glove compartment and threw herself out of the vehicle. She'd have the service station come out and get the old junker running in the morning.

By morning, she would be back in control.

Storm clouds completely blotted out the moon, and the wind had picked up, soughing through the dune grass and the trees that fingered the ridge overlooking the lake. The air was heavy with unshed rain, clinging, smothering. Or maybe it was the house itself. Quickly leaving the soft glow of room lights behind, Echo raced down the drive, remembering to flip on the flashlight when she was half way to the property entrance.

The bulb flickered and immediately grew dim. Great! More bad batteries!

She switched it off to save what power was left. There would be areas where she would really need some light. Going east, Water's Edge Road twisted and tacked away from the lake. The cross streets were few, hilly and angled, turning the area into an outdoor maze.

An unlit maze.

She hadn't been this far west on foot, and certainly never in the dark. If she weren't careful, she'd end up in a drainage ditch with a twisted ankle. Or worse.

Once off the property, she checked the road, then stuck the flashlight back into her pocket. Fighting the chilly, ominous wind, she sprinted up a hill. Her skin crawled and she rubbed her arms through the jacket.

She would be all right. She would be all right. *She would be all right.* She repeated the words like a litany until the noise behind her drove them from her head.

An engine. A vehicle approaching.

Glancing over her shoulder, she saw the lights crest the hill behind and ride high above the pavement. A four wheel drive or a truck. She waved so the driver would be certain to see her. The brights flicked on, blinding her.

Squinting against them, she stumbled and caught her self before her hands hit the ground. Startled, it took her a second to think clearly. To realize the vehicle wasn'

slowing. To cut over to the other side of the road to let it
pass.

That's when the lights swerved and came straight for
her.

Chapter Eight

Echo felt like a deer must when surprised by an oncoming car in the dark.

She froze.

Stood rooted to the spot, looking into the face of death. Disbelieving. Horrified. Adrenaline shooting through her like a bullet.

At the last possible second, she flew out of the vehicle's path and rolled into the thicket of growth at the side of the road. Close. So close that she'd felt seared by the heat of the engine and caught in the pull of the draft as the vehicle sped by without slowing.

She lay there stunned for a moment. Her heart was pounding and she was gasping for air. If only the incident hadn't happened so fast, she might have been able to identify the vehicle for the authorities.

"Damn drunk drivers," she muttered, getting to her feet and brushing the sandy soil and dried weeds from her clothing. Nothing a cleaning wouldn't fix.

She was bandy-legged and would probably have a few bruises in the morning, but she felt in one piece. Testing herself, she took a few steps. Then a few more. It was difficult walking against the wind, which seemed to pick up with every pace, but she managed it.

No serious harm done, thank God.

Lucky, that's what she was. She could have been killed, and all because the battery in her wretched station wagon had refused to start. Setting off again, she cursed the occasional fat drop of rain that splashed her face, and she prayed that she would beat the storm home. She never should have agreed to that drink. Odd how fate sometimes conspired against a person.

First the battery dying...

...then almost being hit...

...and now the threat of being soaked as the drops of rain grew more frequent.

Her mind went back to the first two. The battery. The near miss. She attempted to shake off the sudden suspicion that niggled at her.

Still, she was uneasy.

Rounding a curve in the road, Echo heard another engine nearby. Another vehicle coming toward her. She strained to listen. Did the engine really sound familiar or was her imagination playing tricks on her?

She was certain the moment she caught sight of the lights, too high off the ground to belong to a car. The same high-riding vehicle!

This time she didn't freeze. Every nerve in her body came alive even as she tried telling herself the vehicle's return was a coincidence, nothing to do with her. A missed turnoff. Or maybe the driver had been making a delivery and was merely going home.

But as she crossed through the brights to the other side of the road, the vehicle altered course yet again—veering toward her.

And now there was no denying she was a target.

Whoever was behind the wheel must be insane rather than drunk! Travis Ferguson?

This time, she flew into the shelter of some trees whipping around in time to see the vehicle go by. The familiar truck screeched to a stop.

She watched in horror as the rear lights indicated the vehicle was about to retrace its path.

Echo ran.

She heard the vehicle backing up.

Pulling the flashlight from her jacket pocket, she swept the faint light over the wet pavement before her. No cross street near enough to use. No lit houses close enough to offer sanctuary. On her side of the road, a steep ravine its bottom obliterated by the fog rising against the drizzle. On the other side, a gentle incline into wooded territory that would take her vaguely toward the lake.

She crossed the road and plunged into the shelter of the trees, hoping against hope the driver would tire of whatever game he was playing and take off. Glancing over her shoulder, she saw the lights of the truck. The engine idled as if the driver were waiting...watching...deciding what to do next.

Echo paused and caught her breath. This made no sense. Why would someone be playing a deadly game with her? If it was a game.... Surely no one would have reason to harm her.

Unless...

She had been the one to find the button. And she'd been encouraging Bram to find the truth.

When the truck began creeping forward, she found the ability to breathe again. Whoever was after her was giving up. She edged backward, a weight lifting from her spirit. Relief was all too short, however. For the driver found an unpaved road she hadn't spotted and pulled the truck onto it. That, and the brilliant beam from the driver's window, convinced her to move before she was caught.

Too late!

Light washed over her even as she turned to run. She screamed, the sound muffled by the rising fog. She was being hunted like an animal, for God's sake! Who would want to frighten her like this, and to what end?

Reaching a darkened house, she thought to break in to call for help. But what if this was one of those houses abandoned by summer-only residents? The phone would be out. Then she would be really and truly trapped.

Echo stumbled onto a crossroad that angled back west more directly toward the lake. The drizzle had turned to a downpour. She was soaked. A light glowed in the distance, too far for her to run, but close enough that she could barely discern the outline of the dune. The lake was so close she could distinguish the smell of fish, could hear the waves lapping at the shore.

Still moving, sobs breaking from her throat, she squinted against the murky wet. Several closer houses—none of them lit from the inside—stood within view.

Hearing the truck grind gears behind her, Echo pushed herself until her muscles screamed for mercy. She slipped once, slid along the pavement and rolled to her feet all in one motion, her goal a faint light ahead, the drive leading to one of the big homes lining the dune above the lake. Gasping, she whipped around a six-foot decorative hedge and hid behind it, for the moment sheltered from view and the elements.

The truck followed, turning up the drive, the moving beam flashing along both sides of the blacktop.

Heart in her throat, trying to take deep breaths to steady herself, Echo pressed against the foliage, making herself as inconspicuous as possible. For a moment, as it passed beneath the dim yard light, she could see the truck clearly enough to read the legend on the side if not identify the driver. Lakeside Construction. The company doing repairs at Dunescape Cottage. She'd seen the vehicle parked by the boathouse earlier....

Even as she realized someone from Dunescape must be behind that wheel, she rounded the hedge and tore back out to the road and into the near-blinding rain. The truck's brakes squealed—the driver must have spotted her! Following the outer perimeter of the house's grounds, she edged the cul-de-sac that led to the dune ridge, using her flashlight to locate the steep wooden stairway bottoming out on the beach itself.

The truck was still chasing. She couldn't run much longer, and probably not at all on the sand. Besides which, the driver would be fresh.

What else could she do?

Where could she hide?

Reaching the platform at the top of the stairs, she saw her salvation clinging to the side of the dune—the abandoned drainpipe that had once been used to detour rainwater from the land around the house ran straight down to the beach more than thirty feet below.

The corrugated metal was large enough for a body to crawl through!

The truck braked and shuddered to a stop. The noise of the door opening sounded ominous.

Adrenaline renewed, Echo descended a few feet to a ledge even before the door slammed shut. Careful to make no noise that might alert her pursuer, she slithered sideways along the rain-slicked incline, pausing only when she got to the drainpipe's head, which was open and still partially secured to a concrete footing.

Debris had gathered in the mouth of the pipe, but not nough to stop her. Dropping to her knees, she backed in arefully, and as she eased her body along the slight curve of metal, she searched for footing. There seemed to be one. Suddenly, her feet shot out, her lower half following. Throwing out her hands, she grasped the edge of the pipe in time to keep herself from hurtling down the shaft. Her rings caught on the metal edge. Her legs dangled wildly. Only her upper body was supported by the pipe before it dropped off abruptly.

Echo felt light-headed. She hadn't thought that she might be putting herself in even more danger. She adjusted her body, tried to wedge herself in solid, but no matter how hard she tried, she couldn't get a really good foothold.

Footsteps crunched on wet sand.

Echo stopped squirming and held her breath. Tried to ignore the sharp metal pressing into her palms, not to mention the strain on her arm muscles. Instead, she forced herself to concentrate on the sounds outside her shelter, hoping to figure out how close her pursuer was.

And possibly to figure out the person's identity.

She'd assumed the truck driver to be a man, but the footsteps were light. Merely careful? Or might they belong to a woman? She couldn't be sure.

Everything sounded muffled and odd inside the metal housing, even the rain railing down on her. Though the drainpipe had been detached and virtually abandoned as a means of diverting excess rainwater to the lake, water still sloshed down the eroded gully. It came in waves, soaking her, forcing dead leaves and twigs into her face and hair. The debris threatened to smother her, the stream to lift her bodily and wash her down the pipe's length. She fought the increasingly heavy force until her

arms burned, and she clenched her jaw so as not to cr
out.

Suddenly realizing she hadn't been paying attention t
the whereabouts of her pursuer, she listened hard. Wa
that an engine? The truck moving away? Had her pui
suer given up the hunt at last?

She waited until her hands went numb, until her arm
threatened to dislocate from her shoulders. Knowing sh
could hold on no longer, that she had to take the chanc
of exposure, she finally secured her toes against the coi
rugated metal and used the indentations like tiny steps
As she wiggled her body upward, the metal buckled an
roared against the storm like the rail of thunder.

Punchy, she giggled. She searched for a grip outside o
the pipe. Her fingers met wet leaves. Nothing of sub
stance, not even a tree root.

She had to get out of there!

Fighting against panic, Echo tried again, angling he
left hip and right knee against opposite sides of the pipe
Sliding up an inch at a time, she forced her head an
shoulders out. And then, when victory seemed within he
grasp, her foot slipped. Hands shot out again. Found ai
this time. Her body knocked from one side of the pipe t
the other before she gave up, protected her head with he
arms and let herself go.

Down she plunged, the water and slippery decaye
material easing her path. At the only bend in the pipe, sh
jarred her left shoulder, slowing her flight, then smoothl
shot to earth in one last long drop of at least a dozen feet
She landed with bent knees, and on impact, rolled in th
wet sand.

The breath was knocked out of her, and for a momen
she felt numb all over.

Nothing short of agony followed.

Groaning, she tested her limbs. They all worked. Barely. Engrossed in just trying to rise, she nearly had heart failure when light smacked her across the eyes.

"Aa-a-ah!"

"Echo, what the hell is going on?"

Again she felt like a caught deer. Body frozen. Only her mind continuing to work.

The argument. The truck. Now Bram here.

A cold like she'd never felt before crept through her. Exactly what kind of fool had she been? Rimmed by the flare of his flashlight, he appeared mysterious and commanding, an otherwordly presence who could mesmerize a gullible woman into thinking they had more than mere attraction going between them.

She'd wanted to trust Bram more than anything. Had that possibly been the biggest mistake of her life?

Fighting disappointment, crazily wanting to give him the benefit of the doubt, she choked out, "Maybe you ought to be the one doing the explaining!"

BRAM FROWNED DOWN at Echo. What a mess! He tried to help her up without hurting her more than she must be already. She cried out but got to her feet, pushing at his hands. Her own looked cut and bloody.

"Did you come down that drainpipe or am I crazy?"

"Are you? Is that why you followed me?"

"Followed? I was taking a walk on the beach." Trying to work off his anger with her, with himself and with the past. "I heard this racket and came to investigate."

"You were walking in the rain?" Her disbelief was evident.

"It wasn't raining when I set out." And he'd been too preoccupied to heed the warnings. As, obviously, she had been. Echo was soaked, filthy, her sweater jacket shredded. "Are you all right?"

He sensed her calming down. "I will be," she muttered, staggering toward the stairs.

"Not so fast." He caught her around the waist. Her gasp tore at him as if the anguish were his own. "You can hardly stay on your feet."

"I can stay on them long enough to get myself home."

Not so certain, he refused to let go. She looked wild and utterly desirable. He stilled the inclination to kiss her. She might struggle, and he didn't want to hurt her.

"I'll walk you up to your car," he insisted.

"I'm not going back to Dunescape."

He glanced up. "You didn't leave it in the cul-de-sac?"

"The battery was dead."

If she hadn't driven, then she'd been on foot. Why? All she'd had to do was come back to the house and he would have given her a ride. If he'd been there. A moment after she'd left, he'd stormed out himself, not even looking after her. No wonder he'd missed seeing her station wagon in the drive.

"I'll ask you again," he repeated. "What the hell is going on, Echo?"

She seemed to be studying him, her eyes traversing the planes of his face, up to his forehead. He felt the damned scar throbbing as it did only when his deepest emotions were involved.

As if the sight of it convinced her, she sighed, the sound one of relief. "You really don't know."

That did it! "What the hell do you take me for? Some kind of sadist who wants to see you hurt? I care about you, for God's sake!" Not that he'd meant to tell her like this.

She blinked as if trying to take in this new concept. "I—I was walking home when a truck came up behind me. The driver purposely tried to hit me."

"Oh, come now—"

"Twice."

That shut him up. Quickly Echo told him about her ordeal. That someone was out to harm her turned Bram's blood cold. And he could see she was shivering with it. The cold and the wet. At least the rain had stopped, though the fog was rising. He held her close, felt the rapid beating of her heart and wanted to kill whoever had done this to her. Though she'd begun by suspecting him, she now clung to him as though she never wanted to let him go.

"I was so scared," she admitted.

"I'm here now."

She huddled closer, probably all she'd give in the way of admitting she needed him.

"If you don't mind," she mumbled against his shoulder, "I really want to get home."

"I'm taking you." No argument would sway him.

But she didn't protest, didn't object to the arm he wound around her waist as he helped her up the stairs and set off down the mist-covered road at a fast limp. He took as much of her weight as she would allow and was concerned when he felt her tremble.

"You're shivering. My jacket's not exactly dry, but it's in better shape than yours."

"I'm fine."

Perhaps she had herself in control mentally, but her body was another story. She shook. Uncertain if it was a reaction to the cold or the fright, Bram pulled her closer. He'd never felt so protective of a woman before. Neither of them spoke until they reached her home nearly a quarter of an hour later, and none too soon. The road was barely visible now. The night was heavy with a wet fog, the stuff from which sprang tales of horror.

Her experience had been horrific, Bram thought. The driver of that damn truck was a monster!

Echo seemed to be having a bad case of nerves as she untangled herself from him. Her hand was shaking as she stuck it into her jacket pocket. Pulling out her keys, she unlocked her door and said, "Thanks for the escort."

"I'll see you in." Not giving her a chance to protest, he slipped inside and headed for the kitchen. "Go take a hot shower. I'll make you some tea."

She turned and did as he ordered. Shock, no doubt. Otherwise, she probably would have pushed him out the door and told him what to do with himself. By the time he set the kettle on the stove, he heard the shower going.

To distract himself from the enticing images of Echo conjured by that sound, he hung his jacket on a peg and reset fresh logs for a fire. He liked her place. It was warm and cozy. A little sparsely decorated perhaps, but a relief from the dark clutter of Dunescape Cottage. Thinking about it, he loved the estate, anyway. The mansion might be an old mausoleum, but it was his heritage. And he enjoyed the laid-back atmosphere of the small town, a relief from life in the big city.

In the midst of spreading kindling over the logs, Bram stopped. He was getting sentimental about Water's Edge, as if he didn't want to leave. But his practice was in Chicago. His life was in Chicago.

What life?

The whistle of the teakettle interrupted his reverie. He started the fire and returned to the island kitchen where he stared at Echo's tea collection and picked the one called Sleepytime. Hopefully, it would do the trick to ettle her down. Before the tea was finished brewing, Echo joined him. She was dressed in purple sweats, a magenta towel wrapped around her wet head. She'd removed her rings, and Bram was relieved when he realized she had only minor scratches rather than serious cuts in her hands. What he'd thought was blood must have been rust from the pipe.

He picked out two mugs and set them on the counter next to the teapot. "That was fast."

"I had enough water for one day."

"Go sit someplace dry and warm, then." He indicated the teapot. "I can handle this, honest."

She nodded and crossed to the couch where she gathered every one of her bright throw cushions and piled them on the area rug. Filling the mugs, Bram noticed she wasn't limping anymore, though she might be in the morning, from stiffness. Gingerly, she sprawled out in front of the fireplace, settling on the pillows with a groan of satisfaction.

She ruffled her hair with the towel and discarded it. "I thought I might never be warm again."

Taking a seat next to her, he handed Echo a mug. "Who do you know that would want to hurt you?"

"You tell me." She took a long sip, let her eyes flutter to slits and sighed. "There's a couple of things I haven't told you. For one, the truck belonged to Lakeside Construction. The driver must have been waiting for me to leave the estate."

Bram started. Someone from Dunescape had used the truck as a cover to hurt her?

Echo took another swallow of tea. "Someone obviously doesn't like our poking around into the past."

He stared at her. The implication was clear. The driver had a thirty-year-old secret to hide. Theft? Murder? Most likely both.

"So why go after you?" he mused. "Why not me?"

"I was thinking... does everyone at Dunescape know the button is missing?"

"No. I told Aunt Addy. I doubt she would have spread the news."

"I found it. Maybe someone thinks I still have it. If only we knew who was wearing a fancy vest..." Echo's voice trailed off. "Why didn't we think of it before? The photographs!"

"They're still in my jacket."

Bram jumped up and retrieved the pack from the pocket where he'd stuffed it. He laid the pile on the coffee table, and they went through the pictures of costumed party-goers one at a time. In three of them, they found a man wearing a fancy vest. The problem was the lighting and the age of the photos themselves. It was near impossible to see the buttons clearly or to recognize the faces, which were partially covered by masks.

"I have a magnifying glass," Echo said.

Bram insisted on retrieving it for her and received in return a smile of thanks that warmed him more than the tea.

"I only wish we knew for certain that these men were the only ones wearing vests at the party."

He tried to be positive, however. With the help of the magnification, they easily eliminated one of the three men—his buttons were too small and ordinary. That left two to choose from.

"Hard to tell against all that brocade," Echo muttered. "And the masks cover too much of their faces."

Bram didn't answer. He was staring at the other cos-
umed people in the two photos, one of whom he recog-
ized. His mother. Her head was tilted and she was
aughing gaily at something the man was saying.

"Is this guy at all familiar?" he asked Echo.

"No, not really.... Wait." She stared harder. "From
he build... the posture... he kind of looks like Travis
'erguson."

"Who was eight years old at the time."

Her eyes rounded and met his. "His father, then?"

"Just what I was thinking. Unless I'm mistaken, Nor-
ert Ferguson lost a very costly button that night." And
unt Addy's neighbor thought he had some kind of
laim on Dunescape Cottage, Bram remembered. "Still,
don't see the old man chasing you down and almost
illing you to get it back."

"Someone else may be involved," Echo suggested.

But who? Sipping at his tea, Bram considered the cur-
ent residents of the estate. He couldn't imagine one of
hem being a potential killer, either. If murder had been
he person's intent. Perhaps the driver of the truck had
nly meant to scare Echo half to death.

And had succeeded.

"The truck was parked at the boathouse," Bram said,
practically on the Ferguson property line. The button
as Norbert's. And Travis seemed awfully interested in
etting to know you better."

"He was more interested in knowing how much I had
earned about the secrets of Dunescape Cottage than in
e or in buying anything," she admitted. "I also didn't
ell you that he followed us to the library."

Considering how upset he'd been over Mrs. Ahern's
ossip about his father, it wasn't any wonder he'd missed
at.

"Travis always was a bully," Bram told her. "
wouldn't put a trick like this past him. It makes mor
sense than it being someone from Dunescape. Aunt Add
hasn't driven in years. Mother doesn't know a stick shif
from a golf club, and I doubt Lena could drive a truck
either."

"But we don't know about Sibyl or Uriah."

"Uriah?" Bram hadn't warmed to the man, and h
had wondered if the groundskeeper was taking advar
tage of Aunt Addy. "What makes you suspect him
Other than the fact that he's the only male resident othe
than me."

She covered a yawn and shrugged. "He's pretty ho:
tile to me. Then, that could apply to Lena, too."

No, Lena hadn't seemed too fond of Echo. But, a
Bram had told her, that was the housekeeper's way.

"Anything else you haven't told me?"

"Uh..." She gave him a pained expression befor
looking down into her mug. "Someone locked me in on
of those hidden staircases you were harping about."

"What? When?"

"Earlier this evening...when you went to find th
string for the kids. I thought one of them was explorin;
Actually, I thought Jason was playing one of his prank
on me and I went after him. But it wasn't Jason. Som
one pushed me into the stairwell and locked the door."

"Why the hell didn't you tell me?"

"I, uh, got kind of freaked." She wouldn't look :
him, just kept focused on what was left of her tea.

"Go on."

"I found my way to Sibyl's bedroom. That's when
saw the pouch."

Certain she was still holding back, Bram was tempted to press her, until he noticed how tightly she hung on to the mug. As if she were afraid of telling him. With wisps of damp hair curling around her pale face, she appeared vulnerable. Almost fragile. Not adjectives he would normally apply to her. He assumed she was fighting some inner demons. Having demons of his own to deal with, he sympathized and left it alone.

Reminded of how exhausted she must be, he promised, "I'll see what I can find out in the morning. In the meantime, you need a good night's sleep."

"I doubt that I'll be able to close my eyes."

"You will."

They were already closing, whether or not she realized it. Setting down his mug, he inched over to her side of the rug and pulled her into his arms. His kiss was meant to be reassuring. A tenderness that he'd never experienced with another woman filled him as she gazed into his eyes with trust.

"Relax." Taking the mug from her, he placed it on the floor next to the other. "When you're ready, you'll go to bed, and I'll stay out here on the couch."

But in the end, he never made it to the couch. She never made it to the bed. Within minutes, Echo fell asleep in Bram's arms, and he couldn't bear to wake her. His protective instincts again surfaced and held him captive.

He lay wide-awake for a long, long time, staring into the fire. He was mesmerized and halfway to dozing when an unbidden voice pierced his thoughts.

We're in love. A woman's voice. *We have been for a long time.*

And you helped him in this foul scheme?

Bram jerked. Something new. But try as he would, he couldn't focus, couldn't dig further. The voices were as elusive as his memories. He cursed softly and held Echo tighter. He had to remember, for her sake now, as well as his own.

For he suspected that if he could break through the fog that had held him prisoner for the past thirty years, he might see the face of a murderer.

NORBERT FERGUSON STARED out into the fog, certain he saw the flicker of lights around Dunescape Cottage. Did ghosts need help seeing their way in the dark? Or was someone trying to cheat him again? About to investigate for himself, he was startled by his son's sudden appearance.

"Where have you been? Have you gotten to the woman?"

Travis ignored the first question. "Not yet," he said to the second.

"What are you waiting for?"

"The right opportunity."

"No time to wait! You have to make your opportunity. Make it!" he echoed. Would the boy never learn? "Take what you want."

"Words from the master," Travis said dryly.

"Don't smart-mouth me, boy. Too much is riding on this. Too much."

"So you say."

"Too many years of waiting," Norbert went on, muttering to himself. "Now that snot-nosed brat is back, and years of searching could be for nothing."

"Could be for nothing anyway, Dad." Travis sounded disgusted. "Maybe there's nothing left."

"You're wrong. Dead wrong. We're so close, I can smell the jewels."

He'd been saying that off and on for years, but this time he really meant it.

Time. It was running out, especially for him.

He might be an old coot, but he was stubborn. One way or the other, he meant to be rich before he died.

Chapter Nine

Chapter Nine

"Insurance," Echo mumbled in Bram's ear.

He blinked himself awake. They were still snuggled together in front of the fireplace, but the logs had burned down to mere embers. A gray dawn had broken outside the front windows, making him wonder how long he had slept. The room was decidedly chilly, but the woman beside him was warm and inviting . . . and appeared to be talking in her sleep.

"Echo?" he probed softly.

Her lashes fluttered and her eyes opened. For a moment she appeared confused. Then she frowned, murmuring, "The insurance to cover the Haunted Mansion. I forgot all about it." She sat straight up as if she were going to rectify the situation right that moment.

Feeling the loss of her closeness already, Bram stayed her. "I already took care of it."

She finally focused on him. "You what? But you said I had to . . . When?"

"Two days ago. I figured you had enough on your hands. Consider it my contribution to the youth group."

She stared at him for a moment as the implication of his words sank in. "You're full of surprises."

"The feeling is mutual."

He reached out to run his fingertips along her cheek. Her eyes widened slightly and her lips parted, a small exhalation the only sound. With her hair a vivid tangle, and the bloom of early morning flushing her cheeks, she looked utterly desirable. His physical response was immediate and painful. This wasn't like any past experience. Other women would pale beside her.

Slipping his hand behind Echo's neck, Bram recognized a softness in her she didn't often let the world see. He hadn't been tempted to take advantage of her the night before, when she had been so afraid and vulnerable. He'd only wanted to protect her. But now someone had to protect her against him or...

As if the tension between them suddenly registered, she stared at him. Her eyes remained open as he dipped his head and tasted her lips. He explored cautiously and was gratified when she didn't resist, but melted into him and opened herself. He cared about her and had told her so. She hadn't said how she felt about him. When he broke the tender kiss, he would swear she was blushing.

She shifted away toward the coffee table. Unable to conceal a groan at the movement, she followed with "What time is it?"

Disappointed if not surprised, Bram checked his watch. "Nearly seven." He rose in one fairly smooth movement. Part of his leg was asleep where it had taken her weight. He shook it until the pinpricks subsided. "I should get home, but you could use more shut-eye after what you went through yesterday."

Echo ran shaky fingers through the hair around her face. "So much to do. I have to open the shop this morning. Then everyone involved in the fund-raiser will meet at Dunescape to put the finishing touches on the decorations this afternoon. And my station wagon—"

"I'll check it out when I get back to the estate," he promised, offering his hand and a boost off the floor. He noted the tightening of her facial muscles, though she didn't complain. "Don't worry. Give me your keys and I'll take care of everything."

Though she was smiling, she looked wan and a little frightened still. "You seem to be good at taking care of things." She tested her limbs, did a few gentle stretches. "Thanks for last night. I don't know what I would have done if you hadn't shown."

"You would have walked home," he said with certainty.

Without him there, she would have drawn on her well-developed inner strength. He was only glad he'd been there for her, so she hadn't had to go it alone.

"Probably," she admitted. "But I would have been afraid."

"With reason."

Bram assumed she would be safe in broad daylight, and he planned to do some investigating on his own today, to see if he couldn't ferret out the person responsible for putting her through hell.

"Maybe we should call the sheriff," he suggested.

"No. Not yet."

"Echo—"

"Please. Drop it."

An edge of panic entered her fathomless gray eyes. Bram let it go.

The fog had cleared by the time he set out for home. He chose to walk rather than send for a ride. The fast-paced hike was preferable to a cold shower and would give him time to think. To make some plans. To figure out what he was going to say to his mother.

But when he set foot on the grounds twenty minutes later, he knew he had to take first things first.

The station wagon.

A quick check proved someone had indeed disconnected one of the cables to Echo's battery, leaving it in close proximity to the terminal so it would seem as if it hadn't been properly tightened down. He rectified the situation and got behind the wheel. The vehicle started immediately.

The construction truck was his next stop.

Whoever had driven it the night before had repaired it in front of the boathouse. He descended the stairs from the terrace to take a closer look. Nothing in the driver's compartment to tell him who might have been inside.

But, rounding the nose of the truck to the other side, he noticed one of the cement bags had fallen over, releasing a pile of white powder on the ground. And someone had tracked through the stuff, leaving a trail of sorts on the blacktop. He stooped to finger one of the splotches. Damp, but not fixed. That meant the cement had been spread *after* the rain had stopped, presumably by the person who had tried to run Echo down.

Too bad there weren't actual footprints, or he might be able to tell more about the villain. He followed the traces of cement around the back of the guest wing before the stuff disappeared altogether.

That pretty much cleared the Fergusons, Bram decided, either of whom would have returned to their property. And Aunt Addy and his mother would have used the front door—not that he thought either of them had learned to drive a truck overnight. That left Sibyl, Lena and Uriah.

Uriah. Hmm.

Putting the thought aside for the moment, he entered the house through the ballroom, which had not yet been decorated. Shadows filled the corners of the gloomy room whose scuffed parquet floors and dull paneled walls had been neglected for three decades. Real cobwebs clung to the crystal chandelier and a musty smell permeated the air.

"Perfect as it is," he muttered wryly as he went in search of his mother.

He found her in the east parlor, where many of the valuables from the other rooms had been temporarily stored in boxes. She was sitting in a wing chair, staring at something in her lap. As he drew closer, approaching from the side, Bram got a clear view of the hinged silver frame holding two photographs—the Vanmatre twins. Her fingers smoothed the glass protecting the image of his father, and her mind seemed to be very far away, as if she were lost in the past.

"Mother."

She started. "Oh, Bram. I was just looking through some old things."

She sounded nervous. Tension oozed from her, raising Bram's suspicions. "Nostalgic?"

"Mm," she murmured noncommittally, closing the hinged frame with a metallic slap. "Sometimes I forget how very much you look like your father."

The question slipped out of him. "Is that why you never cared about being my mother?"

"Pardon me?"

He'd never tried to analyze his feelings concerning his relationship with her before, but now they surfaced in a rush.

"You let Lena and Aunt Addy raise me while we lived here."

"I shared you, that's all." Her voice was a shade tight, her posture a tad brittle, as she sat forward in her chair. "You were the only child on the estate, and everyone loved you."

"Then in Chicago, you allowed a series of servants and schools to do your job for you."

"You're exaggerating." She laughed, but the sound was forced. Unnatural.

"I don't think so." The vague feelings he'd suppressed all his life swiftly clarified. He stared down at her, his gaze intense. "How long did you hate my father?"

She appeared surprised—and discomfited—by the accusation. "I didn't hate Donahue. I loved him."

"Then why the divorce?"

The blood drained from her face and she dropped back into the chair. "Adrienne!" she spat. "That woman never could mind her own business."

"Aunt Addy didn't tell me. People gossip." Though his aunt *had* told Lena and possibly Priscilla Courtland. "Not that *I* ever heard it before, because you took me away from here so quickly. If you didn't hate my father, then why the divorce? And why didn't you ever tell me?"

"Because I loved my husband too much to want to share him. And because I killed him."

Stunned, Bram sank into the couch. "*You* killed him." He hadn't been prepared for such a confession; his mind whirled. True, he had suspected his mother might have had reason to want his father dead, but he hadn't wanted to believe it. He still didn't want to. "You were responsible for the accident?" he asked hopefully.

His mother shuddered. "Donahue's death was no accident. It was the divorce. He was shocked when I told him I planned to leave him and take you with me. He told me he couldn't live without us. That he *wouldn't* live without us. He meant you, my darling, not me," she said sorrowfully. "He couldn't bear the thought of losing you."

"And what? You fought? Struggled? And he fell off the terrace into the lake?"

"No, nothing like that. I don't know exactly how it happened." She paused as if trying to put her thoughts together. "Your father made good on his promise. He..." She sucked in a shaky breath and got it out in a rush. "Your father committed suicide. All these years I've lived with the guilt that I drove him to end his own life by threatening to take you away. I hated myself. I didn't want you to know, because I thought you would hate me, too."

Suicide. An alternative to accident or murder that Bram hadn't considered. No one had ever offered the theory before. He hadn't gotten the impression that his father was so weak-spirited. Of course, he'd been so convinced his mother had been having an affair that he'd nearly been willing to think her capable of murder. Though his mind was muddled, he realized she'd spoken of loving his father too much to share him. The lawyer in him surfaced.

"Share father?" he asked. "Who with?" Lena?

His mother laughed, the sound brittle this time. "His other half, of course. Adrienne never wanted Donahue to marry. After all, she herself never married. She thought they were enough for each other. She was so terribly possessive. Donahue was part of her, and she wasn't even willing to share."

Bram was appalled. "Are you telling me that my father and Aunt Addy—"

"No, of course not. There was nothing physical between them. Your father did sleep with other women before me. Adrienne took great pleasure in telling me all about them on our wedding day. She informed me that no matter what kind of physical bond he and I had, it would never be as strong as the spiritual bond they shared. She said he was only marrying me to beget an heir. I didn't believe her, of course, but she was correct. I was young. Foolish. Madly, wildly in love. I thought Donahue felt the same.''

"Father did love you." At least, Bram thought he had.

"As best he could, perhaps. He loved Adrienne better. He deferred to her in all things. They were in truth life partners. To her, I was nothing. To him, I was the beautiful young mother of his child. I needed more."

"So why didn't you tell him?"

"I did. I tried to take him away from this place." Her laugh was bitter. "He wouldn't go to Chicago. He wouldn't even get another house somewhere down the lakefront. Foolishly, I thought that if I got him *and you* away from Adrienne—even a mile away—we three might have a future together. He wouldn't consider it, told me that I needed to grow up." She shook her head. "*I* needed to grow up. Adrienne cheated me of the one thing I wanted more than anything in the world. My own family."

Cheated. Bram's suspicions were not yet allayed. "Is that when you . . . started cheating on him?"

His mother gave him an appalled expression, but her eyes glittered with unshed tears. "There were no other men for me while your father was alive, Bram. You may believe it or not. That's your choice."

I know her as well as I know myself, a voice whispered in his head.

So you know everything about her, eh? Even that she's my mistress?

Liar! She wouldn't do that, not take up with someone like you....

"Bram?" his mother said, her tone disturbed. "Are you all right? You don't look well."

Wasn't it the same female voice saying, *We're in love. We have been for a long time.*

"Bram!" His mother finally broke through his concentration. "Please, tell me you don't hate me."

She looked as if she really cared. In all the years of his life, he'd never seen such naked fear written on her face.

"I don't hate you, Mother."

He wasn't certain if he loved her, either. If all that she had told him was fact, she truly had been cheated. And so had he. His mother had been so afraid of his hate, that she'd held him at arm's length even after they'd left Dunescape Cottage for good.

He needed time to sort things out. To remember what his child's mind had chosen to forget. How much more time, he didn't know. But the memories were coming more often now.

Surely the past would be his, and soon.

He rose. "I have some things to take care of."

"Don't leave now, with this unsettled between us."

"We'll settle things, Mother, and very soon."

Her wounded stare followed him out of the room, as did her claims, which rang in his head. He felt as if he were in an alien environment. Among strangers. Mother. Aunt Addy. Did he really know either of them?

What to do?

Work would take his mind off this newest twist in the puzzle. For a while. Though he'd been up for nearly two hours, a good part of which he'd spent hiking home from Echo's place, he wasn't hungry. His stomach knotted at he thought of food. But he could definitely use a cup of hot, strong coffee.

Stepping into the kitchen, he came face-to-face with Uriah Hawkes, who obviously had the same idea. The groundskeeper was filling a mug for himself.

Uriah...

Thoughts of legal procedures faded as Bram remembered the cement trail and quickly formulated a plan.

"Just the man I wanted to see," Bram told Uriah. "I have some errands I'd like you to run for me. In town."

Far enough away to give him time to search the man's quarters.

"I'm at your disposal, Mr. Bram."

Was there a snide tone in the agreement or was he imagining things? Bram wondered. He didn't know what to think anymore—or how to tell fact from fiction.

"I want you to pick up some supplies from the hardware store." He found a pad of paper and a pencil and began scribbling a fabricated list. "And I need you to check with Carl's Copier to see if any faxes came in for me." Finished writing, he looked up and watched the groundskeeper's face carefully as he added, "And then stop at the library. Ask Mrs. Ahern to make hard copies of some newspaper articles that are on microfilm. Tell her I need everything she can get me about the robbery and my father's death."

He noted the flicker deep in Uriah's eyes. Surprise? Or shock?

"Yes, sir, Mr. Bram" was all he said before setting the mug down on the sink and taking the bogus list. "I'll get on that right away."

If Uriah had nothing to hide, why wouldn't he ask about the articles? Anyone would, just out of natural curiosity for so unusual a request, right?

Bram got his own coffee and stood at the kitchen window until the other man got into his car and drove off th
grounds. After grabbing the master keys from the pan
try, he was out the door, crossing to the coach house
glancing around to make certain no one was watchin
him. He thought he spotted a fleeting movement at th
library window, but on second glance decided it had bee
an illusion.

The interior of the spacious single-room coach hous
was a mess. If Lena was allowed inside to clean more tha
a few times a year, Bram would be surprised. Every hor
izontal surface was covered with dusty magazines an
junk mail and odds and ends that had probably com
from Uriah's pockets only to be forgotten once dis
carded. Clothes lay strewn on the couch and chairs, shoe
and boots in the middle of the floor. The bed was un
made, the wildly twisted covers and sheets spilling off th
end.

Wondering why any man chose to live in such a pig
sty, Bram took as deep a look as he could get. The prob
lem was, he didn't know what he was looking for.

Uriah Hawkes seemed to be a man with no persona
taste. And yet many of the magazines and pieces of junl
mail weren't what Bram would consider typical fare fo
a groundskeeper. From the look of it, Uriah had a thin
for travel, hot cars and even hotter women. He guesse
every man had the right to dream.

Quickly scanning the bathroom and the closet, he cam
up with nothing more substantial.

About to leave, he spotted the telephone on the bed
side table and glanced at his watch. Echo should be at he
shop by now. Maybe he ought to call and check on her
Let her know her wagon was running.

Picking up the receiver, he parked himself on the edge
f the mattress and, tapping out the number, leaned back
n one arm. Something hard and sharp bit into his el-
ow. Wondering what the messy groundskeeper might
ot have brought into bed with him, he lifted his elbow.

"Echoes," came the response.

The tiny object slid along the sheet toward Bram's
nee. Eyes widening, he cursed aloud.

At the other end, Echo caught her breath and said, "If
is is an obscene—"

"It's me," Bram interrupted, his pulse speeding up.
You'll never believe what I just found."

Picking up the object between two fingers, he stared at
hat had once been part of the missing button.

A tiny cut emerald.

SMART THAT YOU DIDN'T let Vanmatre cut me out al-
gether," Travis told Echo as they dug into their lunch
the casual restaurant across from her shop. "He'll be
n his way back to Chicago any day now."

A pang shot through Echo. Undoubtedly, he was cor-
ct. No reason she ought to think Bram had any desire
stay in Water's Edge, but she didn't want him to leave.
he way Bram had worked with the kids...his taking care
f her the night before... and his seeing to the insurance
r the youth group... well, she never met a man who
served her trust more.

Thinking Bram would be none too happy if he knew
e'd agreed to spend time with his aunt's neighbor, she
id, "You make me sound like some prize in a compe-
tion."

"That's not what I meant. Vanmatre and me, we don't
e eye to eye on much of anything. I thought maybe he
id some things that might not be flattering."

"I always make up my own mind about people," sh
hedged, taking another spoonful of the spicy chili.

Travis offered a well-practiced grin. Though Bram
finding the button proved Uriah was a thief, Echo fig
ured there was more to the puzzle. For all she knew
Travis might be one of the pieces. The button *had* be
longed to his father. Besides, if Uriah had the jewels, wh
was he still playing caretaker?

"That's good," he was saying. "'Cause you and m
now, we could have something special going."

Not if she could help it. But Echo smiled encoura
ingly. "As in?"

"Whatever your little heart desires...under the rig
circumstances." Dropping his spoon into his half-emp
bowl, he stretched back and eyed her intently. "Va
matre tell you about the last do held at Dunescape?"

"I've heard about the ball, yes."

"Then you know about the jewels."

Aha. Now they were getting somewhere. "The Cour
land jewels were stolen at midnight, never to appe
again. What about them?"

"My guess is they never left the mansion. And yo
have the run of the place," he said pointedly.

Echo remembered their brief encounter in her sho
when he was so interested in the hidden rooms. "Until th
fund-raiser is over."

"Maybe long enough. Think of it," he said, his voi
lowering into a seductive murmur. "A fortune in jewe
just sitting around waiting to be found."

And he thought that if she could hand him the house
secrets, he would be able to find the jewels, Echo rea
ized. Did that mean he knew something the rest of the
didn't? She decided to play along.

"So what exactly do you want of me?"

"If you hear or see anything that could help me find them, I'd make sure it would be worth your while to let me know."

His tone intimated the reward would be personal as well as monetary. Her stomach turned, and having lost her appetite, Echo set down her own spoon.

"Even though the jewels belong to Priscilla Courtland?" she asked.

"Uh-uh." He shook his head. "Her old man collected the insurance. As far as I'm concerned, that made things square with her."

"You do have a point." Though she was certain that both Priscilla and the insurance company would see things differently.

"Then we have a deal?"

"I'll be as straight with you as you've been with me," she said.

Travis obviously didn't get her drift. This smile wasn't practiced. It was the expression of a man who was certain he'd pulled the wool over a gullible woman's eyes.

GULLIBLE, THAT'S WHAT she'd been. And she would be tormented for it for the rest of her life.

Tormented now, Addy paced before her brother. As usual, he refused to speak to her.

He punished her with his silence.

"I'm afraid, Donahue, and I don't know what to do."

Lightning crackled and lit the windows, casting the room with a bluish glow. Her gaze settled on her beloved twin, who sat in his favorite chair in his favorite room, staring into the dancing flames. More than forty years before, she'd bought the identical leather chairs for the two of them—so that each evening they could sit by the fire and share their thoughts as they shared their

lives—but at the moment, a building anxiety kept he
from taking her rightful place in hers.

"Disaster," she intoned, as thunder continued t
rumble low and ominous in the distance. "Sibyl saw it ir
the cards. And I feel it in my heart."

Disaster involving Bram, though she couldn't put tha
horrible thought into words.

Donahue looked worried, too. He'd been broodin;
again. His expression was darker than she'd ever seen it
Darker than the storm clouds gathering over Dunescap
Cottage.

Addy stopped directly in front of him. "You're not stil
angry with me, are you? I never meant to hurt you. Yo
know that, don't you?"

But no matter how many times she'd told him, sh
wasn't certain that he did. She threw herself at his feet
tried to grasp his hand, but Donahue pulled it away be
fore she could touch him. Turning his eyes to her at last
his judgmental gaze burned her very soul.

"I've devoted my life to you to make up for what hap
pened," she said with a sob. "Isn't that enough?"

How could it be enough? Nothing would bring hin
back—not really. As it was, he rarely allowed her hi
company.

"I'll think of something, you'll see. Tomorrow. Al
Hallows' Eve. The anniversary of your death. How ap
propriate. Yes. Somehow, I'll prevent the disaster an
prove my devotion to you."

Lightning and thunder punctuated her heartfelt dec
laration. Donahue seemed unmoved. Sometimes Add
was afraid he would never forgive her, no matter what sh
did.

Deep in her heart, where the responsibility weighe
heaviest, she knew he was right not to.

ESPONSIBILITY PRESSED down on Echo as she realized
that the fund-raiser could be a wash if the storm kept up
through the next day. The skies opened even before the
dozens of people who'd come to put the finishing touches
on the Haunted Mansion were able to head their vehicles
into town. She walked her sister to the front door.

"You're sure you don't want us to follow you home?"
Izzy asked, as cars began moving through the rain.

"No, but tell Roger thanks. I've got some things to
finish up here."

Izzy gave her an exasperated expression. "Everything
looks great. And the worst of this is supposed to blow
over by morning. Get some rest, would you?"

"Yeah, Auntie E., you can use Drac's coffin," Jason
suggested as he jogged the length of the roofed veranda.

"Oh, gross!" Gussy yelled, following on his heels.

A horn blared from the vehicle waiting at the bottom
of the front steps, and Izzy gave Echo's cheek a swift
kiss. "Stop worrying." To the kids she said, "C'mon,
you two, let's get going before Dad gets impatient. He's
hungry."

"Uh-oh," Echo said, laughing as they all braved the
rain.

Roger Medlock was a sweetheart . . . unless his stomach was empty. She waved to him as Izzy and the kids
climbed into the sedan. Then she headed for the ballroom, where Bram would be waiting for her.

Making her way back through the dimly lit house, the
only sounds those of the rain and wind, she did a last-
minute check. Izzy was right. Everything did look great.
And she was feeling pretty good herself, most of her
kinks and soreness had worked themselves out. Only her
left shoulder still hurt where she'd banged it while
scooting down the drainpipe. She'd kept the whole inci-

dent from her sister. The fact bothered her a bit, but Iz:
would go nuts if she thought someone was after her.

Echo was passing the conservatory and almost to tl
ballroom entrance and the stairs that led to the secon
floor guest quarters when a faint scraping sound can
from behind her.

When she turned she saw nothing. No one hidd
among the plants. No one in the hall or the entrance
the kitchen. As the rain beat down harder on the conse
vatory glass panes, the sensation persisted, making h
wonder if the walls themselves didn't have eyes.

How many secrets did the house hold?

Shaking away the creepy awareness that threatened h
calm, she assured herself she hadn't imagined it. Sl
didn't want to think about the invisible presence th
she'd felt several times now.

She didn't want to think she could turn out like Mam

Hurrying to meet Bram, she stopped in the ballroo
doorway. Dozens of carved pumpkins had been left l
the terrace doors. And he was taking care of what was
have been a last-minute task, carefully arranging a co
ple of the would-be jack-o'-lanterns on one of several i
freshment tables.

"Trying for the best effect?" she teased, entering.

"Trying to make good use of my time."

"Uh-huh. I thought you wanted to supervise."

One of his dark brows lifted. "Start hauling pum
kins and I'll stand back and watch."

"We can work together." Thinking they'd been doir
that quite well, whether working on the decorations
the mystery, she picked up two of the smallest carv
pumpkins and carried them to another table. "I did
little sleuthing on my own over lunch."

"Mrs. Ahern?"

"Travis Ferguson."

"I thought I warned you about him." Bram's intense reaction sounded hollow in the cavernous, high-ceilinged room.

She was pleased that he cared enough to be concerned. "Don't you want to know what he was after?"

"You."

The way he said it made her flush with a pleasant warmth. The single word had the tiniest ring of jealousy. She couldn't help but smile.

"The keys to Dunescape," she said, crossing to the terrace doors to fetch a pumpkin. "Rather, its secrets. He believes the jewels never left the manor, and he means to find them."

Bram glowered. "So that explains the lights. One of our other neighbors told me Father was 'walking' again. He saw mysterious lights around the house through the fog. Probably Travis and old Norbert scurrying around, looking for the entrance to a tunnel."

"You have a tunnel, too?"

"Every good rum-running mansion needs at least one," he said wryly. "We have two." He set his pumpkin next to hers. "You're not going to see him again."

Back to Travis. "For heaven's sake, we live in the same town. I can hardly avoid him forever."

"I meant alone."

"I don't want to be alone with him."

"Good."

She got back to work. While they placed jack-o'-lanterns around the foot of the stage, Bram told her about his talk with his mother.

"So she thinks your father committed suicide. Do you?"

"I don't know. I should be angry or relieved or something, but the explanation doesn't wash for me."

"You think she lied to you?"

"No, I think she really believes what she told me."

"Then that clears her."

"Of murder," Bram conceded. "But she wanted to get away so badly.... What if she didn't have the money and stole the jewels to get it?"

Solving a thirty-year-old mystery wasn't easy. Hadn't she thought it an impossible task from the first? "What if you never figure it all out?"

"Then I'll be haunted by those voices until I die."

A chill swept through her at the reference to death.

Lightning over the lake lit the ballroom with blue strobes. She stared out the terrace doors. Other than the faint glimmer of cracks in the dark, she couldn't see farther than a few feet. Added to the rain, she heard sharp pings that could only mean hail. Driving would be a nightmare.

"I think I'd better go before it gets—"

"You're not going anywhere. You'll stay here tonight."

Here? Where the walls had eyes? "I don't think that's a good idea."

"Then I'll go with you. I won't let you leave alone after what happened last night. Alone, you're a target."

Her stomach lumped at the thought. "And in this house—"

"You would be safe. I had Lena freshen one of the guest rooms you haven't already taken over. Lock your door and no one can get to you."

So he'd had it all planned. "And where will you be?"

"Just down the hall . . . within screaming distance."

About to choke out a reply, Echo realized Bram was teasing her. A grin curled the corners of his sensual mouth. "Deal," she said.

Her room was on the second floor above the ballroom, the closest to the stairs and the corridor connecting to the main house. On the way, Bram indicated the door to his own bedroom, indeed, barely a scream away. Not having been in this particular room before, she was pleasantly surprised by the light colors and cherry-wood furniture, though it, too, had a four-poster with heavy drapes as did most of the others.

"Aunt Addy even volunteered to lend you some sleepwear." Bram fingered the old-fashioned nightgown draped over the mattress.

A thrill whispered through Echo, as if he'd touched her skin. "So the whole household must know I'm staying."

"News does spread fast here." Without warning, he touched his lips softly to hers, making her heart thud. "Or you might be less alone yet."

He was smiling at her in a way that softened the angular planes of his face and wormed its way to her heart. When he left the room with a final order to lock the door and keep it that way until morning, she felt his loss.

Dreamily, she showered in the private bathroom and slipped into the ankle-length white nightgown, wondering what Bram would think if he saw her now. Amused by her own reflection, she wandered around the bedroom, inspecting the old prints and framed photographs on the walls, admiring the silver-plated grooming tools and candle holders on the dresser. A fancy little clock told her it was after ten, normally too early for bed. But after what she'd been through the day before, she could hardly keep her eyes open.

Yawning, she turned out all but the bedside light and climbed into the four-poster, then lay back under the down quilt to listen to the storm. The steady beat drumming against the windows lulled her. Her eyes fluttered closed. She was floating. Her body light.

Her exhausted mind was shutting down....

Until a huge crash nearby turned it up again!

Heart hammering, Echo sat straight up in bed and stared into the dark. That noise—what could it have been? And what had happened to the bedside light? Certain she'd left it on, she carefully felt for the base and switch. Dead.

Slipping out of bed, she made her way to the door and felt for the wall switch. But nothing happened when she flipped it on.

The flicker of lightning drew her to the windows. If anything, the storm had worsened. Wind slashed at the trees. Thunder rumbled in the distance. As hard as she looked, she could see no illumination from neighboring homes. Either the storm was too dense ... or the electricity was down throughout the area. Maybe the crash of a tree going down on a line had awakened her.

Remembering the candle holders, she felt her way to the dresser and was relieved when she found not only them, but a pack of matches. The clock caught her eye. A few minutes before midnight. She had slept for almost two hours without realizing it. Leaving one lit candle on the dresser, she picked up the other to set on the night stand.

But as she passed the door, she paused.

Had she heard a furtive noise?

She could certainly hear the thud of her heart. The beat seemed to thunder in her ears. She pressed one to the wood panel and listened hard. Her limbs tingled with the rush of blood stirred up by fright.

No reason to be afraid, she told herself. Bram was right down the hall.

Within screaming distance.

Her sense of humor deserted her. She didn't think it was funny anymore.

All she heard were light footsteps some distance down the hall in the direction of the main house. Cursing her own curiosity, she unlocked the door carefully and, as silently as possible, opened it a crack, ready to throw her weight back on the panel should some unwanted person be on the other side....

The hall was dark and felt empty.

She peered around the jamb and was startled by several limpid pools of light—sconces holding candles near the stairs, along the corridor and in the main house. Relief washed through her. She'd probably heard whoever had been seeing to the emergency.

About to close the door and get back in bed, she hesitated when she thought she saw a movement in the shadows near the stairs. A dark-clothed figure advanced to the landing. Though he was mostly in shadow, she could hardly fail to recognize the angular features and the dark hair uncharacteristically tumbling over his forehead. He was dressed the way he'd been the first time she'd seen him, in a full-sleeved black shirt, pants and boots.

"Bram!" she whispered.

He looked her way.

Looked right through her... and began to descend.

"Bram!" she called a bit more fiercely.

He didn't even hesitate, but kept going as if in a trance. As if he were sleepwalking. Her stomach took a tumble. People got hurt walking in their sleep. What if Bram stumbled and fell down the stairs? He'd told her to stay in her room with the door locked. Indecision froze her to the spot for a moment.

Then, cursing the rampant storm, the failing electricity and her chilled bare feet, Echo groaned in frustration and went after him.

Chapter Ten

Heart thudding in time with her feet, Echo flew to the head of the stairs, wondering if she should call out again. But to whom? As far as she could see, the stairwell was unoccupied.

How had Bram gotten away from her so fast?

Hanging on to her light with one hand and the railing with the other, she sped down the darkened stairs to the first floor, where several more strategically placed emergency candles offered a modicum of light.

"Bram?" she called softly, all senses on alert. A faint noise to her left was the only response.

Whipping toward the ballroom just as a crash of lightning exploded through the terrace doors, she caught a glimpse of Bram and immediately followed. The cavernous room was pitch-black but for the candle she carried.

How could anyone navigate in this dark without one?

"Bram, where are you? What's going on?"

She felt as if she were being watched. Lightning flickered, giving her a glimpse into the gloom. Dozens of hostile faces glowered at her from the decorative pumpkins around the room. She swallowed and took a deep breath but found it impossible to smile at her own imagination.

She spotted movement near the west wall.

Not bothering to call out again, Echo raced in that direction, only to be disappointed. She was alone. Her sole light flickered and she sheltered it with a protective hand. About to turn away, she realized a draft was responsible for the dancing flame. She was across from the terrace doors. So where was the moving air coming from?

She knew before she could see. The imbalance of air pressure was familiar. Drawing closer to the wall, she spotted the crack in the paneling. Heart in her throat, she turned in a circle, holding out the candle to make certain no one waited to overpower her. Still alone. Back at the wall, she pushed with her free hand. The paneling swung inward smoothly and silently, revealing a small landing and stairs leading down to the lower level.

Excitement shot through her. A hidden staircase in the ballroom! No wonder Priscilla Courtland's jewels had vanished so quickly and thoroughly. While the lights were still out, the thief must have used this stairwell. Odd that the newspaper accounts hadn't mentioned it. And she wondered why Bram hadn't told her about it, either. Perhaps he had just discovered it for himself.

What if the villain who'd tried to run her down was waiting for Bram? She knew she couldn't leave him to fate. Quickly grabbing the top off one of the pumpkins on a nearby table, she wedged the thick skin in the hinged side of the door to prevent it from locking behind her.

And down she plunged into a different kind of dark. Clammy. Spooky. Nearly airless.

At the bottom of the stairs, the cement was cold beneath her bare feet, but Echo was too busy taking in her surroundings to be concerned. She was standing in a wine cellar she had never before seen. No one had ever mentioned its existence, either. And as far as she could see, there was no conventional door.

One of the secret rooms!

Tingling with excitement, she held out her light to look around, but still no Bram. He had to be somewhere. He couldn't have disappeared into thin air. Not like the time she'd followed him to the coal bin....

She fought the urge to panic, the desire to run right back up those stairs and not stop until she reached the safety of her own room.

She would be all right.

Afraid to make any noise, Echo remained silent and slipped between the racks of bottles. Everything looked abandoned, the racks thick with dust, as if they had not been touched for decades. Three decades to be exact.

And then she reached the back wall. One edge of the racks there seemed cleaner than the rest. She ran a hand along the verticle surface...felt a change of air pressure...a tiny draft...an opening on the other side. She pushed. Pulled. Tugged. Finally, the rack slid on concealed tracks to reveal another opening!

Her stomach tightened and her breath caught in her chest at the thought of crossing that new and dangerous-looking threshold. Then again, how could she not? She had to find Bram, and where else could he have gone? Her mouth was so dry she could hardly swallow, her feet so cold they would hardly move. But move them toward the opening she did, all the while keeping a vigilant eye for anything else out of place.

No more nasty surprises for her!

The carpeting under the soles of her feet offered a *welcome* surprise, though, as she stepped inside off the icy cement. The room itself was nothing she might have

expected. Her hand-held candle revealed a study pat
terned after the library upstairs. No fireplace or win
dows, of course. No matching high-backed leathe
chairs. But the shelves looked the same, if less numerou
and less filled with books. She set her candle down on a
desk with green glass and a brass lamp that seemed nearly
identical to the one upstairs.

Though she wondered how in the world Bram could
have vanished on her again, that the room was empty and
unthreatening steadied her pulse. That it was virtually
dust-free, unlike the wine cellar, told her someone must
be using it on a regular basis, someone who lived in thi
house.

But who?

And to serve what purpose?

Distracted by her musings, she was oblivious of any
danger until she heard the soft shush of wheels on well
oiled tracks. Spinning around, she faced a moving wall
of books. The opening she'd come through was narrow
ing fast.

Her escape hatch!

"No!" she yelled, her hand knocking into the candl
in her rush to save the opening. "Don't!"

Too late. The wall whispered shut and the soft click o
metal on metal had the ring of finality. A hiss and a
sputter made her whip around to see the flame of he
candle drown in a pool of melted wax.

She was well and truly trapped!

Turning back to the panel, she hammered the book
case with the flat of her hands. "Let me out of here!"

No one would find her here, not even Bram, for he had
never come across the blueprints. Undoubtedly only on
person knew how to access this room—the one who'
trapped her!

The inky blackness cloaked her, threatened to smother her as the certainty of being locked away for good hit home. Her head grew light and her stomach threatened to empty.

She knew what Mama must have felt like in her deepest, darkest moments of despair.

Echo had always known she was like her mother. Her whole life long she'd felt the connection, the bond of inherited genes that hadn't been quite right, no matter what Izzy said. She'd been too close to Mama to escape her fate. That's why she'd never gotten involved with anyone who could do this to her. Lock her away.

Because she'd known.

And the presence she'd felt several times in this house had confirmed her worst suspicions about herself.

The dark spun around her. Echo clung to awareness for all she was worth. But even as her anger grew, her conscious, rational mind slipped away from her, bit by bit. Fate was not merciful. No surprise there. The surprise was how she'd been able to avoid it for so long.

Giving in to her rage, Echo vented her frustration with one explosive, ear-piercing shriek of defiance.

And then she could hold on no longer....

UNABLE TO AVOID doing so any longer, Bram opened the door. Having barely set foot in the attic, he heard something odd, something akin to a distant if blood-curdling scream under the rumble of thunder. For a moment, he stood unmoving and listened intently. No repeat of the odd sound that had raised the flesh on his arms. He couldn't even say if the cry had been real or remembered.

To remember. That's why he was here.

Finally, he'd dared to broach the last bastion of Dunescape Cottage that might hold the key to his past. He'd been avoiding facing the attic. Yes, he admitted he'd been afraid...not only of what he might remember...but of what he might not.

If this didn't work, he had nothing left.

He flashed his battery-operated torch around the room, saw the useless bare bulb on a wire swaying with the drafts. A sensation along the back of his neck made him swipe his palm across the flesh. The familiar feeling plagued him...he wasn't alone.

"If that's you, Father, help me find the truth."

The words were out of his mouth before he had time to think. Asking help from a ghost...he was getting as bad as Aunt Addy.

Or maybe as enlightened.

He took a better look at his surroundings. The attic was a single large room that, from the outside, seemed to balance precariously on barely a fourth of the main house below and added to the building's oddly distinctive silhouette. He inspected the room. Unchanged. All of it. He might have been cast back thirty years, for he could see no discernable differences.

Boxes stacked in neglected piles. Metal air shafts half concealed by discarded furniture shrouded in sheets. A threadbare cot.

Voices had awakened him from his slumber in that cot....

What the hell are you doing down here?

Bram started. Let the memory flow.

I would think that's obvious.

Obvious that you're a thief.

What do you propose to do about it?

Turn you in....

The voice faded. Bram closed his eyes and concentrated, but all he got for his increased effort was the start of a nasty headache.

"Damn!"

Gone. Even so, his hope was renewed. Usually his memories came in disjointed fragments. He hadn't heard the thief bit before. If only he could distinguish voices. But he'd had them all confused at the age of seven, so they weren't about to sort themselves out now.

"'Obvious that you're a thief,'" he murmured to himself.

A reference to the villain who'd stolen Priscilla Courtland's jewels. So the thief had been caught. By whom? Bram had a preferred answer, of course. He wanted his father to be the good guy. If so, what had the thief done about it? Murder?

He had the oddest conviction that he'd hit on the correct answer. He felt...encouraged. As if some unseen force approved and was compelling him to dig further.

Dodging furniture and a rolled-up carpet, he crisscrossed to the window where the slatted shutter now sat crookedly on its hinges. When he swung it open, the wood collapsed further. No sense in leaving it this way. He tore what was left of the shutter free and threw it to the floor, then stared out the window directly onto the terrace.

He looked to the left, in the direction of the indiscernible Ferguson property. He could barely make out the boathouse. For a second or two, ghostly figures seemed to dance around the entrance before vanishing completely.

Imagination or memory?

His head began to throb, but he ignored it for the moment. He hadn't been able to see well that night, either.

Insidious fog rather than rain had shrouded the area. That much he was certain of. He stared. Focused. Couldn't get a fix on any specific image.

And yet . . . he'd seen something that night.

It would come to him. It had to.

Something—instinct?—pushed at him.

Bram pushed back.

Hoping to distract himself before the headache became full-blown, he let his mind relax and browsed through the attic, stopping here to lift a sheet, there to check the contents of a box. And all the while he felt some invisible force driving him to continue. He was nearly back to the cot before an overpowering urge made him stop and lift a sheet trailing from a chest of drawers. A trunk lay buried below.

He stood staring at it for a moment and concentrated on the feelings coursing through him. An urge to open the thing grew until he recognized it as being something more than normal curiosity . . . as if the urging were coming from outside of himself.

"All right, all right, I'll look," he muttered aloud.

The pressure immediately let up.

Stooping, he undid the lock and lifted the lid, unprepared for the contents that greeted him.

Blueprints!

Carefully, he unrolled each sheet, giving a cursory look-see to the various floor plans until he got to the lower level. Then he took a long, hard look, reacquainting himself with the secrets he had once known . . . and others he hadn't.

Three hidden staircases. Two underground tunnels. Four concealed rooms of various sizes, three of which lay in a labyrinth under the guest wing. One looked to be a storage area with massive shelving indicated. Of course.

In the twenties, Dunescape had been the base of an illegal alcohol-running operation. One of the tunnels connected this room to the boathouse.

His mind suddenly flashed on the past.

How do you know about this place?

Bram immediately tuned in....

I followed the sound and—

You came from the tunnel. How did you know about the tunnel?

But Bram couldn't hear the answer. Staring down at the blueprint in his hands, he concentrated, once again ignoring the throbbing at his temple.

"Get me out of here!"

A new voice?

"Don't leave me here! Bram, where are you?"

His head jerked up at the panic-stricken plea. "Echo?" Had he really heard her?

"Please, somebody help me!"

Her voice was hollow, real and not real. Just like the last time. Just like when he was seven.

"Bram! Anyone!"

His gaze shot to the metal ventilation ducts. That's where the voices had come from thirty years before. And why they'd sounded so spooky.

"I'm in here, behind the wine cellar!"

Her frenzied wail made his gut clench. "What wine cellar?" Bram mumbled.

A quick check of the blueprint in his hands and he knew. Not needing further prompting, he dropped the plans, grabbed his torch from where he'd clipped it to his belt and took off like a shot.

"I'm coming, Echo. Hold on," he muttered as he started the long descent.

Passing the second floor, he suddenly wondered why Echo wasn't in bed locked inside the guest room where she was supposed to be. The wine cellar had to be the area with the shelving. If so, she somehow had gotten herself trapped in a room she supposedly knew nothing about.

According to the blueprints, the stairs that led to the labyrinth beneath the wing started in the ballroom and were conveniently tucked under the stairway leading up to the guest rooms. Touching down on the main floor, he raced along the hall and past the conservatory, switching on his torch as he entered the ballroom.

Running his beam over the west wall, he could see no indicator of where the secret door might be...until his light picked up something strange. He stooped to see better. Bits of what appeared to be smashed pumpkin decorated the floor. And a thin line of orange marked the paneling.

But how to spring the secret door?

As he stood, his gaze met the elaborately carved decorative trim at waist level, mostly flowers and leaves. He ran his fingers over the uneven edges, pressing and poking. A moment later, a leaf gave and the door swung open silently.

Bram hesitated long enough to make certain he was alone before plummeting down into the house's depths. If he was to help her, he had to keep his wits about him. He didn't want to think of the alternative.

He realized the staircase was steeper and went farther down than the normal cellar steps. The labyrinth lay *below* ground level, at least several feet lower than the basement, the reason it had been near impossible to find. Arriving at the bottom of the stairs, he slowed and listened hard, but heard nothing. No voices. No cry for help. He couldn't tolerate the thought that Echo might be in even greater trouble, especially when he got his first glimpse of wine bottles and knew he'd reached the right place.

No matter their differences, he had fallen hard for the impossible woman, and even after knowing her for only a few days, he couldn't fathom being without her. Remembering the way he'd found her after she'd plunged down that drainpipe, he fought panic.

If someone had hurt her again...

Under the right circumstances, he could be capable of violence.

Finding a light switch, he tried it. Still no electricity. He scanned the sublevel room with the torch before reattaching it to his belt.

"Echo," he called, wondering whether his voice could penetrate the walls. He didn't want to think she might not be able to hear him. Maybe louder. "Echo!" he shouted.

"Bram, I'm here!"

Relief shot through him. He realized she was shouting, too, though her panicked voice was barely discernable.

His gaze shot to the metal tubing overhead. The windowless rooms were interconnected and obviously got their air supply from the duct starting in the attic and reaching all the way down here.

"Echo, where are you exactly?" he called.

"The back wall," came her faint reply. She was sounding calmer now. *"The shelving slides on a track."*

Bram wended his way through the racks of wine, but when he reached the back wall, he didn't have a clue as to where to start looking.

"Talk to me," he yelled. "Maybe I can hear you through the wall."

Instead, the muffled sound of pounding—her fists meeting wood?—led him to his right.

"That's it! Keep it up!" He followed the muted thumps, and a moment later almost shot by them. "Got it! Any idea of how this works?"

"If I did, I wouldn't be in here!"

Bram couldn't help himself. He grinned. Even trapped, she was ornery. He'd almost forgotten what a fighter she was.

Retrieving his torch, he ran the brilliant beam over the shelving, and with his free hand, moved a few of the bottles around so he could see behind them.

"Anything?"

"Not yet."

He fought frustration as he continued his search.

Until...

His gaze lit on a disturbed coating of dust on a bottle, as if a sleeve had run over it. Filled with a sense of triumph, he removed it from the rack and aimed the light in its space. He experienced a deep disappointment, for he saw no levers or catches, only the wooden cross brace of the rack itself.

And then he was being pushed again. From the outside in. Almost as if someone were whispering in his ear, telling him what to do. For a moment, he fought this...this presence...and sensed a frustration even greater than his own. Then he let go of his own will and allowed this unidentifiable instinct to guide him.

Reaching out, he grasped the cross brace and jerked it upward. A metallic click and a whisper of well-oiled wheels were his reward as the rack shot toward him a few inches.

"You did it!" Echo yelled, her voice immediate rather than being filtered through the air duct.

Equally excited, Bram shoved at the rack, which slid silently to the left. On the other side of the threshold, caught like a frightened doe in his light, Echo stood wide-eyed, trembling, yet rooted to the spot as if she were unable to move. He held out his arms and she threw herself into them with a strangled cry.

"I thought I was trapped forever," she sobbed into his shoulder as he wrapped his arms around her tightly. "I thought I would go out of my mind." And in a smaller voice, she added, "Just like Mama."

"You're fine," he said gruffly. Her flesh was cold beneath the thin nightgown. He tried to rub some warmth into her. "And you're already out of your mind, or you would have stayed where I put you."

With a sniff, she shoved at his chest and glared at him. "If you hadn't been creeping around in the middle of the night, I wouldn't have come after you."

Cupping her cheek, he wiped away a stray tear with his thumb. "You followed me up to the attic?"

"Not up. Down. To the ballroom."

"I wasn't in the ballroom, Echo. Not until just now when I came down to find you."

"Yes, you were," she insisted. "I saw you." Then her gaze settled on his hunter-green sweater. "But you were dressed differently. A black silk shirt..." She looked at his face. "And your hair, it kind of fell over your forehead...."

Bram didn't say anything. He couldn't. Echo hadn't seen *him*. A week ago, he would have called her crazy. Or full of hooey. But something—someone—led him to those blueprints, made him lift the cross brace, allowed him to rescue the woman who'd become infinitely important to him in a few short days.

"It wasn't me," he emphasized.

Her eyes grew rounded. "Maybe I am already out of my mind. The first time I met you... and then the day in the coal bin...and...and that feeling I keep having that I'm not alone in my own skin." She took a shaky breath and announced, "Bram, either I am exactly like my mother... or your father really is haunting Dunescape Cottage!"

ONCE SHE'D ACCEPTED that the place was haunted, Echo was on edge awaiting Bram's reaction. She felt infinitely better when he neither laughed nor shouted at her. His expression seemed so... accepting.

"You believe me?" she asked.

He nodded. "Maybe Aunt Addy has been right all along. Maybe Father's soul hasn't been put to rest. I haven't seen him, but I keep getting this eerie feeling that I'm not alone. That my thoughts aren't my own. That someone's in my skin. It's how I found you so quickly."

Knowing exactly what he meant, Echo took a deep, relieved breath and sagged. Bram immediately put a steadying arm around her. She snuggled in closer, glad for his warmth and comfort.

"We'd better get you back upstairs before you get pneumonia." He tried to move her off.

But she stayed put. She'd panicked earlier, because she hadn't understood. "No, wait. I think he wanted me to find this place."

"Surely you don't think a spirit was able to lock you in here?"

"No. This particular spirit is kind, not cruel," she said, remembering Donahue's comforting presence on the stairs. "Someone of this earth must have followed me. But there was a purpose to your father's leading me here."

"Just as there was a purpose to my searching that trunk." When she looked at him questioningly, he explained, "I was led to the blueprints."

"You see?"

Her heart lightened. She'd disliked Bram's being judgmental, but it seemed he had the capacity for change—giving her hope for the future, especially now that she'd faced her personal demons and had come out whole. She hadn't exactly done so alone, but that didn't matter. Maybe it was a sign that their being together was special. And right.

"What do you expect to find down here?" he asked.

"I wish I knew. I just feel an urgency to search the place. I was too busy yelling my head off to do it alone."

"Then what are we waiting for?"

First they secured the sliding shelves so they wouldn't have any nasty surprises. Then Bram slipped out of his sweater and helped her into it, seemingly oblivious to the cold in his short-sleeved black T-shirt. And when he realized her feet were bare, he forced his socks on her, as well. Echo was certain she must look ridiculous. But warmed outside and in, she set about the task of figuring out what Donahue wanted of her.

A cursory search of every shelf and every drawer in the desk revealed nothing that gave them a clue.

"If we only had some idea of what we were looking for," she said.

"The jewels." Bram's expression was confident. "In the attic, I remembered more. My father caught the thief, Echo, and that must have happened in here—or somewhere in this underground labyrinth—because I heard them that night." He pointed to the metal ducts. "Your raised voice carried up to me in the attic just as theirs did."

"You recognized the voices?"

"Let's just say my gut tells me Father wasn't the thief."

"But if he *caught* the thief, then . . ."

Their gazes locked.

"Ferguson may have been correct when he said the jewels never left the house," Bram said. "There was a third room shown on the blueprints." He stared at a spot behind the desk. "And an entrance right there."

It took some doing, but while Echo held the torch, Bram found a release. A section of the bookcase popped inward and slid along a track. She shone the beam into the room, which was small and lined with metal.

"A vault." Echo followed him inside. "My Lord, look at this!"

Racks along the walls held paintings and sculptures, pottery and silver serving pieces. Everything looked very old and very, very valuable.

Bram whistled. "I'm no expert, but I would say there's some serious money here."

"Then Miss Addy's not destitute, after all."

"Seems not. I'm just glad she didn't know about all this, or it might be gone, too."

Echo was only half listening as the central object on a waist-high shelf caught her eye. "Bram, look."

She pointed the beam at a large jewelry case. It was covered in a plush blue velvet, the color of Bram's eyes, where the dust had been removed by a human hand. Instinctively, she knew it was home to the Courtland collection. Were they about to find the mysterious jewels at last? She waited until Bram stood next to her.

"You do the honors," she said.

His hand trembled as he flipped open the lid. Then a sound of disappointment issued through his lips when they stared into the empty satin-lined interior. Sorry for having built up his hopes, Echo gave him a stricken look.

"I would have sworn you were right," he said.

"Now what?"

Discouraged, she fiddled with some framed oils that stuck out below, looking at but not really seeing the oversize paintings. She'd been so certain....

Letting the artwork drop back into place, she heard an odd scraping sound as Bram said, "Let's get some sleep. Maybe things will be clearer tomorrow."

"Tomorrow," she agreed. Halloween. Like they'd have any time to think at all. Her first step brought her stockinged feet down on a hard object that bit into her already abused flesh. "Ouch!"

"Are you all right?"

"I stepped on a screw or something." She shook her foot and the sharp object went flying through the beam of light. She followed its trajectory, and her attention was caught by a sparkle between two of the paintings. "What's that?" she asked, steadying the beam to see.

"Looks like a piece of glass," Bram said.

Then, in unison, "Diamonds!"

They both went scrambling, but it was Bram who spread the paintings and reached in after the object.

"Got it." Pulling back, he held out his palm to reveal a large canary diamond, the central stone of a ring, winking up at them.

"Whoever removed the jewels from the case must have dropped this in amongst the oils and not noticed," Echo said. "And it had to have been done very, very recently."

"How so?"

"Look at the jewelry box again. The dark blue velvet covering is full of dust except where it's been handled. I noticed it earlier. Someone was at it before you!"

Turning the ring in the lights, Bram raised his brows. "Why would someone steal the jewels and then hang on to them for three decades?"

"Got me. Maybe we'll have to ask the thief."

Thinking they might be able to catch the guilty one yet, they put everything back in order. Echo wondered how long it would be before the person who'd trapped her would return to see how she fared. Of course, once she showed in the morning, the game would take a different turn. She only wished they could manage to turn it in a direction favorable to them.

Carefully they backtracked to the ballroom. No one else seemed to be awake, but the storm still challenged them from the other side of the terrace windows. The crashes of thunder covered the sounds of their stealthy footsteps as they ascended to the second floor, Bram holding on to Echo as if he would never let her go.

Part of her wished he wouldn't have to.

Once in her room, he didn't waste any time in discarding the torch, pulling her to him and kissing her deeply. Snaking her arms up around his neck, she responded with the intensity of the night's experiences. Her senses were heightened by the rain driving against the windows. She'd thought they might talk, but words didn't seem necessary. Only the closeness and the silent emotions raging between them mattered.

Down in that hellish dungeon, she'd thought she might die, or worse, go mad. If she had, she never would have felt this pure, unbridled passion, this lust for life and him. She'd come so close, so very close to the edge. But she'd looked into the abyss and had come back.

And Bram had been waiting for her.

A sign. Surely it was a sign.

Breaking the kiss, he tore at the hem of his sweater and she raised her arms to give him access, at the same time slitting her eyes to watch. The candle on the dresser still burned; the room was a kaleidoscope of flickering warmth and deep shadows. And in his face she recognized that same duality. Light and darkness. For as surely as she did, he had a dark side, a deep black which he fought to avoid. Her hair crackled with the static that bit through the nightgown as he wrested the sweater fully from her, leaving her aroused and breathless.

"You're so beautiful."

"It's the atmosphere," she whispered, trailing her fingers up the side of his face, acquainting herself with every inch of his skin. "The storm. Wind and rain. All heighten the senses."

When she reached the scar, his eyes flickered closed and his breathing deepened. She traced the jagged line that was normally fine and barely discernable but that could throb with his emotions. As it did now. Alive and pulsing, it told her what she needed to know.

He wanted her as much as she wanted him!

Threading her fingers in his hair, she pulled his face to hers and took his mouth, remembering and returning the power of his first kiss out on the beach. While she drew his tongue into her mouth, she pulled at his T-shirt, fought with his belt and challenged his zipper. She wanted to feel his flesh on hers.

In her.

She wanted an affirmation that she was alive and whole and strong enough to take on anything and anyone.

Bram groaned.

Then he took control, throwing her under the canopy
stripping his socks off her feet, rolling Miss Addy'
nightgown up her body. Slowly. Sliding his hands ove
every inch of her flesh. Smoothing away all the fears th
night had brought. She welcomed his passionate mout
that explored her so thoroughly as he slid up between he
thighs, his rougher skin making hers prickle in anticipa
tion. By the time he was fully extended over her, he
hands were pinned above her head, tangled in the mate
rial of the nightgown, and she thought she might drow
in the intensity of her desire.

His smile was sultry as he stroked her with his body
teased her with the tip of his flesh. The storm outsid
raged no more powerfully than she did inside. She move
her hips and captured him. He thrust, filling her. An
then the true storm began, slowly at first . . . then build
ing higher and higher . . . their frenzied movement
matching the beat of the rain against the house, thei
breathing more turbulent than the wind rustling the trees

Their joining was intense. Too intense to be pro
longed. He slipped his hand between their bodies. Th
moment his fingers found her, she knew she was lost
Flooded with an ecstasy that opened her inner skies. He
cries came quick and sharp. He immediately tensed.

At that moment, when all their senses were height
ened to the zenith, lightning struck nearby, painting th
room and him with a blue glow. And at that moment, h
looked ghostly.

Echo knew that for now and forever, no matter wha
direction their lives took, Bram Vanmatre and this nigh
together would haunt her always.

Chapter Eleven

Impatient with being haunted by the past, Bram stroked Echo's back as she lay curled up against him. "If only Father would talk to us," he mused, "maybe he could clear up this whole damn mystery." He could hardly believe he was buying into the ghost of Dunescape Cottage, that his father was still around, but there it was.

Not quite daybreak, the storm had finally let up and the electricity had been restored. The bedside lamp cast a soft glow over the magnificent woman he was certain he loved. He was happier than he'd ever remembered being. Now if only he could shed the burden of his past, everything would be perfect.

Or so he hoped.

Suddenly Echo said, "That's it!" She popped up and rolled over on top of him, her messy red curls trailing across his chest. She was grinning. "We'll stage a séance that will get us some answers."

For a moment, he gave into the immediate physical need she teased from him. He trailed a finger along the curve of her breast. "A what?"

"A séance."

The mention of the word immediately put Bram on edge. Aunt Addy had been taken by too many con artists' promises. "Tell me you're joking."

"No, really," she said, face flushing with excitement. "Don't you see? It's the perfect solution."

"For what?" He was just getting used to the idea of his father's spirit existing in the house. He hadn't made the leap to believing they could make contact through some ridiculous ceremony. "I thought you didn't do that sort of thing."

Echo sobered, rolled off his chest and drew the sheet around herself. "I've never participated in a séance but I have read about them," she said. "And I've seen them done in movies. Look, I don't mean a *real* séance. I'm talking about a performance to trap a criminal."

"I don't like it."

"You don't like a lot of things." She looked away. "Maybe you just don't like me."

Taking the sheet with her, Echo whipped off the bed, but before she could get away, Bram reached out and grabbed her by the wrist, stopping her. "I love you."

Her eyes widened and her jaw dropped, but all she said was "Oh."

No like confession from her. Bram concealed his own disappointment. "Come back to bed." He tugged and she yielded. When she got settled, albeit keeping some distance between them this time, he asked, "So what do you think will come of holding a séance?"

"Forget it. You're not interested."

That tempted him to throttle her. "I'm interested in everything you have to say even if I don't agree with it."

Her gaze met his. "We'll spread the word that we're going to try to crack the mystery of the missing jewels. And we'll send formal invitations to everyone we've been

speculating about. Everyone who might have been in-
volved. Norbert and Travis Ferguson. Lena Rundle and
Uriah Hawkes. Your mother and Aunt Addy. Sibyl
Wilde. And while we're at it, let's include Priscilla
Courtland."

"Then what? You think my father's going to cooperate and appear on command?"

"*You* can pretend to be your own father."

"As if people wouldn't guess."

"Not if you're at that séance table, they won't." Her
expression turned smug. "I have a plan."

He listened, part of him appalled, another part thinking it was brilliant. Maybe she was right, and they would
catch not only a thief, but a murderer, as well.

'WELCOME TO the Haunted Mansion," Miss Addy told
the newcomers later that night.

A clawlike hand darted out from the folds of her voluminous black cape and stole the tickets from the startled young couple dressed in sixties biker gear.

"C'mon," the young man said, steering his giggling
date into the front parlor.

Her face cast in shadow by her deep hood, Miss Addy
cackled, making Echo smile. The elderly woman really
was enjoying interacting with the ghouls and goblins,
cartoon and fantasy characters, famous actors and infamous historical figures that had been parading through
Dunescape Cottage since early that afternoon. Echo
herself was dressed like a gypsy in long, flowing skirts, an
off-the-shoulder blouse and a brightly embroidered and
fringed shawl. Appropriate garb for a medium, she
thought.

"It's going so well, the Water's Edge Youth Group will
have to do something special to thank you."

"No need. This house has been silent like a tomb for too many years." Miss Addy cackled again. "Now it's been turned into a tomb and it's filled with happy sounds."

Indeed, everyone seemed to be in high spirits, if the squeals and shrieks and laughter floating through the air over the beat of rock music from the ballroom were any indication.

"Besides," the elderly woman went on, "the séance you arranged is adequate reward. I promised Donahue I would prove myself to him and now I can."

Echo wondered what Miss Addy meant by that, but she didn't have time to dwell on the comment before Bram found her and pulled her aside past the velvet rope that kept customers from the quarters that were off limits. He stopped near the library door.

"Everything set?"

"Roger will meet you in your room ten minutes before twelve," she murmured for his ears only. Midnight being the appointed time for the séance to begin.

"You really think this will work?"

She gave his Phantom of the Opera hat, mask and cape a once-over. She'd conned Roger Medlock into sharing the costume. "My brother-in-law might be a bit heftier than you, but under that cape no one will notice." Once the participants knew what Bram was wearing, the two men would switch places.

"What if someone talks to him?"

"His coming in late will help. And I'll discourage conversation."

"And you? No stage fright?"

"I'm fighting it. This has *got* to work."

"What's gotta work, Auntie E.?" came a muffled question from behind her.

Jason and his date came up from the basement. Echo ould hardly look at her nephew without shivering. He as dressed as Dr. Hannibal Lecter from *The Silence of e Lambs*, wearing not only the face mask with holes, ut a straitjacket that reminded her of that time with ama.

She forced a smile and fibbed. "I was talking about all e gadgets, especially the fans and strobes in the maze. /e wouldn't want to disappoint any customers."

"Don't worry," Cheryl said. Dressed as Clarice from e same movie, she wielded a toy gun in one hand and oved her "prisoner" around with the other. "Everying's going way cool."

"We just came up to get some eats."

"Better hurry before they're all gone," Bram sug- sted.

"Mom said she'd save us some. Later."

"Later." Echo waited until they were out of view. You'd better circulate. Make sure everyone who will be the séance sees you in this costume."

"Priscilla Courtland arrived a short while ago. Very rvous. Said she wanted to get a look at the ballroom here the infamous theft happened."

"That means everyone is here but the Fergusons."

And Echo knew they had gotten their formal invita- on hand-delivered by Jason late that morning. Norbert mself had been home to take it from her nephew.

"Good-luck kiss, my fair gypsy?" he murmured.

Though she hadn't completely gotten over her hurt elings of that morning, Echo lifted her face. The coins wn to the scarf half covering her head jingled. Bram's ngers stroked her throat as he took her lips. For a mo- ent, she forgot all the strife and stress of the past few ys. He said he loved her, and she knew she loved him, too. She felt abandoned when he moved back and tipp⟩ his opera hat.

"Luck," she whispered, watching him walk off.

She spent the next half hour circulating from first flo⟩ to second, from ballroom to basement, trying to walk o⟩ the jitters she'd hedged about having. What had she go⟩ ten herself into? If their plan failed, things went wron⟩ and Bram got caught, they'd look like absolute fool⟩ Then, again, she supposed they could pretend the fal⟩ séance was merely a part of the planned festivities.

Checking the ballroom a second time, she stood nea⟩ the entrance to watch the costumed dancers. Than⟩ goodness the weather had let up, though fog shrouded t⟩ lake and crept over the terrace in spooky fingers, whi⟩ thunder rumbled in the distance. Surreptitiously, sl⟩ looked over to the paneling concealing the hidden doo⟩

"Worried about something?"

Startled, Echo whipped around to see Sibyl staring⟩ her assessingly. The nurse had fashioned a provocati⟩ outfit of exotically patterned fabrics. Her head was co⟩ ered as Grandmama Tisa's had been in the photograp⟩ And she was wearing the shell-and-bone necklace.

"I'm making sure everything is going smoothly."

Sibyl's gaze went to the elaborate silver, crystal an⟩ amethyst pendant Echo wore. "The latest for cryst⟩ gazing?" she asked.

"I don't read crystal balls or tea leaves or tarot."

"But you think you know how to hold a séance?⟩ Sibyl gave her a familiar slanted look. "Ever conduct o⟩ before?"

"There always has to be a first time. Let's call this ⟩ experiment."

"An amusing one, I am certain." Attention wand⟩ ing, Sibyl glanced around the room. "Ah, the Phanto⟩

of the Opera," she said, already walking away from Echo and toward Bram. "I wonder if he dances as beautifully as he sings."

Glancing at the watch she'd stuffed in a pocket, Echo realized it was a quarter to twelve. Bram had only had five minutes before he was supposed to meet Roger upstairs. She hoped he wouldn't find it difficult to get away from Sibyl. No doubt the nurse would think they should enter the library together. But she couldn't worry about it. She had to prepare herself and the room, had to set the mood.

Passing the kitchen, where trays were being replenished with refreshments, she waved to Izzy, who gave her a worried look. Her sister knew she was up to something, conning Roger out of his costume as she had, but Echo had chosen to leave the explanations for later.

Her body was buzzing with heightened adrenaline as she entered the library. The fire burned low, exactly as she'd requested, and a single candle in a brass holder sat in the middle of the table Bram had ordered moved in. She turned off the room lights and walked over to the twin chairs before the fireplace.

"Please let this work," she whispered.

Gradually, her stomach settled and her adrenaline level normalized. She had that feeling again of not being alone, but when she looked around she saw no one. No ghosts making guest appearances on this of all nights. How ironic.

"If you truly are here somewhere, Donahue, I hope you'll soon be at rest."

A warm breath of air across her bare shoulders told her he had heard, and she felt less foolish.

"CAN I FOOL THEM?" Roger Medlock asked, pulling the cape around himself more tightly.

"You'll do," Bram agreed. Between the mask that covered half his face and the brim of the opera hat shading the rest, he was unrecognizable. "Good luck."

Roger nodded and opened the door a crack. "When this is over, you and my sister-in-law have some explaining to do." With that, he left the bedroom and headed straight for the stairs.

Dressed in black pants and boots and a black silk shirt with full sleeves, his hair tousled and falling over his forehead, Bram waited until a few revelers passed on their way to the guest wing. Then he followed as far as the linen closet. One last look around to make certain no one was watching, and he slipped inside, closed the door and let himself into the hidden staircase.

He was halfway down to the coal bin, passing the secret door at the butler's pantry, when nerves hit him. Would he be able to carry it off? The plan was for him to get to the other stairway that led to the library, Sibyl's bedroom. He would go only as far as the first floor, however, and wait outside the library until Echo called up his father's spirit. And, with her misdirecting the participants, he would be able to slip inside through the hidden door. Simple he thought, stepping into the coal bin. He hoped it would be effective.

Distracted as he was, he heard the scuffle behind him too late. He turned into something hard and ungiving. Dizzy, he fell to his knees. When he tried to rise, his attacker struck again, hitting him on the back of the head with tremendous force.

Bram's world exploded into a blaze of white light and he went under without a sound....

SOMETIME LATER, he groaned and stirred.

What the hell are you doing down here?

I would think that's obvious. What do you propose to do about it?

Turn you in.

The voices dug deep into Bram's subconscious. He fought for a moment, tried to surface, to focus on them, then gave in and let them flow as they would.

... are you willing to turn her in, too?

Her, who? He'd missed it!

She had nothing to do with this. I know her as well as I know myself.

So you know everything about her, eh? Even that she's my mistress?

Liar! She wouldn't do that, not take up with someone like you. A married man.

Right under your own roof—

Bram floated, aware of a woman's voice. Three people now.

We're in love. We have been for a long time.

And you helped him in this foul scheme?

Helped? The woman sounded horrified. *Oh, my God, no! You didn't... You betrayed me!*

I was desperate. I had to have money.

You played me for a fool. You knew about tonight....

Who was she? Mother? Aunt Addy? Lena? If only he could concentrate harder.

Cruel laughter was followed by a scuffle. Heavy breathing. Male grunts as knuckles smacked against flesh. A crash was followed by heavy footsteps running.

And then the footsteps stopped.

You startled me.

And a fourth person. How many were involved?

How do you know about this place?

I followed the sound and—

You came from the tunnel. How did you know abou
the tunnel? The voice paused. Then, *What?*

Behind you!

A thunk and a crash and the voices had no more to sa'
to him. A dragging sound echoed and faded.

Bram tried to awaken. His mind was willing, but hi
body refused. He had to come out of this. Had to get t
the library. To Echo. Though he feared she was in mor
tal danger, he couldn't force his body to obey him.

Was it possible that he was dead?

"WE'RE HERE TO SPEAK to the dead," Echo pro
nounced, staring into the lone candle flame.

Her solemn gaze shifted, flicked from one participar
to the next. All invited had shown, except Travis an
Lena. Had Norbert told his son or had Travis refused
And halfway through the evening, Lena had simply di:
appeared.

Echo tried to read expressions, but most remaine
hidden. Katherine's and Priscilla's, Norbert's, and o
course Robert's, behind elaborate masks. Miss Addy'
under the voluminous hood of her cape. That left Siby
and Uriah. The nurse merely appeared contemptuous
while the groundskeeper did a poor job of hiding hi
hostility. Wearing his own clothing rather than a co:
tume, he'd been the last to arrive and hadn't uttered
word to anyone.

Echo's heart thudded as she imagined Sibyl conjurin
plots far more evil than she and Bram had planned. "L
us all place our hands on the table and create a spiritu
bond with each other by joining them."

A few at a time, the participants obeyed. Priscilla hel
on to Echo's left hand and Norbert's right. With Trav:

and Lena missing, Miss Addy sat alone, her out-stretched arms linking Norbert and Robert in his guise as Bram. Then came Uriah and Sibyl, with Katherine closing the circle on Echo's right.

"Let us open our minds to truth," Echo intoned. "The truth of the present, that Donahue's spirit lingers...of the past, that he knows what happened here thirty years ago...of the future, that with the channeling of his knowledge to us, his spirit will be released."

"Hogwash!" Norbert muttered. "Pure hogwash."

"Let us be of one mind," Echo emphasized, staring at him, "so that our united power will be great enough to expose the evil that happened here three decades ago this very night, this very hour." He dropped his gaze and she went on. "Let us all close our eyes and concentrate on Donahue Vanmatre."

Wishing she could tell if they all complied, she made her voice vibrate, so if they looked at anything, it would be at her, and not at the shadowed area directly across from her and in back of Miss Addy.

"Donahue Vanmatre. Thirty-seven. Darkly handsome and virile. Loving father and husband and brother." Katherine's hand spasmed at that, and Echo noted the catch in Miss Addy's breath across the table. "See him in your mind's eye. Call him. Ask him to come." She waited a theatrical beat before adding, "Donahue Vanmatre, we call on you to resolve an old injustice and gain peace for your everlasting soul."

That was Bram's cue. But though she searched through her lowered lashes, Echo saw no movement in the shadows.

She tried again. "Concentrate. On the man. On who and what he was. Call him with your minds, your spirits. Only if you really want him to appear will he come.

Donahue Vanmatre, keeper of secrets, we call or you—"

A sudden draft swept through the room, dousing the candle and making a log in the fireplace spark. Unrest fluttered around the table, unease spreading like wild fire. Even Sibyl seemed more alert and less amused.

He appeared as if out of nowhere, behind Miss Addy Echo hadn't even seen the bookcase move. She took a deep breath as the dark figure stepped forward, and as i realizing something significant had happened, the oth ers turned their heads, one by one.

"Donahue!" Norbert's voice trembled.

"My God!" Katherine whispered. "It can't be!"

"It is," Priscilla assured her. "He's come back."

"Donahue Vanmatre, we mean you no evil," Echo said, a funny catch in her voice. She was suddenly so nervous, she could hardly remember her rehearsed pat ter. The only light in the room came from the embers i the fireplace, and the shadows seemed to move with him

"What is it you want of us?" Sibyl asked, amber eye wide, as if she were in shock.

He stared right through the nurse, his gaze traveling to the woman next to her.

Mesmerized, Katherine whispered, "We called him and he responded to the dark forces in this room."

"I—I don't like this," whispered Priscilla, tearing he hand free from Echo's.

Not counting on the others adding their two cents Echo lost track of her prepared dialogue and impro vised. "Let us all concentrate and help Donahue Van matre reveal these dark forces. Reveal the thief and murderer."

A nervous murmur swept around the table as he cir cled them, briefly stopping at each person as if reading their souls. Effective, Echo thought. They all seemed a little freaked.

Why not? She was uneasy herself. Something was wrong here. Bram hadn't said a word he'd rehearsed. And she felt the presence.

Were they both in the room, then?

Or...

He stopped between Uriah and the fireplace, and all eyes were drawn to the dark silhouette. Echo couldn't see him clearly, but she felt his gaze on her face. A whisper of warmth enveloped her and she knew. Dear God, that was Donahue staring at her. Not Bram, but his father. Unless she was mad, she had called his spirit forth and he had answered.

"This is some kind of a stupid trick," Uriah growled. "I'm not putting up with it."

He started to rise. Another draft of air swept through the room. A woman screamed.

Echo whipped around in time to see Priscilla Courtland slump in her seat in a dead faint.

"What the hell..." Norbert ground out.

And as Echo followed his gaze, her mouth dropped open. For there in the shadows stood a woman dressed in a flapper's costume, her head capped, her face masked. As she stepped forward, a huge diamond winked from her throat.

"The Courtland jewels," Katherine whispered.

Not having a clue as to what was going on, Echo stared. Had Bram planned a surprise for her?

"The jewels have been here all along," Norbert said, sounding frustrated. "All along, just like I told Travis."

"Who are you?" Echo asked when she found her voice. "What is it you want of us?"

The flapper backed into the shadows, and Echo could see a slit of an opening in the bookcase.

"Don't go!" cried Sibyl.

People were getting to their feet as the mystery woman slipped out of the room.

"Don't let her get away!" Norbert shouted.

It was Robert who lunged for her, caught her wrist just as she was about to make good her escape. She screeched in fury and fought him. But Echo's brother-in-law was hefty and strong and the woman was frail.

"That's no ghost," came a shaky voice. Priscilla had come out of her faint. "But those are my jewels."

The séance participants quickly surrounded the captured woman, who Robert had brought to the table and pushed into a chair. Echo reached out and removed the mystery woman's mask.

Chapter Twelve

"Miss Addy!" Echo cried, turning her shocked gaze from the aging flapper to the hooded witch.

"Adrienne? Then who is *this?*" Katherine reached out and slipped down the hood as the room lights went on. "Lena!"

The housekeeper gave Bram's mother a black glare of defiance and stepped closer to Miss Addy, placing a protective arm around her mistress. Obviously conspirators, the women had exchanged places just as had Robert and Bram. And looking to the doorway, Echo saw Travis Ferguson standing there, eyes narrowed, hand still on the light switch.

"Sorry I'm late," Travis said smoothly. "Looks like I've missed something."

"What's going on here?" an angry voice demanded. "Aunt Addy?"

"Bram!" Echo started along with some of the others. Having been certain she'd called up his father, she was suddenly disoriented.

"I knew it was a hoax," Uriah muttered.

Katherine turned everyone's attention back to her sister-in-law, who sat rocking in the chair. "*You're* the thief. Why am I surprised when you stole my family from me?"

"I promised Donahue I would make it up to him," the elderly woman said. "So he would forgive me. So many secrets. Donahue's death was my fault."

Her revelation was backed by a flash of lightning and a thunderous threat over the lake.

"You killed him?" Appearing stunned, Katherine gripped a chair back. "And I thought he committed suicide. All these years I blamed myself. You hateful woman! You let me believe it was my fault when you're the one!"

"No, no!" Miss Addy protested, as if finally realizing several people looked at her accusingly. "I didn't *kill* him."

Katherine made a sound of disbelief. "Just like you didn't steal the jewels."

"I'm neither a murderer nor a thief. Just a foolish, gullible woman."

"I think it's time you told us what you do know," Echo said kindly.

"Yes." Bram wedged a hip on the table and took one of his aunt's frail hands in his. "Tell us."

Miss Addy pointed a bony finger at Norbert Ferguson. "It was him. He seduced me . . . for the house's secrets. But I didn't give him all." She cackled. "All these years, and you couldn't find the jewels. I know what you've been up to, you and your humorless son, sneaking around on dark, moonless nights, making people think the place is haunted when they haven't ever seen my darling Donahue."

Looking as if he were about to have a heart attack, Norbert sank into another chair, mumbling to himself.

"Don't bother yourself, Dad. She can't prove a thing," Travis stated.

"Norbert Ferguson started it all," Miss Addy announced. "His wife was still alive then, but he swore he loved me!"

"So you showed him the tunnel," Bram said.

"We could be together in secret, that's what he said."

"He needed a way to sneak the jewels out." Echo's gaze connected with Bram's.

"But I didn't know that until I found him with Donahue."

"Father tried to stop him," Bram said. "What happened to the jewels, Aunt Addy?"

"They're right here under your nose, silly boy." She fingered one of the bracelets. "Pretty, pretty baubles."

Realizing the elderly woman's mind was wandering, Echo was desperate to get her back on track so Bram could at last learn the truth.

"Miss Addy," she said, putting a hand on the woman's shoulder. "They are beautiful. Is that why you took them and kept them hidden all these years?"

The elderly woman's expression went slack for a moment. Then her features crumpled. "They were fighting and I was humiliated. Furious. I secured the jewels, but when I returned, Donahue and Norbert were gone. Back to the ball, I thought, so I went, too."

"I was there with my wife. *With my wife,*" Norbert emphasized.

"Pretending nothing happened!" Miss Addy turned a sorrowful expression on Bram. "I looked and looked but couldn't find you, Donahue."

Bram seemed about to correct her, then, deciding to play along to facilitate Addy's revelation, he said, "That's because I was already dead."

"I swear I didn't know!" she wailed.

"But you knew I was dead the next morning when they found my body. Why didn't you return the jewels?"

"People would laugh at me. You knew what to do, Donahue, but you would never tell me," she said sadly, tears rolling down her wrinkled cheeks.

"You've had my jewels for thirty years," Priscilla said, her tone accusing.

"You were insured. Donahue was dead." Miss Addy gasped, "Who cared about diamonds?"

Echo ached for this sad woman who had lived her entire life for her brother, even after his death.

"What about it, Ferguson?" Bram turned on Norbert. "What have you got to say for yourself? Did you kill my father?"

"Don't look to me!" Norbert exploded. "I needed money, yes, and Letitia tempted me into helping her steal her mistress's jewels. But about the other... I didn't know any better, I swear. Didn't know. Donahue knocked me out with a sucker punch. When I came to, he was gone. Gone. I believed your father's drowning was a tragic accident."

"But it wasn't," Bram said with conviction. He rose and circled the room, his gaze pinning each of them in turn. "Someone else entered the tunnels that night. I heard it all."

"But you couldn't have." Miss Addy appeared ever more confused as she mumbled, "You were in the attic."

"Air ducts go from the attic down to the hidden rooms. Great sound conductor. Unfortunately, I blocked out most of what I heard. Until tonight."

Realizing he was filthy with coal dust—and wasn't that blood on his forehead?—Echo wondered what had happened to him. "You finally remembered."

Bram nodded. "First Father was arguing with Ferguson over the theft. Aunt Addy found them and left with the jewels. Father knocked out Ferguson. Then a fourth person arrived."

The only people in the room who hadn't been cleared or named were Lena and Uriah—both Sibyl and Travis had been too young. Then again, might Grandmama Tisa have gone looking for her share of the jewels? Echo wondered. Or had Lena been protecting Miss Addy as she obviously had continued to do through the years?

But when Bram said, "Another man," all eyes turned in unison to a glowering Uriah, who had edged his way to where Echo stood near the entrance to the hidden staircase.

"How did you know about the tunnel?" Bram demanded.

"I knew about everything going on in this house," Uriah said with a lascivious grin. "The walls have ears, ya know, especially a house like this one with all its secret ways. I made it my business to pay attention, especially when Ferguson got friendly with the island woman. I let him steal the jewels for me. Only I didn't expect for Mr. Donahue to be there that night. Didn't expect the jewels would up and disappear, neither."

"So you killed my father for nothing."

"Had to protect myself, just like I do now."

So quickly she didn't see it coming, the groundskeeper whipped an arm around Echo and put a knife to her throat.

"Echo! Omigod!" This from Robert, who stood frozen barely a yard away.

"Uriah, don't do anything stupid," Bram pleaded, looking as if he were holding himself from attacking the man. "Let Echo go. You don't want to hurt her."

The demented laughter in her ear chilled a disbelieving Echo. Uriah Hawkes was capable of anything, as she well knew. Murder was a game to him.

"Please," she croaked, but he only pressed the knife tighter to her throat. A drop of something warm dribbled down to her low-cut blouse.

"I got nothing more to lose," the groundskeeper stated. "I stayed around all these years taking orders so I could be a rich man someday. Today's the day." He glared at Miss Addy. "Take off them jewels, you old bat!"

With trembling hands, Miss Addy followed his order, removing the collar, brooch, earrings and bracelets.

Encouraged by Bram's steadying gaze, which she was certain was meant to reassure her, Echo tried not to panic. She kept her wits about her, looking for an opening to get away. But Uriah wasn't being sloppy. And he was dangerous.

Evil.

The sound of her heartbeat thundered in her ears louder than the approaching storm outside.

Keeping the knife in place, Uriah stuffed the jewels into his pockets. "Finally, I get what I deserve."

"Uriah, so help me, if you hurt her again, I'll kill you," Bram threatened.

"Again?" Miss Addy's voice trembled with the question.

"He tried to run her down with a truck."

"She found Ferguson's button," Uriah growled. "Thought if I got hold of it, I could blackmail the old geezer. She gave me the slip."

"But the button had already been stolen from Echo," Bram insisted. "And I found it in your bed."

Uriah gave Lena a searing, contemptuous look. "I shoulda done a better job on all of you."

Echo heard the murmured concern of the others as if from a distance. The words sounded jumbled. Made no sense. She was numb with fright. Then the distance was growing. She was being dragged backward into the staircase. Unreal. All that she'd gone through. All that she'd overcome.

She'd survived going over the edge in her own mind only to have her fate placed in the hands of a real madman!

"HE'S MAD!" Priscilla shrieked as the shelving slid in place. "Someone help that poor woman!"

Bram was already trying, but he couldn't spring the door. "He jammed it!" His heart lurched as he thought of Echo's possible fate.

"Maybe if we all work together," Robert said, shedding his disguise.

Thinking they could try until doomsday and possibly not succeed, Bram muttered, "I know another way. He's got to be going for one of the tunnels."

Bram flew out of the library and burst into the hall, Roger and Travis Ferguson right behind him.

He charged toward the ballroom, figuring Uriah would go for the boathouse rather than the coach-house tunnel. It meant easier access and fewer witnesses. The maze was still in operation and would provide a handy piece of misdirection. Once in the ballroom, Bram shoved aside some dancers to get to the paneling, where he quickly found the latch that popped open the concealing door. Ignoring the surprised reactions of the surrounding witnesses, he flipped on the light and descended.

"Good Lord, look at this place," Roger said from behind him.

Ferguson didn't say anything. No doubt he'd seen the wine cellar before, when he'd been ransacking the place with his father. A sound ahead alerted Bram. He plunged forward, dodging racks as a section of the wall began moving. Uriah was about to enter on the other side of the widening breach. Echo was still his insurance. Bram felt her terror.

Spotting the impromptu posse, the groundskeeper foiled him again, dragging Echo away by the hair while sliding the shelving closed.

"Let go!" Echo screamed.

Because Uriah didn't take the time to secure it, Bram was able to reopen the wall. Ahead, Uriah forced Echo under a set of boundary ropes and into the maze, moving against the flow of the crowd.

"Hey, mister, wrong way!" one of the teenagers shouted.

Uriah merely shoved the kid to one side and continued on.

Bram was able to narrow the gap between them until he got tangled in a living web spun by two spider-costumed teenagers who blocked his way and wrapped yarn around him.

"Not now!" he yelled, flinging his arms to rid himself of the clinging material.

The kids jumped out of his way. Catching up to him, Roger helped Bram disentangle himself.

"Where did they go?" Bram asked, anxiety building when he couldn't spot the groundskeeper. Uriah had no reason to spare Echo, even if he was able to get clear. The thought of losing her made Bram sick.

"I didn't see," Robert admitted.

Ferguson shook his head. "Me neither."

The three men cut through the costumed revelers, checking the various doorways. Ferguson sounded the alert.

"There he is!"

The mirrored room. Monsters surrounded abductor and captive at the other end. Strobes flashed. Bodies and limbs moved in seemingly slow motion. A slimy creature dripping with moss threatened Uriah. The nightmarish scene turned even more so as the groundskeeper struck out with the knife and the costumed kid screamed and grabbed his shoulder. More screams followed from witnesses who quickly moved out of the maniac's way.

Indicating the wounded kid, Bram called, "Roger—"

"Got it!"

Echo's brother-in-law dropped behind to take care of the crisis. But Ferguson was still with him as, second-guessing the groundskeeper again, Bram cut through the wind tunnel, jumped a barricade and headed for the corridor leading to the third concealed staircase back in the coal bin.

"Uriah, you can't get away!" Bram shouted when he spotted them.

"And you can't take the jewels!" Ferguson added.

Jewels? That's why Ferguson had tagged along? To retrieve the damn diamonds rather than save a woman whose life was in danger?

Working on instinct, Bram whipped around, fist closed and swinging. He decked the bigger man and, without pausing, completed the circle and drove toward the doorway that was even now closing in his face. Desperate that he not be locked out, he shoved his left arm through the quickly narrowing opening, only to have it smashed. Hard.

Biting back the pain, Bram pried the door open with his good hand and steadied himself. His wounded arm felt odd. Maybe useless.

"You can let me go now," he heard Echo plead breathlessly from above. "I'll stop him from coming after you. I promise."

"Get real. You're my ticket outta here."

"No!" Bram yelled. "Take the jewels and leave her!"

Ignoring the wooziness plaguing him from the combination of a head injury and possible broken arm, Bram pushed himself upward, each stair jarring him with new pain. He heard Uriah pass the butler's pantry on the first floor, the linen closet on the second, the attic on the third. Their footsteps still echoed down to him.

The groundskeeper was heading for the trapdoor that would let them out onto the roof!

The realization strengthened Bram's determination. He had finally regained his past—he wasn't about to lose his future. He had to get to Echo, to save her before it was too late! Using the narrow metal repair ladder secured to the back of the building, Uriah wouldn't be able to keep his hold on her. There was only one other way down, and Bram figured the villain was sadistic enough to let her use it.

A vision of Echo falling to her death clear in his mind, Bram gritted his teeth and forced himself to move faster.

URIAH JERKED ECHO through the opening, then slid the hatch back into place. Her stomach fell as she looked down, unable to see the walkways below. Clouds played hide-and-seek with a tired moon, and fog crawled up the sides of the building, presenting the illusion that they were much closer to the ground than she knew them to be.

One false step and Dunescape Cottage would be doubly haunted.

A gust of wind slapped at her, clearing her mind, renewing her energies. The occasional rumbles announcing a coming storm were drawing closer. The storm inside her had subsided, however. She was calmer now, even though Uriah's cruel fingers were still tangled in her hair. Her scalp might be numb, but her mind wasn't. It was working—against him. He didn't know that. He was holding the knife almost casually, as if he thought she was no threat.

More fool he.

"Get a move on," he growled.

"I—I can't. Too tired," she fibbed, making her voice sound weak and trembly.

"Then I guess I gotta drag you is all."

Lightning crashed nearby, and for a moment Echo could see clearly. They were on the highest of the several varied-level roof peaks typical of a Victorian cottage. This and the closest peak directly below both supported the derelict weather vanes she'd seen from the walkway.

Could she make that single-story jump without hurting herself on the pointy rusted metal pole? Maybe if she were very careful. And if she did, then what? Another drop to another peak and she'd still have a far way to get to the ground she couldn't see.

Meanwhile, Uriah was as good as his word. He was pulling her across the slanted roof toward the chimney. She surreptitiously used her own considerable strength to slow him. Not certain of his intentions, she figured she'd better act fast. Feigning clumsiness, she purposely stumbled, taking him off balance. He let go of her hair and threw out both arms to regain his equilibrium.

Echo sprang forward, shoving his knife arm hard. When he swung around with her weight, his wrist whacked the chimney. The knife dropped, skittering along the slate shingles and catching in a gutter.

"You—!"

He grabbed for her, but she ducked out of his way. Her foot slid out from under her and she went down hard. Panting, she half rolled, half crawled out of his reach. He refocused and tried to retrieve the knife.

"Take the damn jewels and get out of here!" Echo yelled above the rising wind.

Back on her feet, she searched for the section of roofing secreting the staircase. No light. The moon was all but hidden. She wasn't even certain she would be able to find the hatch in broad daylight.

"Not until I take care of you first," Uriah threatened. "I don't like mouthy women who interfere with my plans!"

She continued to move around the roof, watching as his hand connected with the knife. "I won't make it easy for you," she promised.

"You won't get away from me!" he thundered. Then, as he straightened, weapon in hand, a section of the roofing in front of Echo began to move.

Knowing it had to be Bram, she inched back farther, yelling, "I thought you wanted to be a rich man!" She hoped to keep Uriah's attention on her until it was too late. "The longer you wait, the more likely you'll be caught."

Uriah hesitated, and the hatch opened completely. The clouds scattered, and the moon revealed Bram as he climbed out. Echo had never been so glad to see anyone in her life... until she realized his left arm was dangling at a funny angle. He was hurt. Dear God, that madman would have the chance to kill them both.

"Bram, back inside!" she cried, hoping they could both get away before Uriah reached them.

Standing between her and the madman, Bram wouldn't listen. He faced his father's murderer. "You should have gone while you had the chance, Uriah. Now it's too late."

The groundskeeper laughed and advanced on them. And though Echo pushed at his good arm, Bram stood his ground. Suddenly the sky split in back of Uriah, and for a moment, Echo thought she was seeing double. For behind the groundskeeper stood a dark-garbed man, his full sleeves billowing in the wind, his thick black hair furling across his forehead. His angular features were twisted into a grimace of hatred.

"Donahue!" she yelled, his appearance filling her with hope.

"Think I'd fall for that one?" Uriah asked.

But when Bram froze and stared, too, muttering, "Father?" the groundskeeper got visibly nervous and glanced over his shoulder.

Lightning crackled and split the sky into a giant puzzle, the central figure of which was the threatening ghost of Dunescape Cottage himself. His scowl aimed at Uriah, Donahue moved toward the groundskeeper, who dropped his knife, twisted around and tried to back off.

"No, not you! You're dead!"

Uriah's feet tangled with one another and he did a little dance on the edge of the roof. Then one foot plunged over the side. Desperate to regain his balance, to save himself, he waved his arms about, like a puppet out of control.

A gust of wind was his undoing. A giant invisible finger, it popped him over the edge. In slow motion, he fell, limbs waving, torso twisting, mouth opening in disbelief.

"A-i-ee!"

The sound pierced the night as sharply as the weather vane's rusty point, which thrust completely through his chest and impaled his black heart. Lightning struck again, this time connecting with the weather vane. Electrified, his limbs jerked in a macabre midair dance.

Averting her eyes, Echo caught one last glimpse of Donahue Vanmatre, who smiled at her and at his son, looking as if he had finally found some rest, before becoming one with the night.

"YOU NEED SOME REST, Echo. You can't keep going like nothing happened," Izzy nagged at her when she showed up at Dunescape Cottage the next afternoon.

Volunteers were already sweeping through the house, some filling garbage bags with refuse and disposable decorations, others packing up the props.

"I couldn't sleep," Echo admitted as she began replacing knickknacks in the parlor. "And I couldn't sit around the house doing nothing but thinking about it, either. Besides, this is my responsibility."

For many of them, the night had stretched on long after the nightmare ended. Echo replayed the scene in her mind's eye: Authorities arriving. Shocked spectators standing in a downpour as the body was removed from the weather vane. The police taking custody of the jewels and then questioning everyone involved.

"I can't believe what was going on right under my nose and I didn't even guess," Izzy complained.

Echo started guiltily. "Hard to believe they all played some part in the crimes."

The only selfless one had been Lena, who had known all the house's secrets and had been protecting them and her mistress for thirty years.

"Priscilla Courtland is certainly in shock."

"She couldn't fathom her husband having had an affair with her little island maid." Echo had thought the portrait of Grover had looked familiar. His granddaughter had the same mole, the same sly eyes. "He'd covered by sending their love child away to be raised by Letitia's aunt."

"Letitia obviously had no choice or she wouldn't have made a pact with that devil, Norbert Ferguson."

"She figured her share would be adequate compensation for bearing and being forced to abandon Grover's daughter. Throughout the decades, she'd never stopped talking about the jewels, and Sibyl had grown up thinking of them as her inheritance."

Echo found the silver-framed photographs of the Vanmatre twins. She stared down into Donahue's image so like his son's.

It had been nearly daybreak before Bram had been whisked off in an ambulance so his wounds could be tended to. Though she'd wanted to go with him, she'd felt obligated to see to the Haunted Mansion's closing—much of the crowd had remained for the entire spectacle. And now she was back to run the cleanup detail.

"You haven't seen Bram, have you?" she asked her sister.

"Ah, so that's it." Izzy grinned. "About time you met Mr. Right."

"Hardly. We were thrown together, but we don't have anything in common." Just the opposite, actually. His work was in the factual, business world, hers in the spiritual realm. His place was in Chicago; her home was here, Water's Edge. "I wanted to know how he was."

"Sorry, I haven't heard. The dour-faced housekeeper let us in and then disappeared. I haven't seen Miss Addy or the nurse, either. It's like this place is inhabited by ghosts or something."

Ghosts.

Echo couldn't help thinking about Donahue as she worked. Had his vindication finally freed him to go on to another spiritual plane? At dusk, she found herself outside the library. Knocking. No answer. What had she expected? She opened the door, anyway.

A deep, seemingly empty gloom met her eyes, reminding her of the first time she'd entered the room. She stepped inside, her gaze penetrating the spooky atmosphere, touching on the walls of old books. But, also like the first time, she wasn't alone.

Over in the farthest, deepest recess of the room, flames danced and crackled in the massive fireplace. And before the hearth, one of the leather chairs was occupied. Settled along the wing was a man's arm draped by a full black silk sleeve.

"Donahue?"

Ever so slowly, he turned in the chair and peered out at her. Deep-set eyes framed by thick black waves met her steady gaze. But though today his eyes no longer seemed haunted, his expression was neither welcoming nor disapproving.

He seemed to be ... waiting. Again.

"I wanted to say goodbye," Echo told him. "Actually I had hoped you'd already be gone. I thought maybe with Uriah Hawkes dead and the jewels recovered ... Well, I hoped that since you've been vindicated, you night be happy at last." She smiled. "I guess Miss Addy would miss you, though."

"So you won't be coming back?" he asked softly.

"I—I don't know. It doesn't seem likely. I mean, Bram told me he loved me, but his life is in Chicago and mine's here. And he really doesn't approve of me, anyway."

"You're wrong. The question is, do you love him?"

"With all my heart...."

Her eyes widened as she suddenly realized Donahue was speaking to her. For the first time. While she'd often felt his presence and had seen him several times, he had never said a word, not even at the séance.

Her emotions surged and she backed toward the door. "You're not..."

"Not so fast!"

When he shot out of the chair, she made a run for it, but he was quicker, slamming the door and resting his back against it. His left arm was secured against his body in a sling, and she noticed the bruises on his forehead.

"Happy you made me look foolish?" she asked, glaring at Bram.

He ignored the peevish question. "Tell me about the 'with all my heart' part."

"There's nothing to tell. You're leaving."

"Who says?"

"But your law practice—"

"I can commute on the new ferry service across the lake until I'm able to open an office in this area."

The statement practically took her breath away. "And you'll live here, in this house?"

"Until I get a better offer." His gaze mesmerized her as he said, "A neat cottage in a forested area with a wood-chip walk sounds appealing. Know any place available that fits the description?"

"Maybe." Her heart was thundering. With emotion. And a new kind of fear. "But what about Miss Addy?"

"After I hire a new nurse, we'll see. She was telling me how much she loved having people in the house again. I've been thinking this place would make a spectacular bed and breakfast. All that loot in the basement can be converted to cash to pay for repairs...and taxes. Yep, who could resist a lakeside Victorian mansion complete with an eccentric mistress, not to mention its own ghost?"

Echo realized her mouth was open. Bram did, too. He feathered his fingers around her neck as he took advantage of the fact and kissed her soundly. He stole what little breath she had left.

Ghost.

But was there one? Echo wasn't certain anymore. The room really did feel different. Lighter. Less troubled.

Or maybe it was her own heart.

For Echo knew she had finally met a man she could not only love, but one she could trust. With her heart. With her life. With her sanity.

Not that she was worried about that issue anymore. Her mother had been fragile, too easily pushed over the edge into a nervous breakdown, but she hadn't been insane. And Echo realized her own fear of losing her mind—and therefore control over her own destiny—had grown out of a strong identification with Mama and being traumatized by her grandparents' actions.

So when Bram broke the kiss and asked, "Do we have a chance to make a life together?" Echo put her entire being into her answering smile.

"If I have anything to say about it, we do."

"I love you, Echo. With all my heart," he added, echoing her sentiments. "I never thought it would hap

en, that I could feel like this. You've given me a chance
t a real life. You've banished my ghosts."

"We did that together. You. Me. Donahue."

Bram nodded. "He tried helping me long ago in the
ttic right after his murder. He appeared to me then, but
was too scared to want to believe what I was seeing. I
iped the memory away. I wonder if I wasn't responsi-
le for trapping him here."

"I think there were greater forces at work, Bram. Like
he need for vindication. He has that now."

A frantic banging startled them away from the door
aat popped open, hiding Bram from the intruder's view.

"Auntie E., come quick!" cried an excited Jason.
We've got the ghost cornered in the butler's pantry!"

Echo narrowed her gaze and surreptitiously kicked
Bram's ankle. "But that's impossible, because the ghost
s right here."

Jason peered around the door to see Bram glowering
t him. "Aah!" Her nephew jumped.

Then Echo pulled Bram by his good arm, revealing the
ing. "Gotcha!" she said, and for once had a good laugh
t her prankster nephew's expense.

E LOVED THE WAY their laughter made the walls sing
ith happiness again. And this time when they left the
oom, it didn't feel empty and dead.

Echo St. Clair had brought life to this house. To this
oom. To his son.

He'd lived his own life to the fullest for thirty-seven
ears before it had been cut short. Bram was now thirty-
even. But, cheated by the past that had haunted him,
e'd never really lived at all. Not until now.

He only hoped Bram would never make the mistake he
ad—to put anything or anyone before the woman he

loved. As his twin, Adrienne had been part of him. Bu
in the end, their dependence on each other had stole
happiness from them both.

Emotions he'd forgotten he'd once had surfaced as he
realized he was ready to leave Dunescape Cottage be
hind. As Echo had said, he'd been vindicated.

It was time to move on.

.... And here's more of the best in romantic suspense!

Turn the page for a bonus look at what's in store for you next month, in Harlequin Intrigue #253 WHAT CHILD IS THIS?—a special Christmas edition in Rebecca York's 43 Light Street series.

In the hallowed halls of this charming building, danger has been averted and romance has blossomed. Now Christmas comes to 43 Light Street—and in its stocking is all the action, suspense and romance that your heart can hold.

Chapter One

Guilty until proven innocent.

Erin Morgan squinted into the fog that turned the buildings on either side of Light Street into a canyon of dimly realized apparitions.

"Guilty until proven innocent," she repeated aloud.

It wasn't supposed to work that way. Yet that was how Erin had felt since the Graveyard Murders had rocked Baltimore. Ever since the killer had tricked her into framing her friend Sabrina Barkley.

Sabrina had forgiven her. But she hadn't forgiven herself, and she was never going to let something like that happen again.

She glanced at the purse beside her on the passenger seat and felt her stomach knot. It was stuffed with five thousand dollars in contributions for Santa's Toy and Clothing Fund. Most were checks, but she was carrying more than eight hundred dollars in cash. And she wasn't going to keep it in her possession a moment longer than necessary.

Erin pressed her foot down on the accelerator and then eased up again as a dense patch of white swallowed up the car. She couldn't even see the Christmas decorations she knew were festooned from many of the downtown office windows.

"'Tis the season to be jolly..." She sang a few lines of the carol to cheer herself up, but her voice trailed off in the gloom.

Forty-three Light Street glided into view through the mist like a huge underwater rock formation.

Erin drove around to the back of the building where she could get in and out as quickly as possible. Pulling the collar of her coat closed against the icy wind, she hurried toward the back door—the key ready in her hand.

It felt good to get out of the cold. But there was nothing welcoming about the dank, dimly lit back entrance—so different from the fading grandeur of the marble foyer. Here there were no pretensions of gentility, only institutional-gray walls and a bare concrete floor.

Clutching her purse more tightly, she strained her ears and peered into the darkness. She heard nothing but the familiar sound of the steam pipes rattling. And she saw nothing moving in the shadows. Still, the fine hairs on the back of her neck stirred as she bolted into the service elevator and pressed the button.

Upstairs the paint was brighter, and the tile floors were polished. But at this time of night, only a few dim lights held back the shadows, and the clicking of her high heels echoed back at her like water dripping in an underground cavern.

Feeling strangely exposed in the darkness, Erin kept her eyes focused on the glass panel of her office door. She was almost running by the time she reached it.

Her hand closed around the knob. It was solid and reassuring against her moist palm, and she felt some of the knots in her stomach untie themselves. With a sigh of relief, she kicked the door closed behind her, shutting out the unseen phantoms of the hall.

Reaching over one of the mismatched couches donated by a local rental company, she flipped the light switch. Nothing happened. Darn. The bulb must be out.

In the darkness, she took a few steps toward the file room and stopped.

Something else was wrong. Maybe it was the smell. Not the clean pine scent of the little Christmas tree she'd set up by the window, but the dank odor of sweat.

She was backing quietly toward the door when fingers as hard and lean as a handcuff shot out and closed around her wrist.

A scream of terror rose in her throat. The sound was choked off by a rubber glove against her lips.

Someone was in her office. In the dark.

Her mind registered no more than that. But her body was already struggling—trying to twist away.

"No. Please." Even as she pleaded, she knew she was wasting her breath.

He was strong. And ruthless.

Her free hand came up to pummel his shoulder and neck. He grunted and shook her so hard that her vision blurred.

She tried to work her teeth against the rubbery palm that covered her mouth.

His grip adroitly shifted to her throat. He began to squeeze, and she felt the breath turn to stone in her lungs.

He bent her backward over his arm, and she stared up into a face covered by a ski mask, the features a strange parody of something human.

The dark circles around the eyes, the red circle around the mouth, the two dots of color on his cheeks—all wavered in her vision like coins in the bottom of a fountain.

The pressure increased. Her lungs were going to explode.

No. Please. Let me go home. I have a little boy. He needs me.

The words were choked off like her life breath.

Like the rapidly fading light. She was dying. And the scenes of her life flashed before her eyes. Climbing into bed with her parents on Sunday morning. First grade. High school graduation. Her marriage to Bruce. Kenny's birth. Her husband's death. Betraying Sabrina. Finishing college. Her new job with Silver Miracle Charities. The holiday fund-raiser tonight.

The events of her life trickled through her mind like the last grains of sand rolling down the sloping sides of an hourglass. Then there was only blackness.

*Don't miss this next 43 Light Street tale—
#253 WHAT CHILD IS THIS?—coming
December 1993—only from Rebecca York and
Harlequin Intrigue!*

Relive the romance...
Harlequin and Silhouette
are proud to present

by Request™

A program of collections of three complete novels by the most-requested
authors with the most-requested themes. Be sure to look for one volume each
month with three complete novels by top-name authors.

In September: **BAD BOYS**   Dixie Browning
                                          Ann Major
                                          Ginna Gray
No heart is safe when these hot-blooded hunks are in town!

In October: **DREAMSCAPE**   Jayne Ann Krentz
                                          Anne Stuart
                                          Bobby Hutchinson
Something's happening! But is it love or magic?

In December: **SOLUTION: MARRIAGE**   Debbie Macomber
                                          Annette Broadrick
                                          Heather Graham Pozzessere
Marriages in name only have a way of leading to love....

Available at your favorite retail outlet.

REQ-G

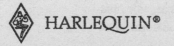

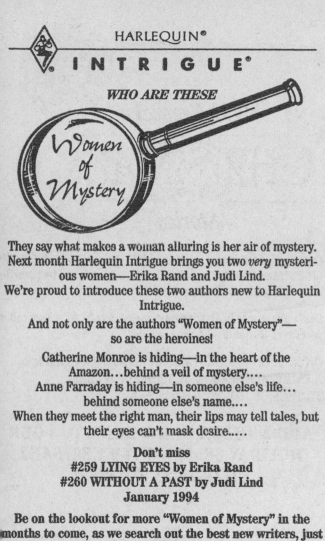

HARLEQUIN®

INTRIGUE®

WHO ARE THESE

Women of Mystery

They say what makes a woman alluring is her air of mystery.
Next month Harlequin Intrigue brings you two *very* mysterious women—Erika Rand and Judi Lind.
We're proud to introduce these two authors new to Harlequin Intrigue.

And not only are the authors "Women of Mystery"—
so are the heroines!

Catherine Monroe is hiding—in the heart of the
Amazon...behind a veil of mystery....
Anne Farraday is hiding—in someone else's life...
behind someone else's name....
When they meet the right man, their lips may tell tales, but
their eyes can't mask desire.....

**Don't miss
#259 LYING EYES by Erika Rand
#260 WITHOUT A PAST by Judi Lind
January 1994**

Be on the lookout for more "Women of Mystery" in the
months to come, as we search out the best new writers, just
for you—only from Harlequin Intrigue!   WOMEN

1993 Keepsake

CHRISTMAS

Stories

Capture the spirit and romance of Christmas with KEEPSAKE CHRISTMAS STORIES, a collection of three stories by favorite historical authors. The perfect Christmas gift!

Don't miss these heartwarming stories, available in November wherever Harlequin books are sold:

ONCE UPON A CHRISTMAS by Curtiss Ann Matlock
A FAIRYTALE SEASON by Marianne Willman
TIDINGS OF JOY by Victoria Pade

ADD A TOUCH OF ROMANCE TO YOUR HOLIDAY SEASON WITH KEEPSAKE CHRISTMAS STORIES!

HX93